Hex
ON THE BEACH

THE MAGIC IN MIXOLOGY SERIES *BOOK ONE*

GINA LAMANNA

For updates on new releases, please sign up for
my newsletter at www.ginalamanna.com.

Feel free to get in touch anytime via email
at gina.m.lamanna@gmail.com!

SYNOPSIS

L ILY LOCKE HAS NEVER BELIEVED in witches and wizards, ghosts and magic, shifters and vampires—especially cute blond vamps with blood-intolerance issues. A rising star at a hotshot marketing agency in Minneapolis, Minnesota, all Lily knows is she's a PowerPoint guru, an Excel ninja, and a coffee-maker extraordinaire. Not to mention she's next in line for a *huge* promotion.

All that changes when Lily's assistant delivers a strange quiz to her, one titled *A Magical Assessment for Normal Folks*. With it comes the promise of a land Lily's never known existed. A land where Lily not only discovers her biological family for the first time, but a place where she can make a difference, change people's lives, and step into the role she's destined to fulfill.

But first, Lily must admit she's a witch.

Welcome to *The Isle.*

ACKNOWLEDGEMENTS

To you, my readers! Thank you for your friendship and support.

I appreciate each and every one of you who helped with this book in some shape or form!

Joy – For being the best "boss" I could ever ask for

Stacia – Thank you for helping me breathe easier with your edits

To Connie – Happy Birthday!

Kim – for all the special secrets

Dianne & Barb for all your help making this book better

SMO'7 – and all seven kiddos! For making me feel very loved

To Mom & Dad — For giving me a 'magical' childhood to daydream about islands that don't exist

To Alex. For making every day feel like it's magic. я тебя люблю!

To Meg & Kristi— For calling me to say hi… sometimes.

To my Oceans Apart ladies— To the best long-distance sisters a girl could ask for

To Sprinkles On Top Studios, my awesome cover designer. Photo Courtesy of Deposit Photos

And last but not least, to all my family and friends, thanks for making me laugh.

CHAPTER 1

"IT'S BEEN CONFIRMED THERE *HAS* been another sighting of The Isle. Nestled against the shores of the frigid Lake Superior, right off the coast of Grand Marais, we have one man who claims he's seen the mystical island just this past weekend. Still, we've no record of any human stepping foot on the—"

"What does she mean by 'no human'?" I asked, interrupting the radio program. "As opposed to what, aliens?"

My assistant scowled. "*Shhh.* I'm listening."

"The Isle is rumored to have all sorts of creatures wandering its lands, traipsing The Forests beside the volcano…"

I tuned out, giving said assistant, Ainsley, a few more minutes to listen before I broke up the party.

When I couldn't ignore it any longer, I stood and forced myself to take charge. "Okay, can we please shut it off? I can't listen to this drivel right now. You know I don't like to be the big, bad boss, Ains, but… this presentation is a big deal. *The* big deal."

"But this show is all *true*," Ainsley said. "There is an island. You know it."

"I don't know it. And this reporter lady is a kook!"

"I want to hear the rest of the program." Ainsley reached for the radio, gulping the last of her virgin piña colada, a drink she said "added to the ambiance" of her weekly listening session. "Let me keep it on until the ending. Pretty please? I'll work twenty minutes late and come in twenty minutes early tomorrow."

"But you know the end of the show. You listen to it every week."

"I like it."

"You're really telling me you believe there's an island with magical powers nobody has ever seen? You know all these people she interviews are lying, right?"

"Ana is *not* lying."

Anastasia, the host of the show, reminded me of Luna Lovegood and her belief in all things Nargles. Long blond hair, hippie skirts, big round eyes, and a belief in the unusual.

"I'm not saying Ana is a liar. I'm just saying she's—"

"Different? What's wrong with different?" Ainsley sat back, displaying arms streaked with tattoos and a rainbow head of hair. "Huh?"

"Nothing." I lifted my hand from the radio. "Fine. Twenty more minutes, but I'm going for a walk. I have to get in the right mindset for tomorrow. Then shut it off, *please*. You're making my job difficult."

"I try." Ainsley smiled, giving me a wink as she held her pink piña colada straw between her teeth and turned up the volume.

As Ana's voice filled the room with her theories on witches and wizards, trolls and fairies, and sorts of creatures that didn't—and could never—exist, I took off down the hallway, taking long, deep breaths.

At Lions Marketing, Inc., my official title was Senior Director of Marketing, though I was only twenty-six years old. I'd been promoted four times in as many years and wore many hats: Excel ninja, spreadsheet guru, coffee-maker extraordinaire. But after four years of grueling labor with long hours and little pay, tomorrow was my time to do or die.

After a lengthy stroll around the office, I ended up back at my desk. Shutting down my computer, I twisted my necklace into knots before I hurried out to my car, distracted by thoughts of the looming presentation.

If I aced this presentation, Lions Marketing was looking at an additional five million dollars of revenue by the end of this year, with the potential for more to come. Not only would that put us in the black for the first time, but it would line me up for my next big promotion.

If it went terribly wrong…

I didn't want to think about that.

As I drove home, I told myself I'd practiced so many times, nothing could go wrong.

But somehow, I wasn't convinced.

CHAPTER 2

I CLICKED MY PENCIL ONCE.
Twice.
Three times.

Standing with a sigh, I stretched my neck in a slow roll, cracked my knuckles for good measure, then strolled around the conference room and tried not to look nervous.

Where is everyone?

Stopping in front of the floor-to-ceiling window, I pretended to stare at the skyscrapers of downtown Minneapolis. But instead of seeing the buildings, I double-checked my hair, which I'd done up in a bun for today's special occasion. My makeup, though minimal, remained intact, and there were no coffee stains on my white shirt. Overall, a success.

Except for one thing.

An audience.

I shuffled, for the zillionth time, through my sheaf of papers and flicked through one slide after the next. I'd thought of nothing except this presentation for the last three weeks, and frankly, I wondered if I might be going a bit crazy. These slides appeared in my dreams. They haunted my shower thoughts. The grocery clerk had heard at least six percent of my presentation while I checked out last night.

My mind drifted as I scanned the surrounding tall buildings, the mini concrete jungle of the downtown Twin Cities. I loved the hustle and bustle through the skyways, the *whoosh* of city bus exhaust pipes, the meetings of strangers day in and day out.

Then all of a sudden, a flash in the distance caught my eye. At first glance, it looked as if a bolt of lightning had struck ground just outside the city limits. Leaning closer to the window, my nose nearly touching the glass, I squinted, trying to see if, in fact, a storm was a-brewing.

"Uh, boss?" Ainsley knocked on the door and poked her head in the room as I jumped backward, self-consciously brushing off my fanciest pencil skirt. I wore one white blouse and had brought another to the office today, just in case. She raised her eyebrows, her messy bun bobbing along with her head. A tattoo peeked out on her shoulder. "Everything okay? You know, if you're considering jumping from the building instead of giving your presentation, there's an easier way. The roof doesn't have windows."

I scrunched my nose. "That's enough. Not now, Ainsley. The clients will be here any minute."

"Loosen up." Ainsley took a few steps into the room, adjusting her stylish leather jacket. "You're way too uptight. I've never seen anyone prepare more for *anything*. You've got this presentation down. Remember last week when I caught you sleeping at your desk?"

I nodded. I'd worked into the wee hours of the morning making sure the graphics of my PowerPoint were spot on. Around three or four, I must have nodded off, because the next thing I knew, Ainsley was making fun of an odd glob of drool on my desk while handing me a cup of coffee.

"Yeah, well, you were reciting it in your sleep." She handed me a slip of paper. "So relax, okay, boss? You got this."

I smiled. "Thanks, Ains, I appreciate it."

"Whatever." She turned and left without a glance back.

Ainsley, a whirlwind of tattoos, piercings, and colorful hair, had stumbled into the position of my secretary years before. I'd originally hired her as a favor to my own boss, but when she proved to be whip smart and insanely creative, I not only kept her on, I promoted her and did everything in my power to keep her around.

We were polar opposites. My hair was mahogany brown and fastened in a tight chignon, and I wore black and gray and white almost exclusively. I had not a tattoo in sight, and I'd never even considered highlighting my hair. But I liked her because she wasn't afraid to tell me when I was being crazy.

Like now.

Except—I wasn't crazy.

Where were they?

Remembering the slip of paper in my hand, I glanced down, expecting it to be a memo that the group was running late. Rush-hour traffic had held up more than one client meeting, so I wouldn't be surprised, except… it wasn't a note from Ainsley.

It was a quiz. Some sort of strange, bizarro magic test.

"What in the world?" I read the note once, twice, three times. I walked across the room and opened the door then shouted down the hall, "Ainsley? What is this?"

Ainsley, however, was long gone—probably out for a smoke break.

One more glance around the lobby told me the client hadn't yet arrived. I reread my presentation one more time, but even in my head I was beginning to sound like a cardboard cutout. I turned my attention to Ainsley's note and found myself shaking my head.

This must be her idea of a joke, something to get me to loosen up so I'd be more *go with the flow* for the meeting. It was sweet, in Ainsley's unique style.

I clicked my pencil once more and doodled in the corner while I read the quiz.

Magic Assessment for Normal Folks

Have you ever found yourself wondering if you are a witch? If so, now is your chance to find out in ten easy questions!

Have you experienced one (or more) strange happenings that are impossible to explain with science?
* No, I'm a completely boring fuddy-duddy, and nothing interesting happens
* Yes, but I pretend it didn't happen

What color are your knickers?
* Hot Pink
* Glittery
* Get out of town, they're called underwear.
* Why wear underwear, anyway?

Did you wash your socks this week?
* Yes
* No
* I'm a barefoot beauty

Do you believe in magic?
* Duh, I'm a witch
* Magic is nonsense

The questions continued, all just as silly as the first few. Ainsley had succeeded in getting a smile out of me, I thought as I skimmed the rest of the article. But she'd forgotten a key, or a point system, or some way to tally my answers.

I circled random responses, as outrageous as I could get, planning to tuck it under Ainsley's keyboard to show her that I had a sense of humor, and I wasn't a total *fuddy-duddy*.

But when I got to the bottom, one of the lines caught me off guard.

** ** Surprise** **

If you can read this quiz, you are a witch. To everyone else, this piece of paper looks like a picture of David Hasselhoff in a polka-dot bikini.

So congratulations! You have magic in your blood. We'll be in touch soon!

** ** Sincerely, Members of The Isle ** **

My pencil hovered over the page.

"Clever girl," I muttered. Even Ainsley's jokes were witty, not the average "tape-the-bottom-of-your-mouse" prank. I'd have to get her back good for this one...

My blood froze as someone cleared their throat behind me and an unfamiliar voice said, "Ms. Locke?"

I turned to see a dapper gentleman looking uber-professional in an expensive suit, tie, and polished shoes extend his hand. His eyes glanced toward the witchy quiz on the table before sliding back to mine.

"Hello, Mr. Davenport, it's good to finally meet you in person. I'm Lily, Lily Locke." I gestured toward the table where the paper sat in clear view, my cheeks warm with a furious blush. "My assistant thought she'd play a cute joke on me."

"Cute?" A woman appeared next to Mr. Davenport. She too wore an expensive, form-fitting business suit and high heels that stated elegant. "I consider that rude. David Hasselhoff, didn't he go to rehab? And why on earth is he wearing that bathing suit? He must be drunk again."

My mind went blank. "Excuse me? David..."

"Your photo." The woman sniffed. "I'd have my secretary fired if she considered something like that *humorous*."

The hairs on the back of my neck prickled at her stuffy tone. Whether or not Ainsley should have tried to lighten the mood, the woman didn't need such an attitude. Ains hadn't meant any harm.

"She was just trying to make me smile," I said. "It's a joke quiz."

"Quiz?" The woman furrowed her brow. "That's not a *quiz*. It's a raunchy photo. I'm all for a joke, but this…"

Mr. Davenport glanced at the photo, but he looked away just as fast. The tinge of red in his ears told me he was embarrassed by whatever he'd seen. He ran a hand through his gray hair. "Well, should we begin?"

"Yes, yes, of course," I said, relieved.

I flipped the quiz over, still wondering how on earth Ainsley had pulled off that trick. I'd really need to have a word with her. A pretend quiz was one thing, but a rude photo that offended our potential clients was another entirely.

I focused on the presentation, pushing the odd events out of my mind. Grabbing water and coffee for everyone, I waited as another six or seven people filtered into the conference room. Eventually, my boss arrived as well and gave me a curt nod, his face stern as usual.

I nodded back, my nerves ramping up. Taking a couple deep breaths, I paused before holding up the clicker for the presentation.

"Welcome, and thank you for coming this morning." I remembered to smile at the last minute, forcing myself to remain *loose* as Ainsley had cautioned. My fingers trembled slightly as I depressed the button to begin the first slide.

"Here at Lions Marketing, we provide the best, the most thorough, the most effective strategies in the industry. As our name suggests, we are the king of the marketing jungle, and…" My voice faltered as I glanced from one face to the next.

Not a single person was paying attention to me.

My first slide didn't contain anything interesting on it, nothing at all except for our company name and logo—a roaring lion. Yet everyone was staring with rapt attention at the screen. As if it were David Hasselhoff in a polka-dot bikini.

My boss's mouth hung open in an unflattering manner, which

most certainly meant bad news. He looked surprised. And shocked. My boss was *never* surprised. I'd once told him a tornado had touched down five minutes away, and he hadn't flinched.

Sensing something had gone terribly, terribly wrong, I made a slow turn until I faced the screen. Then my face fell slack. I dropped the clicker. And I squinted.

"What is that?" I asked in a hushed tone.

On the screen, what should have been our logo had completely disappeared. Er, *sort of* disappeared. The lion from our logo looked as if it'd come to life in a 2-D image, prancing around the screen, opening its mouth in silent roars, swishing its tail.

"Is this another *joke*?" The stuffy woman crossed her arms, but I didn't sense as much hostility. More curiosity than anything else.

Join the club. I had no idea what was happening on the slide, and curiosity didn't begin to explain it.

"No, uh, we here at Lions Marketing are all about new, out-of-the-box, forward-thinking marketing." My boss stood, giving me a quick glare before putting on his "business hat" and facing the clients.

How he remained so calm, so collected, I had no idea. I was quivering in my knock-off boots.

"Do tell," the woman said. "I don't understand."

"It captured your attention, did it not?" My boss gestured to the screen where, at the moment, the lion had apparently decided to take a leak on the company name.

I winced. Poor time for a bathroom break.

"We will catch your consumer's eye like nobody before. I can guarantee that our tactics are on the cutting edge of the industry. Studies in China right now are proving that this sort of viral marketing is what's new and hot." My boss gave me another quick *glare*.

Lucky thing he was there, because I'd never have come up with that fake China study. That was probably the same reason he was my boss, and I was one of many minions below him.

"Interesting," Mr. Davenport said, taking over for his female counterpart. "And how do you see this helping us?"

"Well, I will let Lily move on with her presentation. I know she has a wonderful explanation ready for you with plenty of numbers and graphs. Right?" My boss turned to me. "Lily?"

"Right." I jumped to attention. "Next."

I clicked the clicker but immediately regretted the move. Instead of advancing the slide, the click seemed to only anger the cartoonish lion. Lions Marketing's logo turned toward us with an all-too-realistic expression and roared at the crowd.

Except this time, the animal wasn't silent.

I felt the breeze, smelled the breath from the lion as the roar nearly deafened the room.

"I'm sorry about that," I said, clicking the clicker once more.

This time, the click enlarged the lion's figure. He grew to half the size of the screen, his roars growing louder and louder.

"Lily, what is this?" My boss's tone was furious. In his defense, he had a pretty good reason to be upset.

"I don't know! This isn't my PowerPoint. I've gone through this a million times, you've seen me," I said with a horrified glance at my boss. "I don't know what's happening or how to get rid of it."

"Shut it off." My boss's tone was clipped, and I was sure that neither he nor I missed the raised eyebrows of Ms. Stuffy Bottoms in the corner.

"I'm trying!" But every time I clicked the power button, the lion grew larger, roared louder, and altogether became more animated.

"I'm leaving." Ms. Stuffy Bottoms stood, nodding at Mr. Davenport. "I do not enjoy the idea of *threatening* my target audience with our marketing."

"It's not what you think, it's…" I raised and lowered my shoulders, unable to explain it.

"A joke?" The woman raised her eyebrows. "I'm not sure if that's better or worse, but either way, I won't tolerate it. I'm sorry, but I have a lot of money at stake, and with this sort of showing, I can't *possibly* put my money in your hands."

Mr. Davenport followed the woman without question. On the way out, his eyes met my boss's gaze, and he murmured, "I'm sorry it didn't work out, Fred. Maybe next time."

The rest of the crew filtered out, none of them making eye contact with me, most of them nodding sadly at my boss. When it was just him and me left, I limply raised one hand.

"I'm so sorry, I don't know what happened." I looked at the floor. "Er... are you going to say something?"

My boss's silence bordered on murderous.

I cleared my throat. "You know, I never knew your name was Fred, Mr. Roberts."

I had no idea where that observation had come from, or why it'd just popped out of my mouth. My legs trembled, my fingers shook, tears pricked my eyes—all signs my nerves were shot. Apparently that toyed with my ability to say appropriate things.

"Get your things." Mr. Roberts's voice rumbled throughout the room with a menacing tone I hadn't known he possessed. "You're fired."

I hung my head. Ainsley would've fought back, argued that it wasn't her fault. Part of me wanted to lash out at Fred, tell him this wasn't my PowerPoint, that someone had screwed with me, played an unfair joke that had gone sour. Maybe it was Leslie from down the hall—she'd been angling for my job for a while. Or Sarah from one floor up—she'd been hankering for a promotion for months.

But I couldn't find it in myself to blame anyone else. I'd put my blood, sweat, and tears into this presentation, and it couldn't have gone worse. I could barely process what had happened, let alone form cohesive thoughts or argue my point. No, for now, I needed to lick my wounds and figure out what to do next.

CHAPTER 3

THERE WAS NO BETTER PLACE to lick my wounds than The Bar. It was, as the name suggested, a simple bar tucked in an out-of-the-way alley in downtown Minneapolis. Only regulars came here, the types of people looking for strong drinks, quiet booths, and dart boards without a waiting line.

I shook up a martini behind the bar, helping myself to the liquor cabinets. Jesse, the bartender, and I had become fast friends a long time ago, back when I'd taught him a few fancy tricks about how to properly salt a margarita. I also made a great wing-girl and had secured him some phone numbers on more than one occasion.

In exchange for our friendship, Jesse allowed me free rein, an all-access pass to the liquor stash. It wasn't the alcohol I enjoyed—at least, not as much as the art of making the perfect drink. Every week, Jesse left a slot for me on the menu to feature a "signature drink," which might be anything from an easy wine spritzer to a fancy Nutella martini.

I never needed a menu, a recipe, or a suggestion from a patron. Making drinks was, quite possibly, the only thing that came naturally to me. Which could be a good thing or a bad thing, depending on the day. Normally I didn't even consume the drinks I invented, but today was an exception.

After pouring a martini so dirty it rivaled the floor of the bar, I slid onto a stool and rested my head between my hands. Next to me sat the stack of papers I'd clutched as I slunk out of the conference room a few hours earlier, pretending I didn't see everyone's curious stares.

On top of the failed presentation slides sat the witch test. My stomach twisted, wondering what would happen to Ainsley now that I'd been fired. Not wanting to think about sad things, I pushed the pile away. Luckily the bar was empty, so nobody else was around to see my fall from start-up marketing grace.

"Wanna talk about it?" Jesse asked, pulling himself a tap beer.

"Not really," I said.

"What happened?" Jesse added a few more olives to my already overflowing drink. "You were so excited about this presentation. It was all you talked about for weeks."

I looked at the overly tattooed man, who was nothing more than a teddy bear inside. I guessed he was about ten years older than me, and our relationship resembled that of a big-brother-little-sister situation.

"I failed." I speared an olive with unnecessary violence. "Miserably."

"It can't be that bad." Jesse leaned over the counter, tilting my chin upward with a gentle tap of his fist. "Even if the presentation didn't go so smoothly, how could they not be charmed by this cute face?"

I forced a smile, glancing in the mirror behind the bar. My tightly knotted hair drooped, a few strands spiraling out of control. My blouse had somehow lost its top button, exposing my camisole underneath, while my stilettos rested underneath the bar stool.

"Because a lion took over." I shrugged one shoulder. "Weird day, huh?"

Jesse took a sip of beer. "I don't understand."

"Me neither."

"Do they give out pictures of David Hasselhoff instead of pink slips these days?" he asked, gesturing toward my stack of papers.

I pointed at the witch quiz. "This is *not* a photo. Why does everyone keep saying that? It's a stupid quiz, a joke from my assistant."

Jesse picked up the paper full of questions and examined it so thoroughly his ears turned as red as the maraschino cherries next to him. "Do you need to talk to someone, Lily?"

"I'm talking to you."

"No, like... *psychically*."

"Psychic? Like ESPN?"

"Isn't it ESP?"

"I don't know." I shrugged. "None of that stuff exists anyway. Either way, do you mean a shrink?"

"I'm just saying, I've heard of some people going through really stressful things and having a mental breakdown."

"I'm not having a breakdown. Something just went wrong with my presentation. I can't explain it."

"Like a breakdown?" He raised an eyebrow, eyeing my drink as if wanting to take it away from the crazy person babbling about a lion.

I hugged it closer. "I'm *not* crazy."

The door to the bar opened, and laughter filtered in. I set my drink down, sat back, and stared.

Two women, who looked as if they'd never set foot on this earth before, tottered into the bar, both of them trying to squeeze through the door at once. One of the ladies wore a lime-green skirt, bright-blue blouse, and hat with a bonnet the size of Saturn's rings. She was the plumper of the two by a long shot and clasped what might be a guinea pig to her chest.

The other woman—tall, thin as a wisp of grass, with a frown puckering her face—waltzed in wearing a mustard-yellow dress with a pattern that belonged on my great-great-grandmother's armchair. In other words, the fabric was ugly.

But the short, plump woman smiled so brightly, the wattage of the room increased, and she trilled a hello to whoever would listen.

It was Jesse's turn to splutter.

"Hello, *dahlings*, how are you?" the shorter one asked. "Oh,

Lily, I see you've brought your exam along with you. Wonderful. I was convinced we'd have to beg you to believe it's real. But you've accepted the truth already—excellent!"

"Um…" My jaw hung open. I probably looked unattractive, but then again, these ladies hadn't walked off the fall fashion catalogue of—well, *any* magazine.

"You didn't introduce us," the tall beanpole chided. "She has no idea who we are."

"Oh, *dahlings*, I'm sorry." The plump woman removed her wide-brimmed hat and took a deep bow, in which her nose nearly touched her toes, before righting herself. "I am Mimsey Magnolia, and this is my guinea pig, Chunk. That's my sister, Trinket."

"Trinket Dixie," the skinny woman said, her mouth still pinched in a frown, gray hair curled tightly to her head.

"I'm, uh, Lily Locke," I said hesitantly. With one quick look at the bartender, I knew he wouldn't be speaking anytime soon. "And this is Jesse."

"We know who you are, dear," Mimsey said. "We're your *aunts*."

"What?"

"Your aunts, dear. You know. *Family*."

I shook my head. "My dad doesn't have any siblings."

"And your mother?"

I hesitated, glancing at Jesse. "I don't know my mother."

Mimsey *tsked*, stroking her guinea pig's head. "Ah. Has your father never talked about her?"

"No." It was a bit of a lie, but I didn't know these women from Adam. My father had mentioned my mother, but only in passing and only to say she'd disappeared before I'd turned a year old.

"I wondered if she'd be too young." Mimsey shook her head, her brightly colored clothes flashing with the motion. "I was right."

"Too young for what?" I asked.

"To remember. Everything," Mimsey said. "That dratted curse."

"What are you talking about, curse?"

"If you come with us, I'll explain everything." Mimsey turned and walked toward the door. "Let's go, Chunkie."

"I'm not going anywhere." I glanced at Jesse for reassurance. "This is crazy, right?"

The bartender's face paled. He leaned toward me and whispered, "I don't understand what's happening."

"Me neither." I shook my head, glancing at the two nutso women who must have wandered away from a psych ward.

"You're looking at us as if we're looney, dear," Mimsey said. "What don't you understand?"

"Everything." I raised a hand. "You. Why you're here. Why you're talking about my mother when I haven't seen her in over a quarter of a century."

"Oh, gosh, time flies." Mimsey turned back at the door. "I told you, come with us and we'll explain everything."

"I don't think so." I tilted my head. "First of all, this is crazy. No offense. Second, I don't know where you're going or where you came from."

"The Isle," Trinket said. "Your home. Where you belong."

"I belong right here. Minneapolis, Minnesota." I tapped the bar for added emphasis. "I have a job. An apartment. My dad. A life."

"You don't have a job anymore," Mimsey said with a tinkling laugh. "And I wouldn't call working eighty hours a week a *life*, dear. We know you only see your dad once a week, and he barely notices when you bring him dinners on Sundays. He prefers to watch that game of footie-balls—"

"Football?" I asked.

"Whatever." Mimsey waved. "He prefers to watch that rather than talk to you. That means you just drop off the food and go back to work. On a Sunday night. Who works on a Sunday night?"

"Me," I said through gritted teeth. "Someone who wants to be successful. Have you two been *stalking* me?"

"Stalking is a bit harsh. Just keeping tabs on you. We promised your mother," Mimsey said.

"How do you know my mother? Why do you keep saying that?"

"Because we're her sisters. She was the oldest. Then Trinket, then me." Mimsey pointed at herself with her thumb while Trinket nodded.

"I—*no*. You're lying." I took a sip of my drink, hoping the alcohol would somehow clear my mind. Maybe Jesse was right and I'd overworked myself and was suffering the consequences—a complete mental breakdown. Maybe I should let these ladies take me back with them to the looney bin.

"Okay, enough, dear." Mimsey put a hand on her hip. "If you come with us, we will explain everything."

"Don't go with them," Jesse said. "They don't seem right in the head."

"You think?" I muttered. I looked between the two and asked, "Is there a number I can call, someone to come pick you up?"

Trinket stepped forward, her wispy frame and serious expression somehow intimidating despite her armchair-patterned clothing. "You took the exam. We need you now more than ever. It's *essential* you come with us."

"What exam?"

Trinket gestured toward the *Magical Assessment for Normal Folks* on the bar. Turning to Jesse, she asked, "What do you see on that piece of paper?"

Jesse blushed.

"Answer me, son," Trinket demanded.

"A photo of David Hasselhoff in a polka-dot bikini," he mumbled.

"Traitor," I whispered across the bar. "You can see the quiz questions."

"He can't, dear," Mimsey said, stepping forward. "Only you.

You have magic in your blood, passed down by your mother. And you're the next Mixologist in line."

"What the heck is a mixologist?" I waved at Jesse and twisted my necklace anxiously. "Are you sure you're not here for him? He's the bartender."

"No, *Mixologist*. With a capital *M*," Trinket said. "Now, get your things. We have no time to waste. We must return to The Isle."

"I don't know about any isle," I said. "This is Minnesota, not Hawaii."

"Correct. Which means you're in the right place," Mimsey said. "And Trinket is not exaggerating. We *need* you, dear. We need you more than you know."

I shook my head. "I belong here. On firm ground. On *land*. I appreciate your concern, but... there's no way you're related to my mother. I work in *marketing*."

"If I show you proof, will you come with us?" Mimsey asked. "I completely forgot. Get the item, Trinket."

Trinket fished in a handbag that looked as though it could contain a whole colony of guinea pigs. I didn't respond, looking on with curiosity.

"What do you say, darling?" Mimsey raised her eyebrows. "If we can prove it, will you come with us?"

"You can't prove anything," I said.

"Trinket?" Mimsey asked. "Show her."

"She didn't agree," Trinket argued. "I'm not showing her anything until she promises."

"If you can convince me..." I rolled my eyes in a big circle. "And that's a *huge* if, then I'll consider coming. But don't count on convincing me. I don't even know anything about my mom."

Trinket looked at Mimsey, who gave a single nod and extended her hand. Trinket deposited something small into her sister's palm then stepped backward.

"I believe you have something around your neck, dear." Mimsey took hesitant steps toward me. "May I see it?"

My fingers reached reflexively for my necklace, twisting the heart charm on the end. It was the one thing I'd been given from my mom, the one thing I'd held onto day in and day out since I was a baby. Without it clasped around my neck, I'd always felt... *off*.

I couldn't describe the feeling, couldn't put my finger on what went *wrong* when I removed the charm. But I'd once removed the necklace for my volleyball state championship. We lost miserably, and I sprained my ankle.

Another time, I'd removed it for a job interview. I didn't get an offer from the company.

I'd taken it off for one blind date Ainsley had set me up on, and the entire evening was a disaster, ending with me acquiring sudden food poisoning and puking during the entire cab ride home.

Call it a superstition, call it luck, call it what you may—I never took the necklace off anymore.

Holding the chain lightly, I glanced down. Though the gold chain appeared thin and delicate, elegant in a less-is-more sort of way, I knew from experience that it was sturdy as an ox. It'd snagged on combs, doorways, sweaters, and I'd never once needed to have it repaired. The heart-shaped locket remained firmly around my neck, for better or for worse.

"Ah, yes." Mimsey gave me a sad smile as she studied the necklace.

Sensing her genuine interest, I relaxed slightly, and I extended the chain as far as possible, leaning forward so she could see the charm on the end. It was just a locket—or rather, half of a locket.

The golden heart was tiny, nearly too small to read the print. But instead of opening and closing like a normal locket, the charm sat open, the message displayed through a small glass panel. I didn't need to look down to know what it said. I'd memorized the inscription long ago.

Follow the Heart.

It'd confused me for a long while now, and for years, I'd pondered the meaning. *The* Heart? *Whose heart?* For a while, I'd wondered if my mom had purchased the necklace in a clearance section at the Dollar Store. Maybe they'd goofed and written the wrong phrase. Maybe it'd been made in China and the meaning was lost in translation.

"Follow the Heart," Mimsey whispered. "It's hers."

I glanced at the plump woman, her colorful outfit in stark contrast with the tears welling in her eyes.

"Praise be, it's *you*." Mimsey clasped her hands on either side of my head, kissing my cheeks with effusive enthusiasm. "I've waited so long to meet you, darling. I didn't have doubt before, not really… but this—it's *you*."

I remained confused. "I thought you knew who I was before you arrived."

"I did, *we* did," Mimsey said. "But until we saw the necklace, there was the smallest chance we could be wrong. For a minute when we first walked in, I thought we might've been mistaken. You're so… unlike her."

"Unlike who?" I asked.

"Your mother." Mimsey shook her head. "You're so…" She gestured to my pencil skirt, the stiff blouse, the bun now a bit in disarray. "Organized. Put together. You've got your life in order, so… so serious."

"She wasn't like me?" I couldn't help myself.

"Whimsical would be a kind way to describe her," Mimsey said through a watery smile, a few of her previously unshed tears sliding freely down her cheeks. "But you look like her, dear."

"What about the necklace?" I looked down.

Jesse watched us, his jaw hanging open but no sound coming out. I *should* be speechless. How I managed to maintain any semblance of a conversation was beyond me.

"It's the Order of the Heart," Mimsey said. "Look. I have the other half."

I hesitated, then leaned forward as Mimsey opened her palm. In her hand lay a gold covering in the shape of a heart. It looked to be the same size and shape as my open locket, as if it would fit snugly over the top.

"May I?" Mimsey clasped my necklace with her other hand. "It's a rite of passage."

"May you what?" I peered closer at the gold piece of jewelry in her palm. "What is a rite of passage?"

"The Order of the Heart is an old witching tradition." Trinket stepped forward from her place by the door. "It goes back hundreds of thousands of years, beginning with the first colony of witches and wizards, led by none other than Hecate."

"Hecate? She's a myth."

Trinket shook her head. "Not a myth, though that's what we like the normal folk to believe."

"It's just easier if the humans don't know we exist, dear." Mimsey's lips twitched. "They don't understand."

"I'm not human?" My voice was a ghost of its former self.

"You're a witch!" Mimsey's laugh tinkled throughout the bar, dancing off the rows of pint glasses and beer boots hanging from the ceiling racks. "That's what we've been telling you."

"The Order..." I fingered my necklace, stepping back from Mimsey. "I don't understand."

"I was telling you before you got all skittish," Trinket said, her sour expression growing deeper. "If you'd just listen."

"I'm listening." I perched on a bar stool, thinking it'd be better if I sat down during this explanation.

"The first witch had a necklace. A locket in the shape of a heart, much like yours," Trinket began. "Except she had both pieces; she'd been given it as a protective charm. The necklace kept her safe, and as long as she wore it, nobody could hurt her."

I swallowed, glancing at Jesse to see how he was taking the news. In short, he wasn't. It appeared he'd begun pulling a draft beer then never stopped. The pint glass sat under the tap while beer overflowed all over the counter.

I cleared my throat, gesturing to the ocean of Bud Light Jesse was creating. He leapt to attention, shutting off the tap and scurrying to grab a rag. He wiped up the mess while whistling and pretending not to listen. Judging by the fact that he ran the washcloth over the same place thirty times in a row, he was hanging onto every word.

Trinket cleared her throat, giving Jesse a disapproving stare before continuing. "This witch had a child. A little girl. And when that baby was born…"

Mimsey fanned herself, her face wet with tears. "This story makes me emotional every time."

"Get a grip, sister," Trinket said, her voice clipped. "You've heard this story a million times."

Trinket, with her stoic face and stiff demeanor, was the exact opposite of her sibling. Whereas Mimsey resembled a cushy bean bag chair with a joyful smile and a warm embrace, Trinket was a dead ringer for a principal I'd had in elementary school—a severe woman who'd worn a gray bun so tight I had worried her brain cells would die an early death. She dressed in all black day in and day out and carried a cane around school that she used to knock students on the knees more than she used it to walk.

Mimsey took a shuddering breath. With a dramatic flourish, she swallowed and waved a hand. "Go on then."

Trinket straightened her shoulders. "When her daughter was born, the first witch felt as if her heart had split in two—part of her heart remained inside her, and part of it would always be with her daughter. She felt raw, exposed, and though she wanted to protect her daughter every minute of every day, she soon realized that was impossible."

Mimsey's gaze softened. "Most children want to grow wings and fly."

"As they should," Trinket said, her voice dry. "All children grow up."

"I don't understand what the necklace has to do with anything."

"The first witch decided to split her heart locket. She knew that if she broke her charm in half, the spell that protected her would be diminished. She'd no longer be invincible. For so long, she'd been the only witch alive. Never reproducing and kept safe by this spell." Trinket stepped forward. "When she separated the locket, she broke the spell."

"She passed away?" I asked.

"Not immediately." Trinket shook her head. "She gave half to her daughter and kept half for herself so that they'd always be linked. They'd both be partially protected, but neither would be invincible."

"Which is how our culture came to be." Mimsey turned back to me. "May I?"

I glanced down as Mimsey's fingers brushed against my collarbone. Inhaling, I held my breath as she pressed her half of the heart to my necklace and paused before she snapped it into place. She looked up, and I gave a nod, not trusting myself to speak. My breath came in uneven bursts as I waited, watched, wondered.

Mimsey's fingers pressed tight, and there was a light *clink* as the two halves snapped into place. As Mimsey stepped backward, my fingers played with the charm, getting used to the feel of a full heart on the end of my necklace.

To my surprise, the charm glowed warm, almost hot.

"Do you feel it?" Mimsey whispered.

I nodded. "What's happening?" I didn't want to pull my fingers from the charm. A warm sensation filled me from the inside out, starting deep in my soul and radiating to the tips of my fingers and the ends of my toes until even my scalp tingled with warmth.

"The spell is locking into place," Mimsey said. "That feeling will only last a few moments."

"If—and this is still a big *if*—I believe you two, then why didn't you give this to me sooner?" I looked between the sisters.

Mimsey sucked in a breath while Trinket glanced at the floor.

"What is it?" I pressed.

"The curse," Mimsey whispered, her voice so soft I had to lean in to hear her.

"What curse?"

"We mustn't speak of it here." Trinket clasped her hands together. "We've done our job, sister. We've determined that she is, in fact, the next Mixologist. We've enacted her Protection. Now we must leave. Lily, are you coming with us?"

"The way you're asking, it doesn't feel like I have a choice," I said.

"Without you, dear, our entire culture is endangered. Already, it's begun," Mimsey said. "It's begun, dear."

"What's begun?" I looked at Jesse, not sure I liked where this was headed.

I was plenty happy with my non-dangerous marketing life, to be completely honest. Witches and nonsense—it was too much. I hadn't had time to process anything, yet there I was, standing with two women who were certifiably *bonkers* and talking about witches as if such a thing actually existed. I really did need a vacation.

"I think I'm staying right here," I said. "I'll look for a new job, wake up tomorrow, and realize all of this was a dream."

"I'm afraid not," Mimsey said. "Please, consider coming with us."

"Or don't," Trinket added. "It doesn't matter. You'll come with us whether you want to or not."

I narrowed my eyes. "Do I have a choice or not?"

"You *do*," Mimsey said as Trinket snapped, "You *don't*."

"And how do you plan on making me come with you?" I crossed

my arms, feeling a surge of confidence as I surveyed the two old ladies, one tall and slender, the other short and pudgy. Surely I could outrun these two women.

Trinket, however, must have thought otherwise. She raised a hand, muttered something, and snapped her fingers. All at once, every single tap behind the bar turned on, flooding the counter, the floor, the drains with beer. All sorts of liquor bottles flew into the air, clanking into one another. I ducked, barely missing a bottle of vodka flying past my head. The bottle of liquor met a sharp ending as it crashed into the wall, the heavy glass cracking and depositing its contents on the floor.

Trinket murmured something else, and a ribbon of fire shot up as the vodka hit the floor, surrounding the woman but somehow not burning her. I stood, my mouth agape, my heart racing, as Trinket stared back at me. With the flames dancing around her figure, she looked more like the devil than a witch.

"Stop it, stop it!" Mimsey shouted, snapping her fingers. She spoke a few sentences too quickly for me to catch, waving her arms as if directing a world-famous orchestra.

The taps shut off, the bottles returned to their shelves, and the flames disappeared just as quickly as they'd come. Even the counter was spotless, no sign of the war that'd just erupted.

"Sorry about that, dear." Mimsey shuffled over to Jesse, who was dripping with alcohol. His drenched clothes were the only remaining sign of the disaster flying through the bar seconds before. "Now, Trinket, we're going to have to use a Memory Magnet on him. Do you know how much *paperwork* that is?"

"Our niece wasn't cooperating." Trinket, though her voice remained firm, averted her eyes with a sheepish expression. "What *should* I have done?"

"I'm not forcing Lily to come live with us," Mimsey snarled.

Even Trinket, with her stuffy, humorless personality, looked a bit terrified.

Mimsey pointed in Trinket's direction. "You have *no right* to threaten our sister's daughter. How dare you?"

To my complete and utter surprise, Trinket's cheeks turned red. "I'm sorry."

"You better be." Mimsey crossed her arms, huffing as she turned back to Jesse. She whispered another phrase, touched Jesse's shoulder, and *poof!* Jesse was dry.

I blinked. "How did you do that?"

"Do you *honestly* not believe in magic yet?" Trinket asked. "You're being unreasonable."

"*Trinket!*" Mimsey positively roared. "Use your manners. The girl has spent twenty-six years thinking she's human. It's not going to happen in a second. We're already lucky she didn't throw us out."

"Magic?" I said weakly, still in shock.

"Magic." Mimsey turned to me, placing her hands on my shoulders. "Now, the choice is yours. We both desperately want you to return to The Isle with us, even if my *sister* doesn't know how to show it."

I focused on inhaling and exhaling and trying to listen to the words I found impossible to believe.

"Our people need your services. *However,* we will not threaten you. You *must* decide for yourself if you'd like to join us. To be part of the culture you were born into." Mimsey's eyes implored me to agree.

"I was born here in St. Paul," I said after a pause.

Mimsey shook her head. "No, you were born on The Isle, darling."

"But my dad…" My back stiffened. "Wait a minute. My dad, does he know?"

"*Hmm,* how to put this…" Mimsey began.

"It's complicated," Trinket said, the shortness still prevalent in her words. "Now, your decision?"

I twisted to look at Jesse and realized he wouldn't be helping me anytime soon. His eyes darted between the three of us, his expression as dazed as if he'd been knocked on the head with a brick.

"Let me take care of him," Trinket said. With brisk steps, she strode across the room and removed a pencil from her purse. Or at least, something that resembled a pencil. When she reached Jesse, she grabbed his arm. "Hold still, boy. This won't hurt."

"Stop!" I cried, leaping toward Jesse as Trinket lifted the pencil and pressed the eraser to the center of Jesse's forehead.

"It doesn't hurt him, dear," Mimsey said, grasping my waist and holding on with the full force of her plump body. Though I was younger and arguably more agile, I found myself stuck in place, running as if I had a bungee cord tied to my waist. "Hold still, dear. It doesn't *hurt*!"

"What does it do?" I stopped struggling, but Mimsey didn't let go of me.

Taking hold of my biceps instead of my waist, she held me steady, gesturing toward Jesse. "She's just erasing any memories of magic."

Jesse's eyes remained open, staring straight at me with a blank, unseeing gaze. My spine prickled with the eerie sensation of being watched. But Jesse didn't move as he looked intently at a memory nobody else could see.

"It's literally an eraser?" I asked, looking around for another pencil. "I never knew a number two pencil was so powerful."

"No, of course not, dear. It's enchanted with a spell. We witches try to enchant things that don't look out of place in human culture. Things like lipstick cases, necklaces—"

"Pencils," I finished. "Huh."

"We run a supply store on The Isle," Mimsey said, hopefulness lacing her voice. "Would you like to come see it?"

I gasped, ignoring her question as Jesse sagged against the bar. Trinket—thin, bony arms and all—somehow managed to drag him onto a stool.

"Do witches have superhuman strength?" I asked. "Jesse is not a small guy."

"A bit." Mimsey sounded distracted. "Trinket, are you finished? We can't hang around all day. Someone will wander in for a drink soon enough. We should be off."

Trinket gave a nod.

Mimsey straightened. "Well, then. Lily?"

I opened my mouth, then I shut it. Then I opened it again. I closed it again as Chunk crawled out from one of Mimsey's pockets. I'd completely forgotten about the guinea pig, what with bottles flying around, fire shooting up the walls, and my friend being knocked unconscious by a pencil.

Mimsey stroked her pet's fur absently. "We need an answer. I don't know the next time we'll be able to come back."

"I can't get there on my own?" I asked.

"Yes or no, are you coming with us?" Trinket asked, her voice flat. "There is no other way."

"But—" I hugged my body as I backed up against the counter.

My mind raced. The scariest thought of all? I was considering going with them. I shivered, wondering what I'd done wrong for Karma to come after me. I'd lost my job, encountered two crazies, and gone off my own rocker—all in one day. I didn't believe in things like witches and wizards. And even if I *did,* there was no way I was one of them.

As much as I liked to believe I was an important, successful twenty-something, I still *knew* there wasn't anything particularly special about me. I worked hard, did my job, and I got promoted. It wasn't magic. *Magic didn't exist.*

So why were my instincts telling me these two women weren't lying? *Why am I listening to them when I don't know them from the homeless guy down the street?* I could blame it on the flying bottles trick, the snapping of their fingers and muttering of strange phrases. I could blame it on the eraser-dealie-bob or the whole necklace warming to the touch. Heck, I could blame the strange happenings of the PowerPoint on them. At least then something would make sense.

"Hey!" I raised my eyes from where I'd been staring at the floor. "Did you two ruin my presentation this morning?"

Mimsey shook her head at the same time Trinket nodded.

"It was you." I pointed an accusatory finger at them. "Why would you do that?"

"We thought you'd come back with us if you had nothing to live for here." Mimsey cringed. "We wanted to make your decision easier."

I shook my head. "I worked all my life for that presentation. You've ruined my whole life."

"I'm sorry about the side effects—" Mimsey started.

"Lily." Trinket stepped forward and rested her hand on my shoulder. "Mimsey is a nice woman. She sugarcoats things."

Mimsey nodded.

"I'm not nice." Trinket's fingers dug into my shoulder like talons. "So listen up and listen closely. I don't repeat myself."

Trinket's gaze held mine so firmly that I found myself nodding.

"You have the potential for so much more." Trinket's grip tightened as if it were difficult for her to administer such a compliment. "In the scheme of things, your presentation should be but a mere blip on your radar. It shouldn't be the pinnacle of your success. Your life is *sad* if that is what you live for."

My jaw hung open. "That's... that's mean."

"*Trinket!*" Mimsey stepped forward, shaking her head. "What she's trying to say is that you're talented, dear. You were born for so much more than a job in marketing."

"That is exactly what I said," Trinket said, her tone annoyed.

"Well, not *exactly*." Mimsey tilted her head while disagreeing with her sister. "Your words were a bit harsher."

"My words weren't *harsh*, were they?" Trinket turned to me, her eyes burning furiously.

I cleared my throat. "Just a tiny bit."

"Well, I don't understand what's harsh about me getting a fire under your petunia. You have potential to do great things, Lily Locke. You have the potential to save lives. To change reality for many people." Trinket shook her head. "This little marketing job is nothing. It doesn't love you back."

Mimsey burst in. "It doesn't reward you with hugs or kisses. Not like a child, not like a grandmother, not like the family you have waiting for you on The Isle."

"Family?" I asked. That idea had always been an elusive one to me.

"*We* are your family," Mimsey said. "We have children, your cousins. The Isle has all sorts of *your* kind. Consider our proposal, dear."

I breathed deeply and debated.

"Jesse, what should I—" Glancing at the bartender, I stopped at his surprised gaze.

"Who is Jesse?" Pointing at me, Jesse pursed his lips. "And who are *you*?"

"What did you do to him?" I asked.

"The confusion fades in a few minutes." Mimsey shifted from one foot to the other. "And we need to be out of here before Jesse comes back to himself, or we'll have to redo the procedure, and if you do it too many times—"

"They start to go a little crazy," Trinket finished. "So?"

"Two questions." I crossed my arms. "If I don't like it on The Isle, may I come back?"

"Yes, but—"

Trinket held up her hand and cut off her sister. "Enough. We can't spill our secrets until she's one of us, Mimsey. We've already said enough. *Yes*, that's the short answer. You can return."

I briefly wondered about the long answer, but as Trinket didn't seem inclined to elaborate, I moved on. "Do I have time to say good-bye to my father? What about Ainsley?"

The sisters looked uncomfortably at one another.

"No," Trinket said. "Not now."

"But what if he worries?" I asked.

"We've taken care of that." Mimsey's lips parted as if she looked surprised at herself. "We used a Writing Replicator charm to mimic your handwriting and sent him a note. It says you aren't working for Lions Marketing any longer and mentions that you're taking a few months off to travel and will write to him when you return. As for Ainsley... you'll see her again. This isn't good-bye for you two."

"But why would you do that?"

"We can't risk you coming into contact with another human at the moment. You're aware of our world now, but you don't yet understand why we keep ourselves secret. That's a dangerous combination." Mimsey wrung her hands. "Of course after some training and orientation, you'll be able to come and go between The Isle and the rest of the world as you see fit."

I blinked. "That doesn't sound so bad."

Mimsey shook her head. "It's not. Not in the slightest."

I had a zillion reasons not to go with Mimsey and Trinket. Things like finding a new job, paying rent, figuring out how to afford my grocery bill. Things like not wanting to leave my friends or the one family member I had left.

But I couldn't push away the nagging feeling in my stomach that asked *What's the point?* of unfulfilling work. Sure, I could go get another marketing gig. But how many people would I be helping?

I wondered what the sisters meant when they said I'd have the potential to help others improve their lives. Even more than that, I wondered what they meant about having a family. Because the thought of having someone to love me back sounded incredible. A dream come true. After years of being on my own, living with my dad, a man with fewer emotions than a turtle, I wanted relationships that lived and breathed. I wanted to feel things that made me cry with joy and weep with sadness. I wanted it all.

And for that reason and that reason alone, I nodded.

"I'll go." My voice, somewhat resigned, belied the tiny spark of excitement leaping to life in my stomach. "I'll go with you, assuming it's understood that I can come and go from The Isle in time."

Mimsey nodded furiously. "Of course. Of course, dear."

Trinket let out a rattling breath. "*Thank you.* We need your services more than you know."

The three of us stood in a bit of an awkward silence, alternating between watching each other and looking at the floor.

Eventually, I looked up. "Shall we?"

Mimsey burst into tears, startling Trinket and I so much so that we both flinched.

"What's wrong?" I asked.

"It's just..." Mimsey rushed forward, tucking her guinea pig onto her shoulder. She brushed a stray hair from my face. "It's *you*. My beautiful niece." Her lips parted as she surveyed my face. "We've waited so long to see you."

My insides warmed, and to my dismay, the unfamiliar prick of tears in my eyes startled me. I hadn't cried in *years*. There'd been nobody to comfort me and, therefore, no reason to cry.

But her gentle touch, the kindness in her eyes... I started wondering. *Maybe my mother is still alive. Out there. Looking for me.* I pushed away my tears, hid my excitement, and set my zillion and one burning questions on the back burner for now.

"Oh, cut the crap," Trinket said. "This meeting has enough gooiness to make a... what do you call it, those sticky candies you humans make over a bonfire?"

"S'more?" I said.

"Yes. So sweet it's making me sick to my stomach." Trinket shook her head.

"Is that you?" Jesse leaned over the bar, squinting in my direction as he interrupted the conversation. "Is that you, Lily? Why do you look funny?"

"You don't look funny." Mimsey patted my arm. "Not really."

"Hey—" I started to argue.

"That's our cue," Mimsey said. "Off to The Isle!"

CHAPTER 4

"YOU COULDN'T HAVE SNAPPED YOUR fingers to get us there or something?" I asked, shifting uncomfortably in the bus seat. "My rear end is *very, very* sore."

"I'm a firm believer in doing things the long way at least once before we go taking shortcuts," Mimsey said. "Otherwise, you don't appreciate the shortcut half as much."

"This is a very long anti-shortcut," I mumbled.

We'd been riding through Minnesota for the last five hours. We caught the last bus out of the Cities and rode straight north for ages. I glanced out the window, noting the surroundings that had changed from the concrete of downtown Minneapolis to sprawling suburbia, with all its manicured lawns, residential homes, and children running about as school let out.

Now as the sun set, I tried to find a comfortable spot in my seat. Despite my aching body, I couldn't ignore the beauty of the North Shore. Greenery spanned as far as the eye could see—treetops stretched around the curling edges of Lake Superior while bushes, shrubbery, and grass lined the sides of the highways, making every turn in the road a luxurious sight.

All of this lush greenery was new for me. I'd grown up in this state, and I'd even gone camping once or twice. However, my dad had never been a proponent of father/daughter trips, which meant that most of my childhood had been in the Cities, surrounded by small patches of green, the type that grew between the cracks on the sidewalk. This, up here, was new territory.

"It's beautiful," I said. "So much life up here."

Mimsey shivered. "I think it's rather chilly. I'm not used to it."

"Don't you live on The Isle?" I asked. "If it's up here, you should be used to it."

"The Isle has a different climate," Mimsey said. "You'll see. We'll be at the launch in thirty minutes."

Thirty minutes. Thirty minutes until I'm officially signing over my foreseeable future to these ladies claiming to be my aunts. I must be going nuts.

Thirty minutes later, however, the tingle of excitement was undeniable. I'd never embarked on such an adventure. I'd gone to school, enrolled in enough extracurricular activities to get into college, then I'd garnered a job like a good girl. I certainly wasn't unique. I certainly wasn't special. But it was fun for a change to believe I might be different.

"Stop daydreaming, girl." Trinket snapped her fingers. "Take this."

I extended a hand, and she pressed something mushy into my palm.

"What is this?" I looked at the gummy bear in my hand. "A snack? I'm not really hungry."

"Of course not," Trinket snapped. "It's a Stopper. We'll exit via the restroom."

"What's a Stopper?" I shook my head. "I don't think I like the sound of that. And I definitely don't like the sound of exiting via the bathroom."

"Oh, honey. You don't think we get off at a regular bus stop, do you?" Mimsey gave a kind smile. "The Stopper allows us to get off the bus... unannounced."

"Through the toilet?" I raised my eyebrows.

"Well, we can't vanish in plain sight, can we?" Trinket asked, her voice cross. "One at a time. I'll go first, then you, Lily. Mimsey can follow to make sure nobody is left behind."

Before I could argue, the two sisters shuffled me toward the back of the bus. I didn't know how they planned to be discreet, since they were dressed like two theater majors let loose on the costume closet after splitting a bottle of wine. Bright, flashy colors, overbearing patterns, hats so huge they barely fit down the aisle—the women did not know how to dress to blend in.

"*Sorry, dear—*"

"*Whoops! Your coffee there, my apologies—*"

"*Move your foot, please—*"

The two ladies bumbled through the bus, inconveniencing absolutely every person they passed. I eventually stopped trying to hide my amusement as I watched Mimsey turn to apologize to one person and knock the guy behind her with an elbow. Then Trinket stepped on a businessman's foot, and when she turned to apologize, she bumped someone else.

The cycle went on for each row of passengers. By the time we reached the back of the aisle, the bus was filled with grumbling, disgruntled passengers.

"Good job being discreet," I said, unable to keep the huge grin off my face.

"They make these dang things so tiny," Mimsey said. "Trinket, I need fresh air. Let's get going."

Without a word, Trinket moved past us into the small one-person restroom. She closed the door but didn't lock it, the little notification always saying Vacant.

"Well, she's not going to lock it, is she?" Mimsey said before I could ask. She must've watched me read the sign over and over. "Otherwise how would you get in? Speaking of, you're up."

A pop as soft as a tiny Fourth of July snapper went off, and I felt my face pale. "Does that mean it's my turn?"

"Yes, of course."

"Okay," I said, my voice squeaky. "What do I do, shove it up my nose?"

"Eat it!"

"Eat it?"

"Yes, yes. Hurry, we only have a certain stretch of highway for this to work correctly." Mimsey nearly shoved me into the bathroom and shut the door. "Now, dear. *Gobble it up!*"

Before I could give myself time to second-guess anything, I popped the gummy bear-looking thing into my mouth, chewed for a second, and swallowed.

I crinkled my nose, the familiar sugary taste not quite right. "That's not a gummy beaaa—"

Before I could finish my sentence, the *snapping* sound went off again, but this time it sounded distant, as if in another room. Something tugged behind my belly button, twisting my insides. It didn't hurt, but everything inside me felt uncomfortable. My ribs felt out of whack, my legs turned to rubber, and my head filled with so much pressure it could've been a balloon.

I barely had time to close my eyes before my feet landed on firm ground, my head spinning so fast I had to sit down.

"First-time jitters," Trinket said, not an ounce of sympathy in her voice. "Are you going to puke?"

I didn't answer. Mostly because I felt like puking.

"Eat this," Trinket said, handing over another gummy bear, this one green. The first one had been red. "It'll help the nausea."

I shook my head. If I so much as opened my mouth, I was worried that everything I'd eaten today would end up on the ground.

A second later, and another *snap* announced the arrival of Mimsey.

"First-time jitters?" Mimsey asked, more to Trinket than me.

"I think so, but she's not talking," Trinket said.

"Give me a minute," I grunted, hardly moving my lips.

"I tried to give her the antidote, but she refused." Trinket shook her head. "Prideful girl."

Mimsey sat next to me, rubbing my back. "You don't need

medicine. Just take deep breaths. You're close enough to The Isle that it should have a relaxing effect on you."

"Why would that *place* relax me?" My voice came out a moan as waves of nausea shot through my body. "It's done nothing for me but cause trouble so far."

"Because you're coming home. Doesn't home calm everyone?" Mimsey looked off into the distance, distracted by something I couldn't see.

I focused on the low *whoosh* of the waves against the shore. Eventually my heartbeat slowed, my stomach settled, and I was able to glance around at the beautiful northern settings. I looked up, hyper-aware that everything here felt… *fresh*.

The air, crisp and cool, brought out images of autumn bonfires and nights spent cozied underneath a blanket. Still, the waning September sun warmed my skin as it descended below the horizon, which in itself was a magnificent thing.

Lake Superior spanned as far as I could see, and I understood why it might be called a *great* lake. The water sparkled and glittered under the sun, the blue so deep and dark it mesmerized me in a dangerous way.

The trees had begun to change to their fall colors, the leaves turning bright yellows, deep reds, and oranges so pure I felt as if I might just be the first person to ever see these sights. My lungs breathed in the clean air, and somehow, my shoulders relaxed. My breathing came easier when my mind was no longer plagued with worries, thoughts, fears. Sure, it was a little odd that I'd eaten a gummy bear and been deposited on the side of the road, but somehow that didn't bother me all that much. In fact, I'd never felt more alive.

"It's beautiful," I said finally.

Mimsey and Trinket turned to me.

"You're feeling better, dear?" Mimsey asked. "I'm surprised; you had a quicker recovery than most."

I nodded, pulling myself to my feet.

"Perfect. Now let's go find that boat. I *told* him to be here," Mimsey said. "Do you see him?"

"If that man is one second late, I'm reporting him," Trinket declared, crossing her arms. "We really do need a more reliable Guide."

"A Guide?" I asked.

"The only witch or wizard on The Isle qualified to connect the human world with the magical world," Mimsey explained. "Basically, there's only one way to The Isle that doesn't require magic."

"And it's a boat?" I asked.

Mimsey nodded.

Pointing over her shoulder, I frowned. "It's not *that* boat, is it?"

Trinket sighed. "Yes, that's the one."

I changed my mind right there on that spot. "I'm not getting on that boat."

I'm not sure what I expected—maybe a speedboat or a luxury cruiser, something to impress the newcomers. Anything would be better than the boat bobbing near the shoreline, a run-down dinghy that looked as if it might collapse at any second.

"I'd rather paddle out to The Isle by myself. In a bathtub. Using my hands as paddles," I said, stepping backward. "You guys couldn't have splurged for a pontoon? Honestly."

"It's uh…" Mimsey struggled to look for a word. "It's safe enough."

"If that's supposed to make me feel better, it doesn't." I crossed my arms. "You're not getting me on there."

Trinket turned her no-nonsense gaze at me. "Either you get on that boat, or you start walking back home. The bus doesn't stop here. Trust me, it's a *long* stroll."

I glanced up and down the highway in deep contemplation. But I had no clue how far the nearest town was, and the sun had nearly disappeared, now an orange halo above the land, fighting the oncoming darkness. I'd be sure to freeze in the chilling night winds.

I sighed a long, loud sigh. "Fine. Do you have an extra life jacket?"

"A life jacket?" Mimsey blinked. "What on earth is that?"

I closed my eyes, wondering why on earth I'd ever agreed to follow these ladies to a mysterious, magical island in the middle of Lake Superior.

CHAPTER 5

"HE DOESN'T TALK MUCH," MIMSEY whispered, patting my knee. She nodded toward the back of the sorry excuse of a boat.

Somewhere between a glorified canoe and a flimsy dinghy, the contraption was just big enough to seat Mimsey, Trinket, and I through the center, while the captain sat at the back. I huddled against the wind, still dressed in my pencil skirt and white blouse, though my chignon had disintegrated into a straggly bun, and my appearance might be described as haggard at best.

"What's your name?" I asked through chattering teeth.

The captain's eyes barely flicked in my direction before he looked forward once more. His brown hair stood on end, the wind rippling through it as he increased the speed at which we flew across the water. He had a baby face, round and a bit pudgy. His cheeks were tinged a ruddy red.

"He won't speak to you," Trinket said, her voice as chilly as the night air. "Just leave him be."

"Is he a witch, er—wizard?" I felt bad speaking about the man when he was right behind us.

"I suppose so. Nobody quite knows anything about his past, dear." Mimsey gave a shrug. "He just showed up one day. Never said a word that I know of."

"Do you have a name?" I asked, my voice soft as I looked at the captain. Then I realized why the silence seemed so heavy out here on the water—the distinct sound of a boat's motor was missing. I filed that tidbit of information away to ask about later, along with a hundred other questions. For now, I sat, waiting to see if the captain would respond.

He heard me—I was certain he heard me. The man's ears burned red, and his eyes twitched once more in my direction before refocusing on the now-choppy waves ahead.

"We call him Kenny," Mimsey said.

"Is that his name?"

She shrugged. "Might be. He's never told us anything different. Someone started calling him that, and it just kind of stuck."

I had so many questions for him, but I suspected not many of them would be answered—at least not by him. *How did he get here?* Had he, like me, grown up in the non-magic world?

I was struck with the realization that magic had become real to me. I'd seen, beyond a shadow of a doubt, unexplainable things today. From the lion coming to life on my PowerPoint, to the vodka bottles nearly breaking my skull, to Jesse going from drenched to dry to losing his memory in a matter of moments, I was running out of reasons not to believe. If magic *wasn't* the answer, then it was an elaborate stunt. And don't even get me started on the whole "popping off a bus" trick.

Ironically, magic was a more reasonable explanation than a stunt. I didn't have a single person in my life who knew me well enough, or cared enough, to plan a stunt. Not out of love, not for fun and games, not even out of spite. I lived such an isolated life—focused solely on work—that I hardly had *enemies.*

My jaw, locked tight to stave off the chattering, was aching from the tension. "How much longer? I'm going to die from cold."

"Sorry, dear, use this." Mimsey handed me a blanket that resembled a ragged beach towel.

"What am I supposed to do with this?" I held it up, the flimsy material flapping in the wind.

"Put it over your shoulders." Mimsey smiled. "It'll help."

Skeptical, I shrugged the flimsy material over my shoulders and pulled it tight around my neck. Relief from the biting breeze was immediate. Surprised, I smiled at Mimsey. "This blanket is incredible. It's magic."

Mimsey averted her eyes, shifting uncomfortably. "It's not *all* magic. It's just *enhanced*."

I bit my lip, holding back a laugh. "I meant it as a saying, but well, that makes a lot more sense."

"Almost there. Can you bring us right 'round to the beach?" Trinket asked.

Kenny didn't respond, but he made a minor adjustment to the steering thingamajig, which I guessed pointed us toward an unseen beach.

"By the way, does this thing have a motor?" I asked, gripping the sides of the boat as Kenny continued to accelerate. We were flying so fast, I wondered if the bottom of the boat was even touching the water.

"No," Mimsey said.

She didn't bother to elaborate, and I didn't have time to ask.

"Watch..." I gasped. "*Watch out!*"

Ahead, the waves grew in size, the white caps nearly overtaking our tiny boat with every swell. We pushed on ahead with no end in sight, each crash bigger than the last. Soon, I'd become so drenched by the spray that the blanket was worthless. My knuckles turned a sickly white as I grasped the edges of it so tightly I thought my fingers would fall right off.

"Sit down, dear," Mimsey called above the roar of the great lake. "Just relax. This is normal."

"We're going to die," I yelled, regret plaguing my body. I should have insisted I be allowed to say *hasta la vista* to my father before trekking across the country with two nutcases. And now I was about to meet my end while sitting next to two witches and a mute.

"Get a grip on yourself, woman," Trinket commanded. "Sit down and relax."

"But…" I couldn't bring myself to finish the sentence. Instead, I raised my arm, my entire body trembling, and I pointed ahead, gasping. "There."

Mere feet in front of us, a wave curled into a perfect tunnel. It loomed before us, the momentum carrying it forward just as Kenny cranked the throttle and urged us directly toward it. The steady roar of the angry water deafened me, sucking my screams straight from my lips.

As the wave grew higher, the pit in my stomach sank. Ten feet, twelve feet, sixteen now, easy. Bits of seaweed dotted the wall of water as the top, tipped in white, curled around our boat.

This was the end.

CHAPTER 6

I HAD NO CLUE HOW LONG the blackness lasted.

But I knew the darkness began when the wave hurled over our little boat, and I knew it ended when I opened my eyes some time later.

I opened one eye slowly, just to test. I had no gauge as to how long I'd been out, how I'd managed to stay alive, or how much water I'd ingested. Taking the tiniest peek imaginable, I tried to get a feel of my surroundings.

The glimpse through my lashes told me that wherever in the world I might be, it was bright outside. Sunlight streamed down and poked me hard in the eyeball. I shut my lid again, leaned my head back on a pillow—*whose pillow?*—and rested.

Outside somewhere, birds chirped lilting, happy songs that improved my mood immediately. The sound of gentle waves relaxed my tense shoulders, the aftermath of a tussle with the lake. A light sway nearly put me back to sleep, but as I didn't feel dead and this place didn't appear terrible, I forced myself to sit up.

Except sitting up wasn't as easy as I expected. "*Whoaaa!*"

Rope ties encircled me, holding my body captive. The contraption jolted me to and fro as I tried to steady myself. I set my feet down, but they missed the ground, and I flopped in a heap, realizing too late that I wasn't in a trap. Just a hammock. Which I should have guessed, thinking back to the gentle sway that'd lulled me to consciousness.

"What're ya, *drunk*?" a deep voice growled. "First night on The Isle, and you can't resist getting schnookered. What a load of dung."

I sat up as an old man mumbled, the *click-clack* of his cane piercing my confused brain as he climbed a nearby staircase.

"Hi." I pulled myself to my feet and laid a hand on the wildly swaying hammock, doing my best to steady it. "And who might you be?"

"You don't ask the questions, *missy*." The man stopped in his tracks, poking me on the shoulder with the end of his cane.

I reached up, more out of surprise than pain, and rubbed my shoulder where he'd clocked me. "I'm sorry, sir. You'll have to excuse me. I'm a little confused."

"Why ya confused?" The man watched me closely, scrunching his nose to push a pair of thick glasses higher onto his face. His hair, coarse and white, was so sturdy it didn't move with the light breeze. The strands coming out of his ears looked just as thick, and a stray hair or two poked out of his nostrils.

"I—I, well, the last thing I remember is a wave crashing over me, then everything went black and, uh… I woke up here." I gestured to the hammock, for the first time taking a moment to absorb the scenery around us.

A white-sand beach stretched in both directions until it curved out of sight. The sand glittered as fiercely as if it'd been ground from diamonds, the glint of the sun reminding me of a snow-covered prairie on a sunny Minnesotan winter day. Palm trees dotted the shoreline, popping up among grassy patches, while the aquamarine water licking the edges of The Isle was a blue so pure it looked like glass.

"This place is gorgeous," I whispered.

"It's all right," the man said gruffly. "But ya didn't come here to sightsee, did ya?"

"I don't know what I came here for, to be honest." I met his gaze, forcing myself not to look away. "I haven't been told much of anything."

"They didn't tell ya nothing?" He looked appalled. "Don't know how I'm supposed to do my job if they dump someone like *you* on my doorstep."

"Someone like me?" I did my best to keep my voice even. Even if my dad hadn't been around much, he'd taught me the power of good manners—something this man had *obviously* never learned.

"You're oblivious. Slow. Clueless." He crossed his arms and leaned against the railing of the staircase. "Some student you'll make."

"Student?" I arched an eyebrow and, for the first time, peered behind me.

The structure there certainly didn't resemble a school. It was a beachy bungalow that looked more along the lines of a B and B on Fiji. The bungalow, for lack of a better word, looked like a gingerbread house. The outside walls boasted pinks and purples and yellows, meeting in corners that held up a slanting roof.

Unlike most beach houses, however, this one was *tall*. Two floors plus an attic tall, the roof towering over the neighboring palm trees. A wraparound porch surrounded the glorified hut, where the hammock on which I'd slept drifted in the easy breeze.

"Unfortunately I'm tasked with teaching you." The man grunted. "Don't worry, I'm not happy about it either."

My stomach sank. I'd given up my entire life for *this?* A crotchety old man who claimed I was more or less stupid?

"You don't have to teach me," I said, stepping backward. "If you could just point me in the direction of Mimsey and Trinket, I'll be out of your way. They were taking care of me up until now."

"As much as I'd like to, I can't. We must get moving. Times are a-changin', and though I hate to admit it, we'll need your skills." The old man frowned. "Get on inside. It's time for our first lesson."

"Lesson in what?" I crossed my arms. "Listen, *sir*. I'm trying to be polite, but I can't help the fact that I'm clueless. I was whisked from my life yesterday, which happened to be *just fine,* thank you very much. Then two witches convinced me that magic was real before they nearly killed me en route to this place. I don't know where I am, what I'm doing here, and I *haven't* had any breakfast. Can I please get some answers?"

"No time—" The man blanched, looking at something over my shoulder.

I turned around. Mimsey was striding across the white sand, her face angry.

"Gus Christopher Shank," she said, puffing heavy breaths as she made her way around the bungalow, "I *told* you the girl hadn't been fed. I *told* you not to come before ten a.m., yet here you are, scaring her away at eight o'clock. What's gotten into you?"

The man called Gus paled, stepping down from the stairs. "Just checking on her."

Apparently I wasn't the only person who thought Mimsey's angry face was terrifying.

"I'm sorry about Gus, dear," Mimsey said, trudging through the last few feet of sand. She stepped onto the bottom stair leading to the porch and, breathing heavily, sized me up. "Did you sleep well?"

"I was dead to the world," I said, glancing around. "Though I'm not sure where in the world we are."

"I'm sorry we didn't explain more. It's terrifying your first time, isn't it? The wave, that is." Mimsey gestured toward the now-calm, crystal-clear waters and climbed the rest of the stairs. "You get used to it."

I scrunched up my nose. "I don't think I want to get used to it."

Mimsey patted my shoulder. "Good. I don't think you'll have to, since this is your home. We hope you won't be leaving."

"Do you live here?" I gestured to the building behind me.

"No, dear. You do. This is *your* home."

"But—" I hesitated. "I didn't bring any money."

"We don't need your money. It doesn't even work here, those flimsy little dollars." Mimsey let out a tinkering, pleasant laugh that lightened the mood. "This home belongs to the Mixologist. See, if you come around to the side…" Mimsey turned and hoofed back down the steps, pausing at the bottom and putting a hand on her hip as she looked over her shoulder. "Come on now, I want to show you something."

I followed her, keeping to the opposite side of the staircase and avoiding Gus as best I could. Tailing Mimsey to the side of the bungalow, I was startled when she stopped abruptly and gestured up.

"This is yours, my dear." Mimsey smiled. "Passed down over generations in your family. *Our* family, I suppose."

Before me stretched a rickety-looking tiki bar tacked onto the side of the house. A crooked sign above the serving area read Magic & Mixology, while a row of circular bar stools sat before the counter.

"You can access it from outside or inside. The first level of the bungalow is a store," Mimsey said. "We only put you to sleep in the hammock last night because fresh air tends to help a newcomer after the wave. The second floor is your living room and kitchen, and the attic is your bedroom. I changed the linens yesterday."

"Thank you," I murmured. "This is incredible."

"You have a great location. Well, mostly great. The dock is right down the beach, so you get all the travelers stopping in for beverages. I live not far away—Trinket and I, we run a supply store just down the road. Just… don't go north. That's dangerous." Mimsey looked uncomfortable even as she gave the warning.

"What's that way?" I looked in the direction I assumed was north, seeing nothing but the curve of the island and a smattering of trees.

"Oh, The Forest. But let's not talk about that now. I'm going to send the girls over later to give you a tour of The Isle. In the meantime, I'm afraid Gus is right—we really should get you started with your lessons. The first week is likely to be orientation mostly, and we need to get you up to speed."

"Lessons for… ? I know how to make drinks. I don't understand why you plucked me out to be a bartender, but I can make all the normal cocktails: gin and tonic, whiskey sour, Sex on the Beach, you name it. But there's nothing special about them."

Mimsey smiled. "You didn't notice it where you come from, dear, but here, we notice your skills. You have Mixology in your blood. Here on The Isle, you'll focus on antidote potions, cures, and specialty spells."

I gawked.

Mimsey ignored my reaction. "Gus is the most experienced instructor we have. If you can see through his cranky exterior, you'll be able to pick up a lot of knowledge."

"Okay," I said, still getting used to this whole *magic is real* thing.

"How about you get started while I cook you some breakfast, then we can take a quick break to eat in an hour?" Mimsey raised her eyebrows. "Can you last that long?"

"Yes, no problem." My stomach, still a bit queasy and seasick, needed time to settle anyway.

"Great, come this way. We'll bring you inside." Mimsey trekked toward the front of the house, her feet kicking up sand like an industrial excavator as we plowed forward.

Gus hadn't moved from his perch. He leaned against the railing of the stairway leading up to the bungalow. "You got your undies unbunched?" Gus asked, looking at Mimsey, his voice low and gravelly. "I'm here as a favor, just tryin' to help."

"Gus, stop being a rude old *ass*." Mimsey got up close and personal with the old man, shaking her finger in his face. "We have to keep Lily here—make her *want* to stay. You're doing a terrible job."

"It's okay," I interrupted, trying to make peace. "Gus is just trying to be up-front with me. I appreciate that."

Gus mumbled an agreement, his face showing surprise.

"Shall we get started?" I asked. "Breakfast is apparently in one hour. I have time to learn a few basics before then."

Gus looked at Mimsey in shock. She raised an eyebrow, her expression saying she was quite pleased with my response.

"Go on." Mimsey patted the instructor on the shoulder. "Better not waste time, or I'll burn your toast. I know you don't like burnt toast, Gussy."

"Don't call me nicknames." Gus pounded his cane with exaggerated thumps as he climbed the staircase. "And don't burn my damn toast."

I smiled to myself, following the pair inside. Though Gus's words came out tough, his whole attitude toward Mimsey was one of genuine affection. He brushed past her a hair closer than necessary. When he looked at her, his eyes belied a twinkle of life that contradicted his words, and when he reached the front of the bungalow, he held the door open for the spritely witch.

"Go on," he said to me once Mimsey had entered. "I'm gonna die soon. Don't got all day to hold this door."

I scurried through.

"Don't say that, you morbid old man," Mimsey called over her shoulder. "I'm burning your toast if you threaten to go dyin' on me one more time today."

"Don't you dare!" Gus shouted after her before turning his fuming eyes on me. "That woman, you watch out for her. She knows how to push your buttons."

"I don't *push buttons*, Gus," Mimsey hollered from the kitchen. "I'm burning your eggs too."

Gus shook his head, leaning in to whisper conspiratorially, "She's bonkers."

I couldn't hide a smile, and instead of responding to the two feuding like cats and dogs, I took the time to absorb the lower level of my new home.

"Don't touch nothin'," Gus warned, seeing me scan the room.

"This is so… dangerous." I turned in a slow circle, examining wall upon wall of glass containers. "One wrong move and…" I made a *kaplooey* motion with my hands.

"That's why I said don't touch nothin'. You've got the best store on The Isle for this stuff. People come from… from as far as the *regular* world to get your goods."

I strolled around the outskirts of the room, trying to take in everything at once. Glass vials filled with tropical blues, greens, and reds took up one shelf, while vases of all shapes and sizes lined another wall, filled to bursting with highlighter pinks, lavender purples, and sunburst yellows so bright I had to squint to see them.

A bucket, also made of glass, contained some sort of mixture that changed color before my eyes, sort of like the lava lamp I'd bought during my teenage years. And that was just the beginning of it all. Cups, bowls, pitchers, shots—all sorts of glass fixtures held gallon upon gallon of liquids in every pastel color and shade of the rainbow.

"What is all this for?" I asked, turning to look at Gus. "All these jars and liquids and everything."

"Stupid question. Try another."

I ignored the old man and continued my stroll along the outskirts of the storeroom. I passed a doorway and quietly twisted the handle to peek inside. It led to the tiki bar.

Closing the door tightly, I continued on to another wall of glass containers. These were thick and sturdy, more like heavy-duty storage bins than fragile vases. They looked like cookie jars filled with all sorts of dried flowers: Rose petals, lilacs, and oregano to name a few.

"So where do we start?" I turned to face Gus, clasping my hands in front of my body.

He blinked. "The beginning."

"Which is?" I looked around for a place to sit. "Where's a good place to set up for training?"

Gus *thunked* over to the door leading to the tiki bar. He pulled it open and gestured toward a stool.

"We have lessons at the bar?" I asked, heading outside. "I could get used to this."

"Sit down."

My feet sank into the sand as I hopped onto a stool. As my toes warmed from the fine grains, I realized that my feet were bare. And that I had on a pale-yellow sundress. I didn't remember changing, which meant someone else might have helped. Talk about a scary thought.

Gus watched as I studied my own appearance. "They used magic. Don't worry, nobody peeked at your knickers. The closet upstairs will be outfitted with clothes to your size and taste. It populates automatically, so if you don't like it, you can change. Simple Styling Spell."

"A whole new wardrobe?" My smile grew. "I really *can* get used to this. New clothes, classes at the bar…"

"*Work.*" Gus stood on the other side of the counter. He reached below it, huffing and puffing as he pulled up a book as thick as ten encyclopedias and plunked it on the bar. Judging by the loud *thud* it made, the thing weighed a ton.

"May I?" Without waiting for a response, I slid the book toward me. It was covered with dust and smelled like a musty old library. I sneezed as I ran a hand along the top of the book.

"Don't ruin it," Gus said, wiping the cover with his sleeve. "It's priceless. And it's *mine*."

The book itself had a cover made of hefty parchment at least half an inch thick. Gold lettering on the front spelled: *The Magic of Mixology.* I turned to the first page and found an inscription. It read:

To the current Mixologist—

Do good.

That was it. No signature. Nothing else.

"Who wrote this?" I asked, gesturing to the handwritten note.

"The first Mixologist." Gus grunted, snapping the book shut. "It's a master list of recipes. Chances you'll need this book much are slim, since you'll inherently understand the combinations. Me, however, I use it all the time. It was gifted to me."

I raised my eyebrow at Gus, then looked back at the inscription. "If this is *yours,* that makes you a Mixologist. Why do you need me then?"

"I'm not *a* Mixologist," Gus said. "Don't you ever say that. You're *The* Mixologist. There's one."

"But the inscription..."

"Fine, maybe the book doesn't *belong* to me technically," he relented. "It was entrusted into my care, and I take that seriously. As for Mixology, that is a power which must run in a person's blood. Me? I'm an assistant. I gathered materials, tested potions, managed the bookkeeping and chores for the previous Mixologist. You'll get to pick your own assistant."

"Can I choose you?" I asked.

Gus looked as if he'd never considered the idea, blinking and turning red. "I, uh... never mind that now." Gus shook his head. "I'll help you 'til you get on your feet, then no doubt you'll want to choose someone else."

I couldn't tell if Gus was disappointed or relieved at the thought. His tone dropped in pitch, and he averted his eyes to the large book between us.

Patting the cover, he eventually met my gaze again. "Like I said, it's in your veins, so you won't need this book. More for me to keep track of everything for you. Only when you get to the powerful stuff will you need the last few

Chapters of the manuscript, but that's years away."

"So if Mixology runs through bloodlines, does that mean the last Mixologist was my mother?" I asked, glancing around at the bar with a newfound perspective. *Did my mother belong to The Isle? If yes, then why did she leave, and how did my father play into the equation?*

"It's complicated." Gus pursed his lips. "The last true Mixologist was your grandfather. He passed away two years ago from old age, peacefully. After that, we had crews searching for the next Mixologist. There were rumors you existed, rumors your mother had taken you to live with the humans, but we didn't know."

"Why didn't you know? It's not like I kept my name a secret."

"The curse." He must've seen a question in my eyes, but he raised a hand to stop me before I could open my mouth. "I can't talk about it more than that. It ain't my place."

"So you went without a Mixologist for the last two years?" I asked.

Gus tilted his head. "Sorta. We had a fill-in, and we called him by the title even though he wasn't the real deal. He didn't have it in his blood. He was talented, but no matter how skilled he became, he wouldn't be able to hold a candle to you. The deal was that as soon as you took over, he'd become your assistant."

I cleared my throat. "When will I meet him? I hope he's not upset that I'm here. I can be the assistant for now, maybe take over in a few years once he's trained me—"

"It don't matter," Gus said. "That's not gonna happen."

I frowned. "Why?"

"He's dead."

"Dead?" My jaw dropped. "Oh my goodness. What happened?"

Gus shook his head and looked down at his fingernails. "Murdered."

CHAPTER 7

"WHAT IF I DON'T HAVE talent?" I asked over breakfast. Gus had refused to go into any more detail about the previous Mixologist's untimely demise, insisting that we get to work. After over an hour of memorizing the names of herbs, plants, and flowers that could be found on The Isle but not in the Twin Cities, I'd needed a break. It was all new to me. And it was very confusing.

For example, Wart Leaf, unlike its name, did not cure warts or curse warts, while a petunia petal had different qualities when used fresh versus dried. If ground into a fine powder, the stuff became deadly. I wondered if the poor Mixologist before me had substituted a Bingle Berry for a Schwarp Buckler on accident, killing himself with deadly fumes. It would certainly be easy enough to do.

"You have talent, dear," Mimsey said, sliding three plates of eggs, bacon, and toast onto the bar. Despite her threats, she *hadn't* burned Gus's toast. "We vetted you before we made the announcement. You have the gift."

"I'm never going to remember all of these herbs," I grumbled. "Never in a million years."

"You'd be surprised." Mimsey smiled. "Now let's finish up. You can have another lesson until lunchtime. Over the lunch break, I'll have the girls give you a tour around The Isle. Then you'll come back for an afternoon lesson."

I sighed. "My brain might explode."

"It seems like a lot now, dear. But it gets easier." Mimsey

squeezed my hand. "The first week is the hardest. Once you get the hang of it, I've heard that being the Mixologist is quite enjoyable."

Gus rolled his eyes.

"Oh, stop it, ya old fart." Mimsey took a bite of toast. "You'd better start enjoying life before you're too old to smack people around with that cane of yours."

Gus shoveled another heaping bite of eggs into his mouth. "Let's git back to class."

"She just started eating, Gus." Mimsey gestured to my nearly untouched plate.

"Oh, it's all right." I took a few quick bites of toast. "My stomach is still unsettled from all that traveling yesterday, anyway."

Gus looked appeased, but when my stomach roared loudly, Mimsey narrowed her eyes at me. "Eat, Lily. Gus can wait five minutes."

I picked up a piece of toast, heaped a spoonful of eggs on top, and set a strip of bacon over the eggs. Wrapping the bread into a taco, I raised it in a salute toward Mimsey. "I'll take this to go. Really, it's delicious. You shouldn't have."

"Apparently not," Mimsey said. "Since I'll be eating alone."

Gus clomped back into the store while I gave her an apologetic expression.

She waved at me as she sat back on the stool and properly cut her bacon with a fork and knife. "I'll be fine, dear. I like to watch the water in the mornings, anyway."

I rushed back into the store. For some reason, I felt the need to impress Gus. The man was rude, bitter, and crass, but I didn't want to let him down.

"This is a precious flower," Gus said, taking up residence at a long table that ran down the center of the room. It appeared to be a measuring, cutting, mixing sort of workshop for raw ingredients. A *Mixologist's Supplies* book lay before him, and Gus tapped the cover.

"Pay attention. It's rare, and we only harvest them once per year on The Isle. We have three left at the moment."

"What is it?" I stepped to the other side of the table, unable to see a flower anywhere.

"We press them for safekeeping." Gus opened the old, weathered book with reverence. "It's called the fleur-de-lis."

The words were written in a language I had never seen before, but it wasn't the words that impressed me. It was the gorgeous bloom, flattened to perfection between the pages. "What did you call it?"

"Fleur-de-lis. It's known for innocence and purity." Gus lovingly stroked the flower's surface. The edges of the bloom glowed a dull white, almost as if it had a halo. "We use it for truth serums, among other things."

Gus's tender touch of the petals filled me with curiosity, and the way he handled the flower with love and care surprised me. I imagined this soft side was one he didn't display for many people. I caught myself staring and quickly looked away. Luckily, he didn't notice me staring; he remained so engrossed in the sheen of the petals that he didn't hear me the first three times I said his name.

"Gus," I said gently for the fourth time. "We have this flower in our world."

He looked up as if surprised I was still around. "I know."

"You know what we call it?" I gave a small, tight smile.

Gus held my gaze as he cleared his throat. "You call it a *lily*. Calla lily."

I bit my lip, uncomfortable with his searching stare. He watched me almost as he had the lily on the table—with interest, as if I were a rare, unique being. I was *anything* but rare—I was so *un*-rare, I bordered on boring.

Feeling a blush redden my cheeks, I turned my attention to the flower. "Will we be working with the fleur-de-lis today?"

"Are you batty?" Gruff Gus returned in a split second. "You're a newbie. I'm not trusting my most precious flower in your hands."

I sighed, almost relieved to have the mean ol' man back.

"You'll be lucky if I let you touch a Stink Bulb," he said, his gravelly words at odds with the gentle way he closed the lily inside the *Mixologist's Supplies* and placed the book high on a shelf. The top level of each shelf brimmed full of books. Other rare flowers were pressed between their pages, if I had to guess. "Sit down."

Gus pulled a chair up to the table and plopped *The Magic of Mixology* in front of me, the golden letters glinting up at me.

"Let's review," he said. "Start over."

"Why don't we learn new things?" I tried my best not to be impatient, but if my job was as important and crucial as everyone thought, then I wanted to get straight to the interesting stuff. Plus, I was itching to stop memorizing names—I'd fall asleep before we reached page fifty in the book.

Gus thought otherwise. Raising his cane, he smacked it a hairsbreadth away from my pinkie finger, shaking the table. "Let's review it… *twice*."

I closed my eyes for a moment, taking a deep breath.

"Do you have anything else to say?" A smirk twisted the corners of Gus's lips, and I could tell he was just *dying* to smack the table and issue me a *third* review.

I shook my head silently.

"*Huh*," he grunted. "Maybe you're not as slow as I thought."

Hiding a small smile, I ducked my head and turned to page one. "*Alohis Morgasetti*, a small, round seed with the hallucinatory properties…"

CHAPTER 8

AFTER A RIGOROUS MORNING SESSION, in which we reviewed the first lesson twice, and finished a second, third, and fourth lesson—all of them more grueling than the last—I was *more* than ready to climb back into my hammock, curl up in a ball, and let the wind lull me to sleep.

I'd worked long hours and many late nights at Lions Marketing, Inc., but I had never been this exhausted—physically, mentally, emotionally. Even my hair sagged. Plus, the salt in the air twisted my locks into wild curls. While normally I would cinch the unruliness back into a bun, I was too tired to raise my arms.

I left my hair down and crumpled up in the hammock to wait out my lunch break, the pale-yellow sundress riding high on my thighs. I was supposed to head on a tour of The Isle, but the chirping of the birds, the splash of the waves, the crispness in the air—all of it got to me, and I fell fast asleep.

Sometime later, I took a deep breath and wondered if everything had been a dream. Maybe I'd wake up at Jesse's bar with a hangover that'd knock me out for days before I'd have to show up at Lions Marketing and grovel for my job back.

But when I sucked in a breath that tasted distinctly salty and felt my body rocking with the steady motion of a hammock, I knew I hadn't made it up. Lying here, the sun warming my face, until…

All at once, the sunlight disappeared and the rocking of the hammock stalled to nothing. My eyes flashed open, my heart pounding.

A face stared down at me—a male face topped with disheveled hair black as a midnight ocean, with eyes to match. They stared at me, and I felt myself tipping, swirling into their depths. I screamed, and my hand came up, swinging a hardcore punch straight to his face. My adrenaline pumped and my palms turned sweaty as I struggled to get my bearings.

Thankfully, the man was quick. Unlike me, he hadn't just awoken from a deep dream, and his fighting moves were less groggy than mine. His hand caught my wrist just millimeters from his nose.

"Who are you?" he asked, his voice a low, soft rumble. "And why the hell are you trying to punch me?"

"Do you make a habit of sticking your nose in strangers' faces as they sleep?" I attempted to wriggle my arm from his grasp, but he held on tight, his grip unforgiving. The best I could manage was to pull myself into a semi-sitting position, uncomfortably folded into a pretzel on the hammock. "What is with people here? Have none of you learned manners?"

A lazy, slow smile overtook his face, turning his already-handsome, deeply tanned visage into a work of art. An imperfect work of art, but nonetheless beautiful. The small scar above his left eye only made him more stunning.

"Manners?" he asked. "You call punching someone before asking their name *manners*?"

"What's your name?" I asked, my sarcasm appearing out of nowhere. "I can punch you again afterward, if that makes it better."

The man's eyes crinkled for a moment, confused, until he threw his head back and laughed. Leaning in, he brushed his lips against my cheek before whispering in my ear, "You can *try*."

"Get away from me," I said, shrinking back. "I still don't know your name."

He finally let go of my arm and backed away until he reached the top of the staircase. He surveyed me, his gaze traveling first from my sea-salt 'fro down to my shoulders, where his eyes lingered on the bare skin.

I self-consciously pulled the sundress straps back up onto my shoulders from where they'd fallen, but not before his gaze traveled down to my legs, which were exposed to mid-thigh, thanks to the breeze. I moved just as fast as I could, trying to pull my dress down to my knees.

But my efforts were in vain. I yanked the fabric toward my knees. But instead of covering my body, the jerking motion flipped the hammock upside down. My arms flailed, searching for firm ground, which I found all too soon. With my face.

Lying smack on the wood, nose pressed into the porch, I groaned. Then a gust of wind sent the edge of my dress sailing up and over my head.

Excellent.

When I managed to get past the embarrassment of flailing like a madwoman, the pain started to hit. I fought my dress down, sat up, and waited to die from mortification.

It didn't happen immediately. And the handsome stud was still there a second later, so instead of facing him, I closed my eyes and willed a gigantic wave to come swallow me whole.

"Go ahead, laugh." I waved, keeping my eyes firmly shut. "Hardy-har."

Silence met my ears.

Mustering up my last ounce of courage, I peeked through one eyelid, seeing nothing but miles and miles of water, a beach, and the steps leading up to the porch. I stood up and moved to the staircase, scanning up and down the beach. No one in sight.

Huh. I shouldn't be surprised he'd disappeared—The Isle was filled with magic of all sorts—but he sort of chose an awkward time to just *leave*. I hated to admit I was a little annoyed. Didn't he like what he saw?

I gasped, holding a hand to my mouth as I realized even I didn't know the answer to that. I'd used the restroom once, but it wasn't as if I'd taken a good long look.

So I did what any sane person would do. I peeked.

"What the heck are you doing?" a female voice asked.

My face flushing red for the zillionth time in the last minute, I let my dress drop back to my knees. "I just…"

"She's *new*, give her a break," a second voice replied. "Cripes, Zinnia. You're so *rude*. What is it with people on this island?"

Two girls stood at the bottom of the staircase, as opposite as opposites could be. Both girls were somewhere around my age, mid-to late-twenties, if I had to guess.

The first voice belonged to a girl who could only be described as dark. Her black hair hung around her chin in a sharp bob, while her cheekbones matched her severe haircut. All angles and pointy features, she looked terrifying in leather pants, smoky eye makeup, and a tight black tank top.

"You're Zinnia?" I asked this badass, rocker-type chick.

She crossed her arms. "Who wants to know?"

The other girl rolled her eyes. "Excuse my cousin. She thinks she's tough. Spoiler alert—she's *not*."

"Am too." Zinnia glared at the other girl.

If Zinnia was all badass dark clothes, hair, and makeup, her cousin was the picture of sunny. Gorgeous blond locks tumbled down her shoulders, bouncing happily as she walked up the stairs. A long, swishy skirt danced about her ankles, covering a one-piece neon-orange bathing suit that showed off her plump physique.

"I'm Poppy, the nice one of the two," she said, extending a hand. "This is our cousin Zinnia, the mean one."

I shook her hand, my face twisting into a confused smile. "Our cousin?"

"Oh, right." Poppy smacked her forehead. "I'm Mimsey's only daughter. Zinnia there, she belongs to Trinket. She's the oldest of seven."

"Your parents are Mimsey and Trinket?" My jaw hung open. "So that means—"

"We're cousins." Poppy nodded, helping me along. "Yep."

"And you..." I looked at Zinnia. "*Six* siblings?"

Zinnia gave an exasperated sigh. "Tell me about it."

"I have a theory that's why she acts all tough, trying to get attention from Auntie Trinket in that herd of children." Poppy pursed her lips. "It's the only explanation."

Zinnia, with a murderous glare, ascended the staircase and gave her cousin a punch on the shoulder.

"Ow!" Poppy cried. Looking over her shoulder at me, she smirked. "I'm just kidding. That didn't hurt. I've got about fifty pounds on Zin the Twig."

Where Poppy was all soft round curves, Zinnia was built from thin, bony features. I fell somewhere in between.

"So we're *related*?" I was still getting used to the idea of having a family. I'd longed for siblings ever since I knew what a sister *was,* but without a mom, that wish had never come true.

"Get used to seeing us around." Poppy enveloped me in a huge hug, a wave of floral perfume drifting pleasantly around us. "Welcome to The Isle. In fact, we're here to give you the official tour."

Still processing all the new information, I managed only to nod.

"What *were* you doing though?" Poppy asked. Lowering her voice, she leaned in close. "Checking your undergarments? I know how that goes. Sometimes I forget if I have on my nice ones or my workin' ones."

"You have working underwear?" Zin asked. "Gross."

"Don't pretend you *don't.*" Poppy rolled her eyes. "Everyone does. Who dresses to look good for work? That's all about comfort. Right, Lily?"

Zin shook her head while my face remained frozen, eyes wide, lips sealed tight.

"See?" Zin said. "You're just weird."

"Yeah, my mom says unique." Poppy grinned. "You know my mom, right? Mimsey?"

"Yes, she's very sweet. She made me breakfast this morning. In fact, she might still be here." I glanced behind me, but the bungalow appeared empty. "Are you hungry?"

"Yeah, I'm ravenous." Poppy peered over my shoulder. "Whaddya got in there?"

"You just ate!" Zin crossed her arms. "And Mother said we only have an hour to do the tour before Lily has to get back to work, so we should really get started."

"I would love to see The Isle," I admitted as Poppy squeezed past me and peered through the windows into the store. "If that's okay with you two."

"Of course it's okay. And Poppy is *always* ravenous, so that's normal." Zin's lips flattened into a straight line. "Let's *go*."

"Fine." Poppy straightened. "Where to first?"

"I haven't seen anything yet." I shrugged.

"Follow me." Zin stormed off, her black everything contrasting against the white sand.

I wondered how she didn't sweat to death in all that leather and latex.

"She puts on a tough show," Poppy whispered as we followed Zin. "But her bark is louder than her bite. Literally."

"Not funny," Zin called over her shoulder. "Just because your *bite* is worse than mine at the moment doesn't mean it'll always be that way. Just you wait…"

"She's mad because she can't control her forms yet." Poppy shook her head. "*Slacker.*"

"I'm not a slacker!" Zin turned to me, her face so white she looked nearly transparent. Ghostly white. Which reminded me…

"Are you guys witches like your moms?" I asked.

Poppy snorted. "No."

Zin spoke through gritted teeth. "Neither of us is a witch, which is why there's no hope for us taking over the Mixology business. They had to bring you in for that."

"So human, then?" I asked.

"Nope, not that either," Poppy said. "But this game is fun. Guess again."

I looked between the two. "Really, this magic stuff is all new to me. I have no idea."

"Sure, you do." Poppy poked my shoulder as we walked down the beach. "Think of all the books you read."

"I mostly read mysteries," I said. "Featuring humans."

"Fairy tales, then," Poppy said.

I thought back to all my fairy tales, but except for the witch in *Hansel and Gretel*, I was drawing a blank. Biting my lip, I ran through a list of supernatural creatures. "Fairies?"

Zin wrinkled her nose in distaste.

"Elves?" I asked.

Poppy stopped, putting her hands on her hips. "Do I *look* like an elf to you?"

"No, but the only other things I can think of are giants and trolls, and you *really* don't look like either of them," I said, my voice weak. "I'm sorry, I need a clue."

Poppy put a finger to her lip as if in thought. Then she withdrew her hand. "Fine, here's your clue."

When she didn't say anything, I looked up from the sandy beach. Poppy had stopped a few feet back, curling her lips into a sneer that chilled my blood. Fangs as long as my middle finger extended from her teeth.

"Holy moly, you're a saber-toothed tiger!" I stumbled backward until I collapsed into a heap.

Poppy burst into laughter, her teeth receding into her mouth. "No, silly. My kind get a... *sparkly* rap thanks to a current pop culture movie."

"A vampire?" I gasped.

"Nailed it!" Poppy held up a hand. "Poppy the vamp, at your service."

I glanced at Zin, who appeared bored with this game and not at all frightened. I looked back at Poppy. "Should I be worried?"

"Oh, no." Poppy waved a hand. "I'm blood-intolerant."

I scrunched up my face in confusion. "Excuse me?"

"Sucking blood gives me real bad gas. Bloating, cramps... you don't wanna hear what else." She winked. "Seriously, it's gross."

"But... won't you die without blood?"

"Your grandfather was the Mixologist when I was born. As soon as my mother realized I was a vampire, she hounded him to come up with a synthetic cocktail that takes care of all of my nutritional needs. She thought eating blood was just *vile,* so she tried to stop me from ever trying it. But I snuck a gulp once, and I got really sick." Poppy grinned. "Anyway, the cocktail's like a Bloody Mary. He always called it my Vamp Vitamins. I suppose that means now you'll be in charge of making it."

"I haven't made anything yet," I said as the three of us resumed walking. "Gus is making me memorize everything before I even touch a mixer or an herb."

"Well, Gus is a crank." Poppy stuck out her tongue at an imaginary Gus. "If I run low on my backup stores of the Vamp Vites, I'll have my mom pester him until he lets you mix up a batch. I think Gus holds some sort of weird torch for her, which is cool and all, since I don't know my dad. Plus, it might be good practice for you. The Vamp Vitamins are easy—that's what the last one said."

"The last one?" I asked, trying to pull information from them without giving away what I knew.

Zin and Poppy exchanged a glance heavy with meaning.

"The last Mixologist," Poppy answered.

"What happened to him?" I asked.

"We'll tell you later," Poppy said breezily.

My inner alarms went off—buzzing with suspicion. So far, Poppy had been forthcoming with all sorts of information—sometimes *too much* information. Her eluding my question had my mind zipping with possibilities.

"You never guessed Zin's type. I'll give you a hint—it's *not* human."

Zin scowled. "I don't have to say my species if I don't want."

Poppy made a face at her cousin. "Lily can guess, then, and I'll just nod when she gets it."

"Also a vampire?" I asked.

Zin looked far more like a vamp than sunny, sweet Poppy. I wouldn't have been surprised if fangs the size of my arms popped out of Zin's mouth. I had the sneaking suspicion that Zin would enjoy terrifying anyone around her with a peek at a set of monster incisors.

"Ha, she wishes," Poppy said.

"I do not," Zin hissed. "And she'll never guess."

"Probably not," I agreed. "Another clue, perhaps?"

"What's furry?" Poppy asked.

"Um... a dog?"

"Bad clue, Poppy," Poppy said to herself. "C'mon, Poppy, think."

"She talks to herself." Zin shook her head. "And people think I'm the strange one."

"They howl at the moon." Poppy raised a finger.

"A werewolf?" I asked, looking at Zin. I didn't want to admit it, but I could see that. Zin seemed vicious enough.

"You're only about half right." Poppy blew her cousin a kiss. "Ain't that right, Zin?"

"Shut up," Zin said, marching forward and leaving us behind.

"What did I say?" I asked.

"Nothing, nothing." Poppy patted my arm. "She's just sore. She's a shifter, but she hasn't managed all her forms yet. She sort of... spontaneously combusts into different forms."

"Oh my gosh, that sounds dangerous," I said. "No wonder she's sensitive about it."

Poppy smirked, shaking her head. "Just the opposite. Zin tries *so* hard to shift into something like a werewolf or a dragon—something badass." Poppy gestured for me to stop walking, watching to make sure that her cousin was out of earshot. "The last three things she's shifted into are, not in this order: a kitten, a mosquito, and a penguin."

I held up a hand to cover my mouth. "That sounds adorable."

"It is." Poppy laughed. "That's why she hates it."

We continued walking.

"You said at some point she'll be able to master it?"

"Most shifters have only one form by the time they come of age—about sixteen years old or so. She's about ten years late and *still* has no idea what her final form will be."

"That's got to be tough. Like getting your driver's license ten years after everyone else."

"Driver's license?" Poppy's eyebrows furrowed. "What's that?"

"Never mind. I just mean… I'm sure it's hard on her."

"Yeah, a bit." Poppy shrugged. "I think that's why she dresses like a warrior princess, but whenever I suggest that theory, she snaps at me. And it's not *always* cute. When she was a mosquito, she bit me right on the ass."

I laughed. "Ouch!"

"Tell me about it." Poppy shook her head. "Enough about that, anyway. How are you adjusting?"

"It's a whirlwind." I hesitated. "A bit overwhelming."

"Yeah, I'd imagine. But it's not that bad once you get used to The Isle—or so I hear. I've always lived here. Never left." A note of wistfulness colored her voice.

"Don't worry." I put a hand on her shoulder. "You're not missing too much out there. And if you do want a tour of the real world—er, at least the Twin Cities—I'd be happy to take you."

"Really?" She raised her eyebrows, clasping her hands to her chest. "I'd *love* that."

I smiled. "It'll be fun. Speaking of, what do you guys do here for fun?"

Poppy opened her mouth to respond but stopped, instead looking over my shoulder. A frown twisted her lips downward.

"What is it?" I asked.

"They need us," Zin called, hurrying back from where she'd gone on ahead. Her serious expression churned my stomach as she glanced in my direction. "It's an emergency. More specifically, they need *you.*"

CHAPTER 9

THE THREE OF US HUFFED and puffed up the front steps of the bungalow, where Mimsey stood waiting, her hands twisted in front of her.

"I'm sorry to interrupt your tour, girls, but we have a bit of an emergency, and I thought it best if Lily was here." She looked at me. "Gus will help you get through it, dear."

"Get through what?" I asked as Mimsey pulled me inside. "I've only had one morning of training. I've been here less than twenty-four hours. I can't help. I don't know anything about anything."

"Chop the Cat's Foot there. I'm grinding the Devil's Bit here," Gus instructed, his arms already working with fury.

"It's not a real... uh, cat's foot, is it?" I asked.

"You call them Stalwart and Ground Ivy," Mimsey said. "It's a plant, not a cat. Hurry along, dear, we have a patient coming in."

I set to work chopping the dried Cat's Foot. "A patient?"

"He needs a cure." Mimsey watched the two of us work. "He says it's the *plague*."

Poppy sucked in a breath. "The plague? But we haven't had an incident in over six months. I thought we were in the clear."

"What's the plague?" I looked up.

"Keep chopping, girl," Gus snapped.

I moved my arms faster. "Is it a disease?"

"Of sorts. A malicious one," Zin said, as if the prospect of a malicious plague interested her. "Very dangerous. Someone created it to kill us all off."

Mimsey frowned. "It's serious, Zin."

"Of course it is." She looked at her fingernails, which resembled talons painted jet black. "I'm just telling Lily the truth."

"You don't have to scare the girl." Mimsey put a hand on her hip. "Just concentrate, darling, and follow Gus's instructions."

I chop, chop, chopped. "I'm concentrating, but I would *also* like to know what I'm dealing with. The truth please, or else I'll never learn."

Mimsey glanced uneasily at her daughter and niece. "It's never been proven to be malicious. It could be one of many things. There're a lot of factors involved."

"Well, I'm not going anywhere." I chopped some more. "I'm listening to any factors you want to tell me about."

"There's a theory," Zin cut in, her voice dropping, "that it's The Faction acting up again."

"The faction?"

Mimsey held up a hand to quiet everyone down. "Here on The Isle, dear, our motto is *Maintain the culture*. What culture, you might ask?"

I nodded.

"The magical culture. Witches, mainly, but as you're aware"— she gestured to her family—"we have an eclectic mix."

"I'm the only vamp here," Poppy piped up. "And Zin's basically the only shifter. If there're others, they live in The Forest. You're the oldest of us all; that's why you're in line for the Mixology gig above Zin's siblings. At least, that's what we think; the whole process is a bit finicky, and sometimes a generation is skipped entirely."

Mimsey nodded. "As I said, mainly witches and wizards. A long time ago, we all lived in peace with the human civilization, magic and non-magic worlds combined. But eventually we started butting heads with one another, first over silly things like rules and regulations. Then more and more, these *tiffs* became dangerous."

I swallowed, torn between the two worlds. I had experienced a piece of both by now, and I could understand why emotions might fly high between the two.

"At some point, so many of our kind were killed off that we said enough is enough. We decided to remove ourselves from human civilization once and for all and set up our own culture, economy, way of life." Mimsey spread her hands wide. "Thus, The Isle was born. A safe haven for magical folks from across the world."

"Why would anyone be after the people here?" I looked up, but I spotted Gus watching me. I immediately went back to work, head down. "It doesn't seem like you're bothering anyone. I lived in human civilization—just hours away—for *years,* and I never knew The Isle's existence was real."

"The Faction isn't made up of humans." Mimsey sighed so hard, her chest rose and fell a few inches. "See, there's a group of people out there, rogue witches and wizards, that formed a small clan. They're the ones who believed we should forget about The Isle and… I'm quoting here, dear, I don't believe it…"

"What my aunt is having a hard time saying," Zin cut in, "is that The Faction thinks we should have taken our rightful place in the world."

"Mixing with the humans?" I asked, confusion probably clouding my eyes. "As in, they wanted to keep things how they were?"

Zin shook her head. "As in… they wanted to wipe out humanity. Or most of it, at least."

Mimsey's eyes darkened. "These people, The Faction, they don't listen to reason, Lily. They're so steadfast in their beliefs that they can't step back and look at their system from an outsider's point of view. It's so difficult to describe, I'm sure you can't understand—"

"I do understand." I stopped chopping, but this time Gus didn't comment. He merely looked at me in curiosity. "We have human groups like that too. Except they don't know you… er, *us* magical folk exist, so they take it out on other humans. Cults, religious extremists, things like that. They've done horrible things. To our own kind."

A quiet moment of silence passed.

"Then you do understand." Mimsey cleared her throat.

I nodded.

"The Faction wants to return to the days of Greek gods and goddesses, when us magical folks sat up on some hill they called Olympus and ruled the world." Mimsey shook her head. "It's appalling."

"Doesn't sound so bad to me," Zin said. "I wouldn't mind being a ruler."

"Stop changing the subject." Poppy tapped the table next to my chopped leaves. "The *plague*."

"Right, right." Mimsey jumped to attention.

Gus smacked my hand, mouthing, "Snap to it."

"So the plague is from The Faction?" I asked, brushing the powder into a small pile. "Trying to get rid of you all?"

"There're lots of theories. Conspiracy theories, mostly," Mimsey said. "They want us to join them. But we haven't budged for hundreds of years, and we never will. Recently, they've been saying we're as bad as the humans and they're going to wipe us out too."

"Everyone thought they started with the last Mixologist, though nothing was ever proven... *ooops*."

The room went still as all eyes swiveled to Poppy.

"I shouldn't have said that," she murmured.

A chill snaked down my spine. "If you think you're keeping a secret from me, you're not. Gus told me about the last Mixologist."

"What did he say?" Mimsey asked.

"That he was murdered."

Mimsey gasped. "That's not true. The Mixologist wasn't a victim of The Faction."

"He *might* have been," Zin said. When Mimsey glared at her, Zin shrugged. "What? It's not like we know what happened."

"What do you know about it?" I asked, my voice nearly silent. I tucked my hands behind my back, afraid they'd shake so hard I'd chop my hand off if I continued working.

"He made a mistake," Mimsey said. "Lyle Walters stopped by in the morning for his daily Caffeine Cup. Supposedly the Mixologist would toss in a pinch of powder that prevented hair loss, which was why Lyle came all the way across The Isle every morning for it."

Gus stood, forgetting his own pile of flower-dust on the table. He straightened his back, his eyes narrowed on Mimsey.

"Poor Lyle, when he came in for his daily cup of joe, found the Mixologist slumped over the bar. It was too late when Lyle arrived, and even if it wasn't, nobody could've helped Neil. Gus is the only person who knows what half this stuff is, and mixing isn't his specialty." Mimsey looked down. "They say the Mixologist had an accident—mixed Hog's Snout and Roaring Lions. A deadly concoction when combined with water."

I recognized the names from my lesson this morning, but I frowned as I struggled to remember if they were toxic together or not.

"Lies." Gus's response slithered across the room, the anger beneath his word chilling me to the bone.

"Ex-excuse me?" Mimsey looked at him, her eyes twinkling with surprise.

"Neil, the Mixologist, wouldn't have made that mistake. Mixing that family of herb with its deadly cousin is well known to cause instant death. Child's play." Gus shook his head, jabbing a thumb in my direction. "She could've told you that."

I nodded, which was only a tiny lie. I'd study harder tonight. I'd only had one day on the job.

"Why didn't you say something?" Mimsey asked. "Gus, you should have spoken up."

"I did. Nobody listened." Gus turned back to his table and continued working.

I looked at Gus, or rather, the top of his head, as he bent over the table. "You should've said something again so they could find who did this to the Mixologist, if it wasn't an accident."

Gus straightened, brandishing the long blade he was using in my direction. "You're new here, girl. You don't know how things go on the island."

Poppy's eyes widened, her gaze darting between the two of us.

The blade quivered inches from my chin. I raised my hands slowly. "You're right. That's why I need someone to teach me."

We sat that way, Gus holding the knife just under my chin, me trying my best not to look away.

"Get that knife out of her face, Gus." Mimsey stepped forward. "Who do you think you are, waving a sharp blade around like that? She doesn't know any better. And anyway, she's got a point. If you didn't think it was an accident, why didn't you speak up *louder*?"

"Nobody would've listened," he grumbled.

"You have to give them a chance," Mimsey said. "For crying out loud, Gus, we all thought it was a mistake. And frankly, unless you have any evidence otherwise, I *still* think it's a mistake. Even the best of us make errors from time to time."

Gus lowered the blade to the table, his muscles flexing as he *chop, chop, chopped* some more. "You're right."

"I'll help you." I took a chance, a huge chance, and laid a hand on Gus's forearm. "I can help you look into his death."

Gus looked at my hand as if he wanted to chop it right off, but when I didn't budge, his shoulders sagged. "No. It was an accident." But the resignation in Gus's voice said he didn't believe it. Only that he didn't want to talk about it *now*.

"Fine," I said, taking the clue. "It was an accident."

"I don't need your help." Gus's shoulders stiffened once more as he gathered the dust into a few separate piles. "Unless you're talking about getting this antidote ready for our customer."

I turned back at the table just as the door burst open.

"The *plague*," a man moaned, stumbling through the door. "They got me. I have the *plague*."

The man in question was shorter and squatter than Mimsey and sweatier than all of us combined. His red face was crinkled with pain, and his arms flailed as he stumbled for the table.

"There, there, Leonard." Mimsey burst to action and led the ailing man to sit on the chair she pulled from... *from nowhere?* I had to learn how this magic business really worked.

"What do you need from me?" I turned to Gus, who looked as if the top of his head might pop off in anger.

"Leonard Fluffleknocker." Gus stepped around the table, the long blade still in his hand. He stomped to where the man sat, head in hands and sweating quite profusely. "What in the tarnation are you doing in here?"

"He has the *plague*," Mimsey said, backing away. "Treat him, Gus. Look at how much pain he's in right now. He's suffering."

Instead of firing instructions in my direction, hustling to make some sort of antidote, or doing anything else that would've made sense, Gus put one hand on his hip and lifted his other hand—the hand with the blade. He slipped the shiny length under the man's chin and forced the man's face up. Gus stepped forward, balancing the knife carefully.

"You've got the plague, eh?" Gus asked.

Leonard's eyes were large as saucers. He started to nod but stopped. Probably since the knife didn't move with his head. He blinked instead. "Yes. Gus, you've got to save me."

After a long, empty silence, in which Gus studied Leonard's eyes, ears, and even took a quick peek up his nostrils, Gus let the knife down from under the man's chin.

"Really?" Gus said skeptically. He strode around the seated man who, if possible, was sweating now more than ever. "Symptoms include stomach cramps, a burning sensation in your throat..."

Leonard nodded with enthusiasm as Gus completed his circle. "Yes, yes. Both those things."

Gus retook his stance in front of the man. "And let me guess—a huge case of embarrassment."

Leonard continued to nod for a second, until he processed Gus's words. "What?"

"That's gas, Leonard, not the plague. Did you combine beer and burritos like *I told you not to*? Heartburn and gas, Mr. Fluffleknocker. That's what you've got. Not the plague. Shame on you for scaring these ladies."

Mimsey gave a long sigh of relief. "Is it true, Leonard? Your doctor told me just last week you've been having intestinal issues."

"Stop talking to my doctor," Leonard said, exasperated. "What happened to confidentiality?"

Mimsey's ears pinkened. "It's a small town. Word gets around."

"Not about my bowels. And it's *not* gas." Leonard's gaze shifted in my direction. "You the new Mixologist?"

I nodded.

"Look at me yourself. You'll see the plague, I guarantee it." Leonard looked miffed that everyone had witnessed his false alarm, and a flash of embarrassment hid behind his wildly darting eyes. "Come, look."

Leonard stuck his tongue out as far as it could go. I winced, having no desire to peek down anyone's throat, especially not a man producing sweat in such quantities. But as everyone's eyes shifted toward me, I took a deep breath.

Stepping forward, I focused on the desperation in Leonard's eyes, the hope that maybe I could save him from a bit of ridicule if I came up with something—anything. I was willing to bet Leonard *hoped* he had the plague, just to save face.

I peeked down his throat, did one full circle around Leonard, then crossed my arms as I stopped in front of him.

"Well?" Leonard growled, almost accusatory. "What is it?"

I narrowed my eyes, tempted to agree with Gus just because I didn't like Leonard's tone. But I couldn't find it in myself to add more salt to the wound. "It's not the plague. It's definitely not the plague, but it is something called *Flatulent-itis*."

"What is *that*?" Leonard's eyes grew wide while Mimsey stepped forward, patting his shoulder reassuringly.

"It's... uh..." I looked at Gus, who snorted in derision.

"Go ahead," Gus said. "Explain to everyone, please. I'm *fascinated*."

"It's a, um, stomach condition with a very easy fix." I gave a serious nod. "It's a good thing you came in when you did. We caught it early."

"See?" Leonard leapt from his chair, pointing at Gus. "That man is an idiot. Good thing we have a *real* Mixologist in town."

"Don't you talk to him like that—" I had half a mind to reverse my fake diagnosis, but Gus interrupted me before I could finish.

"Yes, we're lucky to have her," he said mildly. His tone flat, Gus looked at me. "Let's get Leonard his antidote so he can get on his way."

I nodded, looking wildly around the room. I discovered immediately, however, that I had no clue what herb was where, which were potent, which were harmless.

"Excuse me." I ducked out of the store and moved behind the bar, where I'd noticed a few pitchers of plain water and some fresh fruit.

Working quickly, I poured a glass full of water and set it on the counter while I peeled all sorts of fruits. I figured it was safe to assume that everything was edible since it'd been served for breakfast just hours ago.

Squishing a variety of bright fruits, some of which I knew—oranges, lemons, berries—and others I didn't—something resembling a banana except a whole lot juicier and shaped like a pear, and a pink, heart-shaped berry—I collected the juices and added them to the glass of water. I stirred until the beverage turned an oddly bright color.

Grabbing the glass, I paused as another idea hit me. I poured leftover coffee from breakfast into a mug and, grasping the two drinks, kicked the door open.

"I've come up with a cure," I said.

"Really?" Gus, though heavy on the sarcasm, looked mildly amused. "What page in the book was *this* cure on?"

I cleared my throat. "I, you know… I went with my gut on this one. Listened to my heart."

"Like a true Mixologist." Leonard sneered. "Not like the fake *he* is…"

I held back the glasses. "Apologize to Gus, or you don't get the antidote."

"No." Leonard crossed his arms. "He talked to me as if I were crazy. *Gas!* Can you believe it? I think I'd know if I had gas."

I held the drinks away even farther. "Fine. Then deal with… uh, *Flatulent-itis* by yourself."

"Sorry," Leonard grumbled at Gus. "This place needs new customer service."

I handed over the drinks, thinking that we needed new *customers* since the service was quite fine by my standards. "Drink the tall glass first, then the coffee—er, then the mug."

Mimsey, Zin, and Poppy all stared at me open-mouthed. I shrugged.

Gus's eyes twinkled with humor. "Don't forget the incantation."

I squirmed. "Uh, okay." I whispered a few nonsensical words.

"They have to be at hearing level," Gus prodded.

I glared at him. Now he was just messing with me.

"Fine." I wiped my hands on my sundress. "Uh…"

The room fell silent, and I thought quickly. When I spoke, it was so low, so fast that nobody but me could understand the words, or so I hoped:

Drink from the glass, and then the mug.
You're sweating so much, don't give me a hug.
Gus says you have gas, and I think so too.
So drink the coffee and use the loo.

I blushed a brilliant red, not quite sure where the rhyme came from. It was all I could think of on short notice, and judging by Leonard's serious face, he hadn't understood a word I said. Gus, however, turned his back to me, his shoulders shaking violently in what I assumed was a fit of laughter.

"Go ahead, drink up," I said, a bit cross with Gus for putting me on the spot.

Leonard's face constricted as he swallowed the first beverage. He smacked his lips. "Tastes disgusting. But I can feel it working already."

I nodded. "Good. Now, follow it up with the mug."

"Tastes like a sad excuse for coffee," Leonard said, looking my way. "Must be a deadly disease I have if you're forcing me to drink a pile of dirt."

"Totally." I scanned the room, noticing realization dawn on Mimsey's face. Then anger. After all, she'd made the coffee.

"I'll have you know that coffee—" Mimsey began, shaking a finger at Leonard.

"That coffee you have brewing is about to burn," I interrupted. "Leonard, thanks for stopping by. The effects should work in... about thirty minutes or so. I suggest you get home before then. Take the day off and relax, all right?"

He licked his lips. "Thanks for nothing, Gus. Take a page out of this girl's book." Leonard approached me, reaching to shake my hand.

I shook it, wincing at the stickiness of his palm. "No problem."

"Glad to have a real Mixologist back on the island," Leonard said. "Thanks for saving my life."

"That's my job." I gave a fake smile, withdrawing my hand and making my way to the bathroom to wash my hands before he'd even stepped out of the door.

When I returned to the store a minute later, four sets of eyes stared at me—mostly they were mystified, but Poppy appeared incredulous. Amusement twisted Zin's lips into a smile. Mimsey crossed her arms, probably still miffed about the coffee comment.

Gus shook his head. "Fruit juice and coffee? Maybe you are smarter than you look."

My cheeks warmed. "No. It's nothing. Shall I clean this up?" I hustled to the table, uncomfortable under everyone's watchful gaze.

"My coffee does *not* taste like dirt," Mimsey retorted.

"No, but it does clear your system in about thirty minutes to the dot," Poppy said with a grin, apparently finally understanding why everyone was amused. "That's clever, Lily. I like you."

I couldn't hold back a smile as I scooped the powders from the table into extra jars I found on one of the shelves.

"It wasn't terrible," Gus admitted.

Reaching for labels, I kept my smile hidden as it grew.

"*Now* can we take you on a tour?" Poppy asked.

"It's time for lessons." When he saw me struggling to spell the name of a plant, Gus snatched the jars from me and filled out the labels. "We must get back to work."

"She hasn't had a break all day, you crazy old man," Mimsey said. "Give her an hour. She deserves it after that performance."

Gus looked as if he were about to tell off Mimsey, but he shut his mouth before he responded. He glanced at me then shrugged one shoulder. "Fine. One hour."

CHAPTER 10

THE ISLE TURNED OUT TO be a walkable distance—at least the places we were headed.

"It's not a huge island," Poppy said, holding up a map as we stepped into the sunlight. "Here's where we're at now."

She pointed at the lower of two bridges that spanned a canal that split The Isle into two. My bungalow was on the left side of the island, along with the beach, the dock, and something Poppy referred to as The Forest.

"We don't go up here." Poppy shuddered as she pointed at the cluster of trees just north of the bungalow.

"Why not?" I strolled across the bridge next to Poppy. Zin walked a few feet ahead, still listening.

"It houses all the dangerous things," Zin said, her voice low. "I'll go someday, even though Mother says she'll *kill* me if I do."

"Aunt Trinket's a bit uptight, but I think my mom would kill me too," Poppy added.

I fell silent. I had nobody to kill me if I went to The Forest.

"Oh, I'm sorry." Poppy threw her arm around my shoulder. "I didn't mean anything by it. If anything, you're double loved. If you go into The Forest, both Trinket *and* Mimsey will kill you."

"What a lucky duck," Zin said dryly. "Just what every girl wants."

"What sort of dangerous stuff is in The Forest?" I asked, already comfortable with my cousins.

Something about this place felt *right*. Despite the murder claims and mean ol' Leonard, I no longer doubted if I'd made the right decision. Being here did feel like coming home, and though I wasn't used to the whole idea of *family*, I liked thinking that I had aunts, cousins, people who'd kill me if I broke their rules.

"I don't know." Poppy sighed wistfully. "We've never been allowed to go there. But I suspect there's a handful of fairies, maybe a troll or two. Someone once said they heard a giant thumping around, but I think that's a load of crap. Giants can't swim, and they'd sink a boat. How'd they get here?"

"There's also the volcano," Zin said. "To the very north of The Forest. There're all *sorts* of stories about that. It'd take all day to tell you."

"Has anyone been up there... ever?" I glanced at the water as we crossed the bridge, and my eyes bugged out of my head when I saw the brightly colored fish, dolphins, and sharks swimming peacefully underneath, twisting through seaweed forests.

"Only the Rangers." Poppy's voice fell to a whisper. "They're a private bunch, them."

"What do they look like?" My mind flashed back to the man who'd caught me snoozing in the hammock.

"You'll know one if you see one." Zin gave a nod. "They don't talk a whole bunch. They're big, they're strong, they're smart. Basically, they're the best of the breed."

"What breed?" I asked.

"Magical folks, of course, silly," Poppy said. "They're mostly wizards—we all are here. The shifters are the weird ones."

Zin scowled. "I'm not weird."

"Little bit?" Poppy grinned.

"I'm not *weird*!"

A light *pop* sounded. I looked at Zin, but she was no longer there.

"Zin?" I turned to Poppy. "What did you do? Where'd she go? *Zin!*"

Poppy couldn't respond. She was far too busy giggling out of control. "That's a *new* one."

"You think this is funny?" I put my hands on my hips. "I just met my cousin. I can't have her disappearing already. What is so funny, anyway?" My voice trailed off as Poppy pointed at the ground, laughter racking her body so hard, tears streamed down her face.

I looked toward where she pointed and saw, where Zin had stood moments before, a very large turtle. Unfortunately, the turtle had landed upside-down, its legs wiggling in the air.

"Is that Zin?" I crouched, looking for signs of familiarity. But for all intents and purposes, the animal looked just like any other turtle I'd seen.

"Of course it's Zin." Poppy struggled to control her laughter. "Sometimes she gets so upset, she shifts uncontrollably."

I gently flipped the turtle over so it was right-side up. Immediately, Zin the Turtle waddled as fast as she could toward Poppy and snapped at her toe. Poppy's laughter turned into a howl of pain.

I bent again and did my best to try to loosen Zin's jaw. I failed. Miserably. Standing, I said to Poppy, "I don't know what to do. She won't let go."

But Poppy was looking past me, pointing over my shoulder. "Why'd you do that?"

I turned back, my mouth opening in awe as Zin morphed back to her original size, black clothing intact.

"I told you not to laugh at me." Zin sniffed. "That's what you get."

"You ruined my toe!" Poppy looked at the red mark on her foot.

"Just the polish, you'll be fine. Don't be a baby."

"Maybe this is a strange question," I cut in, trying to diffuse the argument, "but how are your clothes not ripped to shreds?"

"Her mom put a special spell on them so they'd shrink and expand to fit her shifts," Poppy said. "Isn't it neat?"

"So you're saying the turtle was wearing a tiny pair of leather pants?" I asked, trying hard to suppress the smile toying at my lips.

"Yep! Except they go invisible on the first shift, the one into an animal state. Kind of like a chameleon. Then when she shifts back to human form, they return to normal. Clever, huh?" Poppy grinned. "It took her mom three years to perfect it. For a while there, Zin would shift back into her birthday suit, which was pretty embarrassing for her but pretty hilarious to me."

"About The Forest," Zin said, her lips in a thin line. "Maybe you should *both* go there. I hope you get eaten by trolls."

I hid my smile as Poppy rolled her eyes.

"So these Rangers," I said as we resumed the tour, "I think I saw one. Or rather, he saw me."

"Really?" Poppy raised her eyebrows. "You didn't get a name, did you?"

I shook my head.

"Did he say anything?" Zin asked.

"Sort of."

Both of my cousins swiveled to look at me.

"*And?*" Zin prompted.

"Well, he sort of saw my underwear." I scrunched up my face. "It wasn't my fault, I swear. He was standing too close while I was sleeping on the hammock, and I flipped right off."

"I bet he liked *that*," Poppy said. "Ugh, you're so lucky."

"Lucky? It was mortifying!" We stepped off the bridge, and I glanced around the right side of the island. Houses, small businesses, and storefronts lined the shore of the canal.

"Yeah, but it's not like they get that view a lot." I must have looked confused, because Zin explained, "Rangers can't get married. Their jobs are too dangerous."

I swallowed. "Dangerous?"

She nodded.

"That doesn't mean they never see *butts*," Poppy said. "They can't get married, but that doesn't mean they've joined a convent."

Zin's face turned a shade paler. "How would *you* know?"

"They're studs. They can have whoever they want." Poppy fanned herself as she turned to me. "I should know. I work as their dispatcher. Mom and Trinket own a supply store, so I work there some days and other days I'm at Ranger Headquarters."

"How would you even know? I'm sure their girlfriends aren't calling Headquarters," Zin scoffed. "How unprofessional."

"You wouldn't *imagine* the requests I get." Poppy rolled her eyes, transforming her voice into a high-pitched squeak. "*Is Ranger X there? I'm in* danger. *Can you patch me through? There's a spider in my bed.*"

"No!" I gasped, laughter creeping into my voice. "Really?"

"Something about those men makes the ladies go nuts." Poppy grinned. "I'm surprised you spotted one so quickly. Usually they stick to their own territories—the volcano, The Forest, the barracks. They only venture out into civilization when they have to deal with stuff the normal patrols can't handle."

"He was probably curious to see the new Mixologist," Zin said. "Which Ranger was it?"

I shrugged. "Big guy. Dark hair. Scar next to his eye."

Zin and Poppy stopped walking and shared a knowing glance.

"What?" I stopped a few feet ahead of them.

"If that's true…" Poppy blinked at Zin. "You met Ranger X. Do you know how lucky that makes you?"

I shook my head. "Not in the slightest. Who's Ranger X?"

"That's a great question." Zin marched onward. "Nobody knows who he is, or how he got here, or even his real name."

Poppy shook her head. "The lifespan of a Ranger is about five minutes. They all quit immediately, or end up… well, you know. Dead. But not him."

Zin raised an eyebrow. "He worked his way to the top of the

clan. Ranger X is the leader of the group, the boss, their alpha guy. It's hard to describe."

"The other Rangers think he's a god." Poppy shrugged. "I don't know what happened, but they unanimously voted him to lead their crew. The Rangers are not a friendly bunch, so to have them all unified behind one person—well, it hadn't been like that for years."

"Plus, he's young," Zin said. "What is he, thirty-two?"

Poppy nodded. "I get the most phone calls for him. But as far as I know, he's never even touched a girl."

"False," I said with a shiver, remembering his lips brushing against my cheek. "He touched me, and I'm certain there've been others."

Poppy inhaled sharply. "Did you *kiss* him?"

"No!" I bobbled my head back and forth. "Of course not, I just… he seems experienced."

Zin narrowed her eyes at me. "You're not telling us something."

"No!" I struggled to find less incriminating words. "It's just a gut feeling."

"We're messing with you." Poppy lightly punched my shoulder. "Anyway, we could talk about him forever, but at the end of the day, he's a giant mystery. Nobody knows anything, but the rumors are always flowing. Oh, let's pop in here for a minute."

I looked up. "A tea shop?"

"It's not just any tea shop," Poppy murmured. "And if you plan on having any more *run-ins* with Ranger X, you'll want to get a cup of the *Glow*. It's ginger tea with a dash of glow worm—sounds gross, but it makes you shine like a rainbow."

"Rainbows shine?" I asked.

"Oh, just come inside." Poppy grabbed my hand and pulled me forward. "You can thank me later."

"Don't drink anything," Zin whispered. "It's all a lie."

"What's all a lie?" I asked, but it was too late.

All three of us stepped through the door. The tea shop was

dark and musty, the exact opposite of the fresh, bright outside. Tea barrels lined the walls from floor to ceiling, a light herbal scent tickling my nostrils.

The store appeared empty except for the stash of tea leaves.

"Should we leave?" I asked in a hushed voice. "This place kind of freaks me out."

"Oh, there's no need to leave, Lily." An unfamiliar voice filled the room, as if coming from the barrels themselves. "In fact, I've been waiting ages to meet you. Step farther into the store. Let me see the new Mixologist."

My spine tingled, my senses burned, and my freak-alarm rang all sorts of bells.

But despite all my misgivings, when Poppy grabbed my hand and pulled me forward, I went with her.

CHAPTER 11

"COME OUT FROM THERE, HARPIN," Poppy said. "I want to introduce you to the new Mixologist."

A man stepped from behind a thick drape that hung over a door at the back of the store. He wore a long black robe that swished when he walked. His hair—just as long and just as black—hung over his shoulders. His voice was smooth as silk. "So you're *the one*."

"Hi." I offered a quick smile. He gave me the creeps—the sheen of his hair, the translucence of his skin, the way his green eyes watched me with a cat-like intensity. "I'm Lily."

"I know exactly who you are." Harpin emerged from behind the counter as if he were gliding, due to the lightness of his footsteps and the soft rustle of his robes. "As I said, I've been waiting a long time."

"What, twenty-four hours?" Poppy rolled her eyes. "She just got here."

Harpin's eyes flashed in annoyance. "I've known about her for some time now."

"Right," Poppy said, leaning on the desk. "Okay, then."

Harpin stalked forward and came within an inch of my face. He made eye contact for far too long, studying me as if he could see into my soul. A hint of garlic came from his person—his breath or his robes, I couldn't tell. But it made my eyes water.

"Are you crying?" he asked.

I shook my head. "Just got something in my eye." I didn't want to say it was a whiff of garlic.

Harpin moved his eyes down my face, studying my nose, my ears, my chin in turn. When he looked at my lips, I couldn't handle it anymore.

"Can I help you?" I asked.

"Just studying what a *true* Mixologist is made of," he said, stepping behind the counter.

I detected bitterness in his voice. He appeared to hate me right off the bat. I had no idea why, especially as I wasn't the one who smelled like garlic.

"How is the training going?" He raised one shiny eyebrow so high it nearly disappeared into his hairline.

"It's fine." I glanced at my cousins, hoping they'd help me out. "Difficult. Interesting. It's hard to say if I'll be any good at it, since I've only been here one day." I gave a light laugh, but the humor died immediately in the damp, musty air.

"But you've already begun handing out antidotes, I hear." Harpin rested long, thin fingers on the counter. "How very confident of you."

"I haven't handed out anything."

"Lies," he hissed. "Leonard Fluffleknocker?"

I barely managed to hold my tongue. Better for him to think I was confident than to have him spreading rumors about me handing out fake potions. "How did you find out so quickly? Leonard only stopped by thirty minutes ago, or so."

"I have *gifts*."

"You can see the future?" I asked.

"My *gifts* are impossible to explain."

"No, your *gifts* are a whole load of bull-dung." Zin *tsked*. "Don't go telling the new girl lies, Harpin. She's green to the whole magic thing, doesn't know up from down yet."

Harpin looked annoyed. "It's not lies. I *can* see the future."

Poppy stepped forward. "Harpin, listen here. You got gifts, that's for sure. Your ginger tea makes me glow like I ain't never glowed before. I attract men like flies to honey after one cup of that stuff. Your Gass-Pass helps digestion more than anything I've ever seen. But you don't have any seeing-the-future powers."

"But I knew about Leonard. How do you explain *that*?" Harpin leaned forward, a challenge in his eye.

"Oh, lordy. It's called living in a small town." Poppy met him nose to nose. "When you live in a place the size of a postage stamp, word gets around pretty quick. I'll bet he stopped in here on his way home, bragging about how he was cured of the plague, am I right?"

Harpin shook his head, but the red hue in his ears said differently.

"So stop telling the new girl your nonsense stories, and instead give me some Glow teabags. I might as well take Gass-Pass while I'm at it. I plan on overindulging on dinner. It's sloppy joes tonight." Poppy reached into her pockets. "I don't have money right now. Put it on my tab."

Harpin disappeared as quickly as he'd arrived, the sound of muttering coming from behind the tea barrels.

Zin stepped close enough that our shoulders touched. "Don't take it personally. He's been hankering for your job since he came out of the womb."

"The Mixology job? Why didn't he get it?"

"It isn't in his blood," Poppy said.

"Yes, but it wasn't in Neil's blood either, and he served as a replacement after the last Mixologist. So why did Neil get the job, but not Harpin?"

"Because Harpin sucks at being magical." Zin's nose twitched. "His teas are nothing but that—tea. The whole 'glow' thing is all in Poppy's head."

"Is not," Poppy said. "I *do* glow. Like a lava lamp."

"Because he puts in powdered glow worm. But that's not magic.

Or Mixology. That's just... I don't know... cooking." Zin shrugged. "The same thing would happen if you sprinkled glow worm into your pasta sauce."

"I take it you don't shop here?" I grinned at Zin.

She shook her head. "But it's good Poppy believes in Harpin's crap. One of us has to keep him on our good side, and I'd rather she spend the money trying to glow."

"Why do you care if he's on your good side?" I wouldn't much mind if I never stepped foot in here again.

Zin shrugged. "Small town life. It's just politics. Plus, I wouldn't want him to poison Poppy with his teas, so I try not to cause too many waves."

"He'd do that?" I asked, my voice hushed.

Zin shrugged, but before she could answer, Harpin emerged from the back room. "There's the tea."

"Oh, thanks," Poppy said, scooping up her haul. She nodded in my direction. "Now, Harpin, we'd love to stay and chat, but we've got to get her back to her studies."

"I thought it was in her blood." Harpin made a note on a piece of parchment. He spread it across his desk, all sorts of numbers and figures making it look like a ledger. "I didn't know she needed to *work* at it... I assumed it came naturally."

"Harpin, stop being a troll," Zin snapped. "You know how difficult her job is. Even if the talent does run in her veins, it doesn't mean we can just snap our fingers and fill her head with the names and properties of each plant."

"Then what does she have that I don't?" Harpin's lips tipped into a smile. "You'll understand I'm just curious as to why my application has been rejected so many times. I'd like to learn... for next time."

"With any luck, there won't be a next time in *your* lifetime." Poppy took a sniff of her teas, nodding with satisfaction. "Lily's here to stay. Right, Lily? And as long as she's not going anywhere, you're out of luck, Harpin."

"Yes, exactly." I tried to look confident. "I'm staying."

"You don't sound so sure." Harpin pressed the tips of his fingers together. "Life often has a funny way of interrupting one's plans."

"Stop it. Lily's a West Isle Witch now, which means if you want to annoy her, you're going to bother all of us. Do you want me to tell Mimsey on you?" Poppy grasped my wrist and pulled me toward the door. "You mess with her, you mess with the rest of us."

"Pay your tab, Poppy!" Harpin called as she pushed open the door. "You're overdue."

"Am not!" Poppy singsonged back. To me, she whispered, "I'm *so* overdue, but I'll get it to him on my next paycheck. Jeesh, he's so uptight about bills and timeliness. It's *annoying.*"

"Your receipts are falling off my desk!" Harpin shouted. "I'm using them as a placemat *and* a rug."

I thought back to the massive roll of parchment on his desk, wondering if it was a record of all of Poppy's recent purchases. If so, she liked her tea. That was a *lot* of leaves.

"You're welcome," Poppy said. "Without me, you'd never have a rug. Now you've got a rug *and* a placemat."

The sunlight came as a welcome relief. The inside of the damp tea shop had made breathing difficult. I took a deep inhalation of fresh, sea-salty air and exhaled slowly.

"West Isle Witches?" I asked. "Is that some sort of a club?"

Zin had reverted to her sullen self, giving us a scowl before she dropped behind us. I'd be scowling too if I had on the amount of black clothing that she did. My airy sundress allowed for a nice breeze on my legs, but her leather pants had to be sticking to the backs of her knees. The sun burned my shoulders, and the balmy, humid air didn't do much to keep us cool.

Poppy held her teabags with delight, taking a whiff of the fresh leaves now and again as we trekked back across the sandy path toward the bungalow. "Not a club. Just family."

"Whose family, specifically?"

"Ours!" Poppy stepped onto the bridge. "Look, see here? There're two bridges that cross the canal. The Upper and the Lower Bridges, but only the Lower is in use."

"Why's that?"

"Because the Upper Bridge leads nearly straight into The Forest. The only people who use it are the Rangers. They have barracks up there, but a normal person would go halfway around The Isle just to use the lower bridge—too dangerous otherwise."

"A normal person?" I blinked.

"You know, *magic* normal." Poppy shrugged. "We have normal witches and weirdo witches too. Just like humans have normal folks and weirdo folks."

"Since you all live on the west side, that's where the name comes from?" I asked.

"It's how we refer to ourselves," Poppy said. "Me, Zin, my mom, Auntie Trinket, the rest of Zin's siblings… and now you." She beamed. "Since we're all females, we have different last names, so we just dubbed ourselves the West Isle Witches. It's easier."

"But don't other witches live on the west side too?"

Zin shook her head. "We're the only witches brave enough. Everyone else lives along the canal. There's a salon on the west side, but they don't live there."

"You can see it there, to the left of the beach." Poppy pointed. "Otherwise, it's just us. Well, us and the jail."

"You have a jail here?" I hadn't expected a jail. I supposed I'd figured the magical community had a different way of dealing with rule-breakers. "Is the other side of The Isle safer?"

"Yep. A lot." Poppy grinned. "The bridges have barriers—spells and protective hexes—to keep away the creatures who live in The Forest."

"That makes me feel *real* safe," I said dryly. "Since I can see The Forest from my front porch."

"But you've got the Rangers just a few minutes away. That's a bonus," Poppy said.

"But I don't know how to *call* them if I need help. It's not like you guys gave me a cell phone."

"Oh, I wasn't even talking about the *help* part." Poppy winked. "I just meant you have a better chance of catching a view of them in the wild. The Rangers hate going to the East Isle. Too commercial. In fact, some of the witches looking to catch a husband come sunbathe on your beach just to try to catch their attention."

"Great," I muttered. "But I thought they couldn't get married?"

"They can't," Poppy said. "But a girl can try. Everyone wants to be the witch who can take a Ranger off the market. But as far as I know, it hasn't happened yet."

"Have you tried?" I shot a mischievous glance in my cousin's direction.

"Of course not!" Poppy looked appalled. "They're like brothers to me. I don't even find them cute. I just like talking shop with other girls, so I pretend to find them attractive."

"How quaint," I said with a smile.

Poppy gave my shoulder a good-natured punch. I had to admit I liked it. I liked the joking. I liked everything that went along with having a family, even if it meant I really *was* a witch.

As we hoofed it back to the bungalow, I found myself hoping more and more that I would be able to do the Mixologist's job and do it well. Because I could handle losing another job, but it'd be much harder to lose the family I'd already begun to love.

"Is that Kenny?" I asked, nodding toward a flash of movement down by the docks.

"Yeah. I forgot about him." Poppy took another loud sniff of the tea leaves. "He might live over here. Nobody's really sure. I assume you met him on the journey here?"

I nodded. "Do you know why he doesn't talk?"

"You know, he hasn't *told* me," Poppy deadpanned. "Seeing how he doesn't talk and all."

"Ha-ha. You're funny." I grinned.

"Hey, you're part of the family now. It's your duty to laugh at my lame jokes." Poppy patted my shoulder. "Look, your Mister Grumps is waiting on the porch. And he looks a bit angry, so I'm going to leave you here."

I groaned. Gus didn't look happy as he scanned the beach, his eyes locking on mine as we neared the bungalow. "Why does everyone hate me already? Harpin, Gus…" I turned to face my cousin, but she was too busy burying her head in the bag of Glow tea. "Poppy, you are *glowing.*" I turned to Zin. "Is that safe?"

"Oh, good. It's working." Poppy smiled. Her face had a greenish tinge, sort of like a nauseated version of the Hulk or a glow stick sold at Fourth of July parades.

"Isn't it supposed to just, uh, enhance your skin?" I asked.

"Yes, isn't it?" Poppy frowned. "It's supposed to make you radiant."

"Well, you're certainly radiating… something." I nodded. "Like toxic waste."

"His teas are crap," Zin said. "Come on, Poppy, stop sniffing it. You're going to turn into a pile of neon goop if you don't get your head out of that bag."

"Is she okay?" I asked, stepping toward the porch.

"She's fine, just one too many sniffs of the tea leaves," Zin said with a shake of her head. "Go on. We'll meet you later."

I nodded. "I'll see you around."

"We'll be at Grannie's," Poppy shouted as Zin yanked her in the opposite direction. "Grannie likes to sniff the tea leaves too. You can join if you want!"

"Sounds lovely," I called with a wave. But the smile fell from my face, replaced by a sensation of dread, when I turned around.

Gus stared daggers at me.

I gave him a curt nod. "Oh, hello, Gus."

"Having a good time *sniffing leaves?*" Gus's voice was low. "Did you forget about your studies?"

"No."

"Blowing off your lessons to frolic around The Isle?" Gus followed me inside. "I tell you an hour, you take an hour and five minutes."

"I took a lunch break." I faced him, trying hard not to let my voice wobble. "This is hard work, and I had a nice time with my cousins. I'm ready to get started."

I strode over to the table in the center of the room. The *Magic of Mixology* lay open to the last page I'd read. I sat down and skimmed the words, revisiting the herbs and flowers I'd learned earlier in the day. When I glanced up a few moments later, Gus was standing along the far wall, his lips slightly parted in confusion.

"Yes?" I asked sweetly.

Gus leapt to attention as if I'd startled him. "Read. Stop talking."

Ten hours later, I rose from the table. My legs ached, my arms drooped like weary noodles, and my head spun like a top. I'd barely moved for the rest of the day, learning flower name after flower name, studying herb property after herb property, and memorizing which herbs could be mixed with which flowers.

Dinner had been provided at the table. A glass of water refilled magically whenever I sipped it. If I moved so much as an inch, Gus stopped whatever he was doing—organizing the shelves, grinding powders, measuring stem lengths—to glare at me until I continued reading. I only got to stretch my legs during two bathroom breaks all day.

Strenuous and long were the two words I'd use to describe the day. If every day was like this, I didn't know how long I could hold up before I crashed.

"One more page," Gus said, and I sat back in my chair. "Now."

"I'm not retaining anything." I collapsed against the table, leaning my head in my arms. "I'm exhausted, and my legs are cramping."

Gus grunted, and I took that as a sign I was dismissed.

Part of me wanted to join the girls and Grannie and sniff some tea leaves, but I had a feeling that ship had sailed hours ago. It was late now, almost one in the morning. I could stop by tomorrow instead—if Gus didn't keep me captive all day again. The only date I had for the rest of the evening was with my bed.

I dragged myself up the stairs, wishing I had the power to fly. Then I remembered I was a witch. I had no idea how to work a spell, but I was tired enough to cross my fingers and try.

"My legs are tired, I'd like to cheat—
So give me wings instead of feet.
Make me fly on up to bed,
Where I can lay and rest my head."

My heart sank when it didn't work. But the steps looked too challenging for my sore legs, and I wasn't ready to give up yet.

"Give me wings and make me fly,
Take me high up in the sky.
Gus is mean, and grumpy too.
Making me fly is the least he can do."

"How are those spells going for you?" Gus asked, standing below me on the staircase. "Any luck?"

I groaned. "Did you hear the last part?"

"I heard all the parts."

"I didn't really mean it..." I breathed. "I'm too tired to even apologize. Sorry. I'll be nicer tomorrow."

Gus cleared his throat. "Good night."

I turned back in surprise. "Good night, Gus."

He turned away. As I climbed the stairs, the sound of his futzing in the store filtered upstairs, comforting in its familiarity. Though he put on a hard shell, I had the feeling Gus cared more about Mixology than anyone on this Isle.

I found the bedroom in the attic, a room with slanted ceilings that met in a peak at the center. The space was big, formed from airy windows and high raftered ceilings. The bed sat in the middle of the room, all white, fluffy, and welcoming.

Stumbling toward the bed, I took a moment to bask in the bright moonlight and twinkling starlight streaming through the windows. In the Twin Cities, we could hardly see any stars due to the amount of lights, but here, the night was pure and crystalline.

After a quick shower, I slipped into the first nightie I could find hanging in my magically enhanced closet, and I climbed into bed. The smell of freshly laundered sheets, scented with sunlight and salty sea air, enveloped my body as the silky fabrics lay smooth against my skin.

I sighed in bliss. As I closed my eyes, listening to Gus tinkering in the store below—glass lids tinkling as jars were opened and shut, the swish of a broom's bristles against the wooden floor, the creak of a chair as Gus finally sat down—the stress of the day seeped away, and I was left with a sense of contentment I'd rarely known.

My fingers found the heart charm dangling above my chest, the necklace still warm to my touch. Though it was just a simple piece of jewelry, I remembered what my aunts had told me—it was protection, a piece of my mother passed on to me.

And as I drifted to sleep on the magical Isle, I couldn't help but feel grateful for the family I'd come to know and already love.

CHAPTER 12

"*WAKE UP!*"

The shout startled me from a peaceful, dreamless slumber. I rolled over, savoring the last few minutes in the heavenly comfort of my bed. Gus's grating voice served as the harsh reminder that I had another long day ahead of me, one filled with more reading, sitting, studying, reciting—so much work that my head ached just thinking about it.

"*What do you think this is, a bed and breakfast?*" From the sound of it, Gus was standing at the bottom of the staircase, shouting his lungs out. "*Get your rear end out of bed and come downstairs. Now.*"

I shut my eyes, thinking that had to be the most obnoxious alarm clock in the land. I bet the East Isle could hear every word.

"I'm coming!" I called back. My words cracked, my voice still rusty with sleep. *How long had I been out?*

Squinting, I spotted a clock on an old, antique-style dresser, and it blinked seven o'clock. I had barely managed six hours of shut-eye before it was time to get back at it.

As much as my body didn't want to sit and study for another twelve hours, a part of me fluttered with excitement. At some point, the studying had to slow and the mixing had to begin. That was what I looked forward to learning. But my excitement was interrupted by more of Gus's bellowing echoing up the stairs.

"I'm *coming.*"

I stood, selected another sundress from the closet for simplicity's sake, and stepped into it. The fabric was soft against my skin, an off-white with a hint of lace on the sleeves. It felt nice against my slightly burned skin—my body wasn't used to the strong sun on The Isle. This magic closet was something I could get used to, for sure. It was better than a personal stylist and far less expensive.

I shuffled downstairs after pairing a set of fluffy, pastel-yellow slippers with my white dress, since I didn't have anyone to impress. I would bet a lot of money Gus didn't give a rat's behind about shoe style.

"It's early." I rubbed my eyes as I stepped into the store. "We couldn't have started at eight?"

"No." Gus, though he'd had less sleep than me, looked as if he'd clocked a full twelve hours of snoozing and gotten a massage at a spa. His eyes were clear, and he managed to speak in complete sentences, unlike myself.

"Do we have coffee?"

"You can make some." Gus bustled about the shelves, pulling down a few jars. "I've got out the ingredients for a Caffeine Cup. Go ahead."

"Can't I just make regular coffee?" I asked.

"Why would you want to?" Gus's eyes flashed with confusion as he gestured around the store. "That's like going to a gourmet buffet and asking for a piece of plain toast."

"How am I supposed to know? Mimsey made regular coffee yesterday," I grumbled, still cranky at getting pulled out of bed so early. "Coffee's been working for me for the past decade."

"Yes, well, she doesn't need the practice. You do."

"Do you have instructions?" I scratched my head, looking with dismay at the ingredients spread across the counter. "I don't know how any of these things work."

"Then I suggest you figure it out." Gus shook his head. "Do you expect me to do your work for you? I only pulled the jars from the shelves so you wouldn't kill yourself with your first mix. Nothing there is toxic. You might get sick, but you'll recover."

"How very kind of you." I peered closer at the jars, this time recognizing one or two of them. "Will you watch to make sure I do it right?"

"No. I have an errand to run—need to sweep up some more Nightshade from the supply shop." Gus grabbed a hat from a peg beside the door and put it on his head. "I'll be back. You have ten minutes to complete it, or no caffeine for you."

"That's not fair," I moaned.

"Ten minutes."

Ten minutes later, I had somehow concocted a bubbling mass of something that looked similar to coffee but had a bit of a foreign scent to it.

"I have no idea what I'm doing," I mumbled. "No instructions and expecting me to work before coffee. Now that's just cruel."

Glancing around the store and making sure that Gus hadn't crept back unnoticed, I leaned over my miniature mixing cauldron. It sat on a stand above a tea lamp, which according to the *Magic of Mixology*, was the best way to heat a Caffeine Cup.

I waved my hand, feeling like an idiot as I recited another made-up incantation.

Bubble, bubble, toil, and trouble
Can't think of a rhyme except for Hubble.
I need some coffee, and I need it fast,
Else my patience for Gus will never last.

I gave the mixture a moment to react, hoping against hope I'd unlocked the secret of magic. Unfortunately, I hadn't.

"Dang it," I murmured as the mixture remained exactly the same. "Why does that never work?"

The creak of a porch stair alerted me to Gus's presence just outside the store, but I was too late to do anything about it. He leaned against the edge of the door, his face impossible to read.

"I didn't mean it. Again. I promise," I stammered. "I was just testing to see if I could come up with a spell, but... wait a second. What's wrong? Why do you look so sad?"

He didn't respond.

"Gus, is everything okay?" I stepped from behind the table.

Again, he didn't move to answer my question. But before I could prod him for information, Aunt Trinket flew past him into the room, a whirl of pink pantsuit, puffed-up hair, and angry lips.

"What did you *do?*" Striding straight up to me, her eyes wide and her body shaking in what I guessed was either surprise or rage, she looked me in the eye. "What were you *thinking, Lily?*"

"What are you talking about?" I stepped back. Trinket's perfume smelled perfectly fine on a normal day, but this morning, it overwhelmed me and made me claustrophobic as she waved her arms in front of my face.

"Leonard Fluffleknocker," she said. "What on earth did you do to him?"

"Absolutely nothing." I glanced over her shoulder at Gus, hoping he'd confirm my story. "He wasn't even sick to begin with. I gave him coffee and juice, that's it."

Trinket breathed heavily, her eyes still brimming with crazy. "You did nothing. Are you sure?"

"Not a thing," I said again. "I'm positive. Gus can back me up, I promise."

More heavy breathing from Trinket, and no confirmation from Gus.

"Why?" I asked. "What's wrong?"

Aunt Trinket eyed me up and down, her face contorting in thought. Eventually, her expression turned from upset to resigned. She shook her head.

"What?" I pressed.

Trinket lowered her gaze, her shoulders slumping as if the anger had seeped right from her and evaporated into thin air, leaving only a trace of sadness in its wake. "He's gone."

"Leonard's gone? He ran away?" I asked. "Where did he go?"

"No. Leonard was found dead this morning." She looked at me, her eyes bright with warning, analyzing my face. "He's died, Lily. And everyone's wondering why."

CHAPTER 13

I GASPED, MY HEAD REELING AS I tried to process Trinket's words.

"Do you know anything about this?" she asked.

I shook my head. "I… I'm wondering why too."

"You know *nothing* about this." Trinket's hands came up, her bony fingers clasping my shoulders.

"Nothing," I confirmed. "I promise you."

"Trinket, let her *go!*" Mimsey stormed into the room, a wildly patterned dress fluttering as she stomped by, her clothing so bright it stung my eyes. "Get your hands off our niece."

I breathed a sigh of relief as Trinket let go. I glanced at Mimsey.

"I don't know *anything*," I said, stepping back and looking between my aunts. "I promise you."

"Of course you don't, dear," Mimsey said with a flick of her eyes in my direction. "You've only just arrived. I saw that spell you did yesterday. It was nonsense. Nonsense incantations don't work. Come on, Trinket, you know better than that."

Gus's gaze burned holes in my head as I glanced at my shoes.

"Well, of course. It's just… people talk, and…" Trinket stuck her pointy nose in the air. "I just had to be sure."

"Of course people talk!" Mimsey threw her hands up in exasperation. "When have people *not* talked about the West Isle Witches? We're different, Mimsey. We live between the jail and The Forest, and people like to start rumors. They need to unify their hate against someone, and it's usually us. That's never bothered you before, so why are you going nuts now?"

Trinket sucked in a breath. "Well, Lily is new here. Maybe it was an accident, maybe—"

Her words faded as Mimsey walked right up to her sister. Though Mimsey was a good several inches shorter than her sister, her eyes beamed with intensity, making her seem taller, bigger, and more powerful than anyone else in the room. "Don't you dare finish that sentence, Trinket. Lily is as much of a West Isle Witch as *any* of us."

Trinket's chest heaved, but she didn't comment.

"Don't you dare insult her mother—*our sister*—by saying anything else, you hear me?" Mimsey said. "Lily had nothing to do with Leonard's death. Leonard was rude to her, just as he is to everyone else, and she saved him from embarrassment. She didn't have to do that, but she did it to be nice."

"But maybe—" Trinket started.

"Maybe nothing! Don't you trust me? Don't you trust Gus?" Mimsey shook her head. "We were both here. Nothing happened. His death is unrelated to whatever he moaned about yesterday. Leonard had gas, and that's final. It's only because of Lily that the entire Isle didn't find out."

"But the Rangers are saying he didn't die from natural causes," Trinket said.

"That doesn't point the blame to our niece!" Mimsey threw her head back, rolling her eyes to the ceiling. "Leonard was a real jackarse. You know that. I know that. Everyone knows that. The only person who *didn't* know what a turd he could be was Lily."

Trinket murmured in agreement.

"Now I'm not saying I wanted him dead," Mimsey said. "I'm just saying that plenty of people didn't like him, and I'm ashamed of you for storming in here like that and pointing your bony little finger."

"Mimsey, it's okay," I said, finding the guts to step forward. I rested a hand on her arm. "You have no idea how much I appreciate you sticking up for me, saying all that stuff."

Mimsey's gaze was still livid, but her eyes softened slightly. "You didn't deserve to be accused, honey."

"I didn't do anything to Leonard. I have no reason to lie. I don't know him from Adam, and I have no reason to wish him harm." I turned to Trinket. "But I understand why someone might think... might be skeptical, since I'm new here. Don't get mad at your sister."

Mimsey waved in dismissal. "We get mad at each other all the time. That's what sisters do. And Trinket needed to be put in her place this time. What I'm really confused about is Adam. Who the heck is Adam?"

"Adam?" I looked around, confused.

"You said you didn't know Leonard from Adam." Mimsey pursed her lips. "I don't know Adam either. Why is he important?"

"Oh!" I said. "It's a saying."

"A saying?"

"Never mind," Trinket said. "Adam isn't relevant."

I sat heavily in the chair before the table. "If it wasn't me, then what could've happened?"

Silence fell over the room.

After a long beat, Trinket spoke, stiffening her shoulders. "I owe you an apology, I suppose."

"I, uh, suppose I accept?" I looked at Mimsey.

"You do owe her an apology, Trinket," Mimsey fumed. "But we're moving on. It's just that sometimes being the talk of the town is hard. It's stressful. And when we're the first people everyone thinks of when it comes to strange occurrences, well... tempers flare."

"My temper didn't flare," Trinket corrected, tilting her chin up. "But I *suppose* I may have jumped to conclusions. As Mimsey said, the West Isle Witches are often the subject of gossip. I like to be ahead of the gossip, and this morning, I was behind the curve. I don't like that."

"Why are you—er, *we*—the source of gossip?" I asked. "You guys don't seem strange to me. I mean, except for the whole magic thing. But everyone here is used to that."

Mimsey started to speak, but Trinket cut her off. "Now is not the time to go into family history. If you aren't responsible for Leonard's death, then I need to go speak to the Rangers."

"It's not your business," Mimsey said. "Leave it alone, Trinket."

"I'm just asking questions. And I'm making sure they have no reason to suspect Lily." Trinket turned and flounced out of the room.

"Is she okay?" I pointed after my aunt.

"Trinket's just being nosy. Leonard's death will be the talk of the town in about two minutes." Mimsey wrinkled her nose. "In the meantime, we're cancelling your lessons for today. I'd like you to come to the supply shop with us."

"You're not cancelling her lessons," Gus growled. "It's more important than ever that she learns her trade."

"This place is going to be swarmed by busybodies and nosy onlookers. Everyone is going to stop by to get a looky-loo at my niece." Mimsey placed her hands on her hips. "She won't get any work done here. If we take her to the supply shop, we can at least give her some peace and quiet, a bit of protection from the gossip."

"I don't need to be protected," I said. "I can handle it. I'll stay here and study."

Gus's eyes burned with what I hoped was approval.

"No, dear. I'm sorry, I'm putting my foot down." Mimsey stomped to cement her words. "You're coming with me."

"But if I didn't do anything wrong, why should I hide?" I asked.

"You're not *hiding*, you're avoiding a bad situation." Mimsey huffed. "There's a difference."

"How long can we avoid the bad situations?" Gus stepped into the store, pacing in a slow circle around Mimsey. "How long are we going to close our eyes to the bad things happening around us?"

"You're making a correlation where there is none." Mimsey's shoulders trembled as she spoke. "This was an unfortunate accident. The Rangers will find the culprit and lock him away. End of story."

The silence in the room after Mimsey's statement spoke volumes. She averted her gaze from either of us as if she didn't quite believe it herself.

"How long are you going to keep telling yourself that?" Gus moved so close to Mimsey I could see the breath from his words ruffling her hair. "You know it as well as I do, Miss Mimsey. The winds are changing."

She straightened her shoulders.

"It's more important now than it's ever been that we have an experienced Mixologist on our side. We need her prepared, and time's a-ticking. If we wait any longer, it'll be a danger to us all."

My heart rate picked up as I listened to the pair speak as if I weren't standing right next to them.

"Fine." Mimsey's lips fell into a thin line. "She can study. Bring your book, Lily. We're not going away to hide."

I scooped up *The Magic of Mixology* at Gus's grudging nod. "Then why are we leaving?"

"We're going to meet your grandmother."

CHAPTER 14

"SO WHAT'S SHE LIKE?" I asked, scurrying across the sandy walkway after Mimsey. My aunt's legs were far shorter than my own, yet somehow, I couldn't keep up.

"You'll see soon enough."

"Does she know about me?" I half-jogged to match her pace.

"Of course she does."

Mimsey clearly wasn't in the mood for small talk, so I concentrated on the surroundings. We sailed down a small path I hadn't noticed before. It ran along the north side of the bungalow, its entrance masked by shrubbery and overflowing flowers. If Mimsey hadn't pushed back a branch and shown me the way, I might never have found it.

"Is this a shortcut?" I asked.

"You could say that." Mimsey pushed past a bush with pink flowers as large as my head.

I fell silent again, watching my step as we twisted and turned through the foliage.

"What is this place?" I ducked underneath a tree wrapped with vines.

It felt as if a tropical jungle had sprouted up out of nowhere, except it was like no rainforest I'd seen before. Orange blossoms as big as chairs lined the path, while a prickly plant bloomed with white petals as large as umbrellas, the leaves coated with fur. Ruby-red fruits dripped juice, large sticky gobs of the stuff, from overhead.

"The Twist," Mimsey said, breaking the silence. "It's called The

Twist. A long series of gardens that doubles as a labyrinth. Your grandmother is… paranoid."

I dodged a huge drop of the sap-like substance as I darted around a vine that moved as if it were a thinking, breathing entity. "So you're saying we're in a maze right now?"

"Only those with West Isle Witch blood can find their way to Grannie's. We're almost there now, just a few more feet and… here we are." Mimsey pushed one last berry-filled branch out of the way as she stepped into sunlight.

A moment later, I emerged behind her, trading the semi-darkness for a bright, manicured lawn. The sun's rays warmed my skin as I sucked in a breath. I held it in as I took in the grounds.

Eventually, Mimsey realized I'd stopped. She turned around. "You like it?"

"This is incredible." I felt as if I'd stepped out of the real world and into a fairy garden. Granted, I'd already stepped out of the real world the moment I began believing in magic and found myself on an enchanted island, but this was something else.

Far in the distance, I spotted a cozy stone cottage, built in a crooked, charming sort of fashion. Leading up to the cottage was a gravel path that wound through gardens with blossoms so vibrant, they made Minnesota's greenery pale in comparison. The scent of roses and lilacs hung heavy in the air, drifting with a lazy breeze that kept the temperature cool—a nice change of pace from the humid jungle that'd led us here. I closed my eyes and detected a whiff of lilies and a hint of apple blossom.

"Yes, it's nice." Mimsey appeared significantly less dazzled by the ambiance than me. Then again, maybe if I'd grown up here, I'd have gotten used to it too.

But the newish cookie-cutter house I'd grown up in on the outskirts of St. Paul had lacked the quaintness that this place had in spades. Bushes spilled onto the pathways, and a brook babbled in cheerful spirals around the gardens. Birds and small animals hopped and scurried about. I even saw a pair of swans on the water, which was as clear as glass. Bright pebbles lined the riverbed, giving the water a mystical, almost ethereal quality.

I blinked at Mimsey's definition of *nice*, forcing myself to snap to attention. The yard, the cottage, the maze—everything was gorgeous. But I wasn't on a walking tour. I had come to meet my grandmother.

"Now, I'm going to give you one warning," Mimsey said, sliding her arm through mine as I joined her on a small bridge crossing over the stream. "Your grandmother is a bit... kooky."

"Kooky?" I raised an eyebrow.

Mimsey sighed. "I can't explain it. You'll see. Just don't take offense to anything she says."

"Of course not," I assured Mimsey with a pat on her forearm as she led me to the front door, but my stomach churned with nerves.

"Relax, dear. It'll be all right." Mimsey raised a hand to a knocker as round as a dinner plate. She took in a deep breath, clasped the handle, and leaned back with all her weight.

I stepped back to give her space.

"It's quite... *heavy*, this door knocker." Mimsey grunted as she let the handle fall against the door.

A church-like bell radiated from each and every window and out over the trickling stream, the reverberations rattling my skull. A few birds took off, and another few animals rustled through the underbrush.

"Wow." I stuck a finger in my ear, trying to clear some of the leftover *ringing* sensation. "That's quite loud."

"Your grandmother's quite deaf." Mimsey crossed her arms. "Well, she's selectively deaf. She doesn't like visitors and tends to ignore a *normal* knock on the door, so Trinket and I had this installed. There's no way she can ignore a sound like that."

I heartily agreed, wondering if I'd gone partially deaf myself. I'd had to read Mimsey's lips to understand half of what she was saying. As the last of the reverbs dampened, we waited patiently for someone to let us inside.

When nobody came, Mimsey raised her fist and pounded on the door. "Don't make me do that again, Hettie! Because I will, and you know it."

Nothing but silence greeted Mimsey's threat.

"Maybe she didn't hear you?" I suggested.

"Of course she did," Mimsey mumbled. "Everyone inside The Twist can hear this knocker. That's part of the charm."

I was fairly certain Mimsey meant *literal* charm instead of figurative.

"Well, she asked for it." Mimsey fastened her hands around the knocker once again and leaned back with all her weight. "She wants to ignore me? I'll make that old woman deaf before I let her ignore me."

Just before Mimsey released the deafening knocker, a voice floated through the heavy wood of the door. "Put that thing down, and set it gently. Who do you think you are, molesting your own mother's ears with that racket?"

Mimsey rolled her eyes at me, slowly releasing the knocker. The smallest of sound waves bounced off and disappeared into The Twist. "About time, Mother."

Amid grumbles, shuffles, and a cloud of dust, the door eventually opened outward, almost wiping us clear off the steps. I leapt out of the way, as did Mimsey.

"Mother, we switched your door to open *inward*, like every other normal person's in the world." Mimsey stepped off the front steps. "Why did you change it back?"

"I prefer to make sure my visitors remain on their toes." A tiny, bird-like woman stood behind the door, her hair curled into a miniature Afro. "Y'all get knocked off my stairs, it ain't my problem."

"That's not how you make a good first impression on your granddaughter." Mimsey gestured toward me. "Meet Lily."

The woman I guessed to be my grandmother squinted, analyzing me. She wore a velour tracksuit with diamond-studded pockets, more bling on her fingers than most jewelry stores owned in their entirety, and a headband that said *Fabulous* pushing back her hair. To top it off, her carefully styled 'fro glistened with a shimmery purple-and-blue mixture carefully layered over her gray locks.

"Hello," I said with a small wave. "Like she said, I'm Lily."

My grandmother remained silent. Eventually she stepped outside and walked in a slow circle around me. She squeezed my nostrils shut then yanked on a lock of my hair. When she reached the back of my body, she gave my butt a pinch.

"Yep, you're a West Isle witch," she confirmed.

"Of course she is, Mother. Stop being facetious." Mimsey lightly smacked her mother's hand as the woman began to stick her finger in my ear. "Stop it."

"I'm analyzing my granddaughter. Aren't I allowed to do that?" Hettie turned to Mimsey, narrowing her eyes. "Just making sure she's healthy."

"You're messing with her," Mimsey said. "Leave her alone, and invite us inside."

I stood stock-still, very confused. I now understood what Mimsey meant by my grandmother being kooky. If anything, I thought kooky might be an understatement.

"So do I look healthy?" I asked, playing along. After all, I only got the chance to make a good first impression on my long-lost grandmother once.

"What is this nonsense you're wearing? Look at this." Hettie snapped the spaghetti straps of my sundress against my shoulders.

"It's a sundress," I said. "Supplied by my new closet here."

"It's a baby-making dress. You're practically walking around *inviting* half the town to frolic underneath your frock."

"*Mother!*" Mimsey jumped in, looking appalled. "Stop it. She looks beautiful, and the dress is completely respectable."

"Oh, I know, I'm just kidding. I was just about to ask where I can get one of them," Hettie said. "It'd be nice to flaunt these ol' legs of mine."

"Well, I found it in my closet." I gestured to where I thought the bungalow might be. At the moment, we were so far deep in The Twist that the only sign of the water surrounding us was a light misty layer in the distance, hovering over the treetops.

Mimsey crossed her arms. "Invite us in, or we're off. We stopped by for... well, reasons."

"Ah, right. Come in." Hettie waved an arm at us. "You must wait for an invitation inside; otherwise my tiger will attack you. He's trained to attack anyone who enters without my personal invitation."

I glanced at Mimsey. "Is that real?"

"Of course it's real," Hettie growled, striding ahead of us. "Or is it? Better not test me, 'cause you never know."

Mimsey spun her finger in circles next to her temple. I nodded.

Without glancing back, Hettie raised one finger that was right in the middle of all the others. "I can see you back there. I'm not *crazy*."

My mouth parted, but I didn't say anything.

"I have eyes in the back of my head." Hettie looked over her shoulder and winked. "*Or do I?* Better not test me."

"Stop being difficult, Mother," Mimsey said. "Let's sit down for a cup of tea. We have things to discuss."

"This way." Hettie made a sharp left down a stone walkway.

Though Hettie's home looked like a quaint cottage on the outside, the inside was much more spacious, complete with spiral staircases leading off the main hallway in every direction, big fireplaces sporadically placed between rooms, and even a few exotic birds flitting above. But when Hettie stopped and opened a heavy-looking wooden door with a snap of her fingers, she led us into a room that fit perfectly with the "hidden cottage" theme.

Plush chairs lined an oak table marred by imperfections—probably handmade and very old. A fireplace large enough to drive a car through lined one wall. In front of it sat a simple two-person table with matching chairs, a quaint tea set complete with a steaming pot and stacks upon stacks of cookies already prepared in the center.

"Here, dear." Mimsey pulled out a chair for me with a wave of her hand and nodded for me to sit down. She followed suit, then Hettie sat.

"So..." Hettie wiggled her fingers over the cookie selection, eventually choosing a macaroon and popping it whole into her mouth. She raised her eyes to me and cocked her head sideways. "I hear you've been on The Isle for one day and already killed someone."

I'd been eying the cookies as well, too afraid to reach for one, when my jaw dropped at her words. "What? No! I haven't killed anyone."

"Shame. That Leonard was a real donkey patootie." Hettie looked somewhat disinterested now that I'd admitted to *not* killing anyone, and she reached for another cookie.

"*Mother*. Stop that. Leonard didn't deserve to die, even if he was rude." Mimsey crossed her arms, ignoring the cookies. "After all, your manners leave something to be desired."

"I'm old. I'm allowed to be rude."

"You're completely capable of living a normal, non-rude life," Mimsey said. "You only say you're old when it suits you. Otherwise, your age doesn't affect you in the slightest."

"That's where you're wrong, daughter. I'm a bit saggier than I was in my prime." Hettie glanced down at herself. "Can't do much about that."

"Magic?" I asked.

"We don't alter our own appearances, and illusions are a

lie," Mimsey quickly explained. "We don't encourage magic that harms others, even if it's just a small lie. Slippery slope, you know. And *Mom*, I don't want to hear about *your sagginess*. You're still my mother."

"Yes, I suppose so." Hettie looked deep in thought. "You know, I like that. From now on, please refer to me as Your Sagginess."

"Mother—" Mimsey started.

"That's *Your Sagginess* to you." Hettie pointed at her daughter, waving her finger back and forth as if chastising a child. "I will refuse to answer to anything else."

"Mother, please. This is serious. We need to discuss Leonard." Mimsey stared resolutely at her.

Hettie, however, dunked a sugared cookie into her tea and took a bite.

"Stop acting like a child." Mimsey slid her mother's teacup away from her.

Unfazed, Hettie raised her hand and, as if fishing with an invisible line, hooked the teacup with a quick flick of her fingers and slid it back across the table in front of her.

"Mother," Mimsey began again, the exasperation growing in her voice. When Hettie didn't respond, Mimsey *harrumphed*. "Fine, Your Sagginess."

"Was that so difficult?" Hettie's gaze flicked between the two of us. "Now, speak. What did you come to tell me?"

"Well, I didn't come to *tell* you much of anything," Mimsey admitted. "I came to ask if you'd let Lily stay here until we sort things out."

I swiveled my head to look at Mimsey. "What?"

Hettie looked amused by my reaction.

"I don't want to stay here." Hearing how that sounded almost as quickly as I finished speaking, I turned to Hettie. "Not that I don't love this place. The house is adorable, and you seem... well, it'd be nice to get to know you, but I don't want to hide away. I want to help."

I looked back at Mimsey, who looked down. "I think you should relax here and study. The Rangers will take care of everything."

Hettie threw her hands in the air. "It was just Leonard. What's the big fuss? Can't they do the typical autopsy?"

"Foul play was involved, Mother—"

"Your Sagginess," Hettie corrected.

"Your Sagginess," Mimsey said with an eye roll. "We can't have the new Mixologist's name attached to a murder, especially before most of The Isle has even met the girl."

"They may not have met her, but everyone's watching." Hettie turned eerily knowing eyes in my direction. "You're already famous, new girl."

A shiver ran down my spine. "I'm not sure I like the sound of that."

Hettie shrugged. "That's not my problem. I just thought I'd let you know."

"Anyway, *mothe*—Your Sagginess, can Lily stay here for a few days? Just until things are sorted out." Mimsey turned to me, her gaze imploring. "You'll be safe here. Nobody can reach this cottage without West Isle Witch blood, as I said. And frankly, nobody much wants to come here."

"What's that supposed to mean?" Hettie narrowed her eyes at Mimsey.

"If you insist people call you Your Sagginess and you refuse to answer the door, Mother, that's what happens. You've told half The Isle a tiger will attack them if they ever knock on your door." Mimsey massaged her temples. "You've done this to yourself."

"Oh, I like my peace and quiet." Hettie sat back with a satisfied expression. "In fact, I should do more to make sure people are scared of this place. Maybe a real tiger is in order…"

"I'm leaving. Lily, please stay here," Mimsey said.

"Excuse me." I raised a finger. "Um, Aunt Mimsey, I'm sorry, but I don't want to stay here." I glanced at Hettie. "Again, nothing against you or the house… uh, Your Sagginess."

Hettie bowed her head. "No offense taken, Your Perkiness."

"Stop it, Mother," Mimsey said. "And Lily, why on earth would you say that? Even Gus didn't have a problem with you studying from here for a few days. And Gus has a problem with everything."

"Right old crank, he is," Hettie said. "His Grouchiness."

Mimsey ignored her mother. "You'll be safe here. Away from questions, the public eye, nosy busybodies stopping by to see what you're all about. They'd just disturb your studies, dear."

"I concur." Hettie pounded her fist on the table as if she were a judge. "As a busybody myself, I can say that my daughter, Her Know-It-All, is correct. I would definitely be stopping by to order a drink and test the new Mixologist, if you stayed at your home."

I flexed my fingers. Getting assessed by one nosy islander after another did not sound appealing. "But staying here would be the easy way out. Plus, I don't really want to see if that tiger actually exists."

Hettie beamed.

"I have to go back home." I shook my head, pushing my untouched teacup toward the center of the table. "If I'm truly to become the next Mixologist, or at least give it a shot, I have to give it a full shot. And that doesn't mean hiding away."

"You won't be hiding forever," Mimsey said.

"I may be new here, and I don't fully understand magic yet. Maybe I never will. But I do understand the message I'm sending if I hunker down here until this passes. I don't want to be known as the person who hides when things get difficult."

Silence fell on the table.

After a long moment, Hettie punched the air. "Zing! One point for my granddaughter, zero points for my daughter."

Mimsey frowned at Hettie. When she returned her gaze to me,

the frown was replaced by a resigned look. "Are you sure about this? We want to protect you, dear. If you choose to go back to the shop, we can help some, but we might not be able to shield you from everything."

"I don't want to be shielded." Gaining confidence, I swallowed, trying that whole *fake it 'til you make it* mentality. "I want to go back to my shop."

"That settles it." Hettie pushed back from the table and stood. "For what it's worth, I'm glad I don't have a tomato for a granddaughter."

"A tomato?" I asked.

"Mother, that's not the saying." Mimsey shook her head. "A tomato—"

"A tomato is squishy. It goes rotten quickly, and it collapses under the smallest amount of pressure. The skin is thin, soft—it's malleable." Hettie cleared her throat. "I think it's a perfectly good expression, and if it's not one, then write it down and *make* it one."

I looked away, uncomfortable being the topic of conversation. I tried to hide the flush in my cheeks at being called *not* a tomato. In a strange way, it was the nicest thing anyone had ever said to me.

"You're right." Mimsey looked at me, a hint of pride in her eyes. "She is *not* a tomato. Her mother would be proud."

An odd silence fell on the room, and I busied myself looking deep into the fireplace, though it remained empty. I had so many questions about my lineage, but now wasn't the time to ask.

Mimsey cleared her throat. "Well, I must be getting off. If it's settled that you won't be staying here, then we should leave together. The Twist is difficult to navigate, even for those with West Isle Witch blood."

"May I offer a piece of advice?" Hettie raised her finger.

Mimsey shook her head. "No. Enough advice from you today."

"Well, I'm going to offer it anyway, just like any good parent does." My grandmother turned to me. "Don't be a tomato when it comes to Leonard either. Understand?"

I frowned. "I'm not sure I do. Aren't the Rangers looking into things?"

"Isn't your name on the line?" Hettie raised an eyebrow. "I wouldn't leave my reputation in anyone's hands but myself."

"Maybe you should," muttered Mimsey. "You might have a slightly less *crazy* reputation if you did."

"That's exactly what I'm talking about." Hettie smiled broadly. "My reputation is the fault of nobody except myself. And if people want to think I'm bonkers, so be it. I'd rather be underestimated than overestimated, ain't that right?"

I crossed my arms. "So is this whole '*out there*' reputation a ruse? An act?"

"Not at all. She really is nuts, just give it some time." Mimsey pursed her lips. "Are you ready? Is the lecture finished, Your Sagginess?"

"For now." Hettie looked at her fingernails. "Don't worry, there's more where that came from."

"We'll be holding our breath," Mimsey said with a tight smile. "Lily?"

"I'm happy I got to meet you," I said. "Maybe I can come back and visit sometime?"

"Don't get eaten by the tiger." Hettie waltzed away without another word, leaving the door swinging on her way through it.

"That was..." I turned to Mimsey. "Interesting."

"You're far, far too kind." Mimsey took my hand and led me through the house. "You're guaranteed *interesting* with my mother, that's for certain."

CHAPTER 15

"YOU'RE A *MURDERER?*" ZIN, FOR the first time since I arrived, showed actual approval toward me. "Wow, you're making waves on what... day two on the island? Three? I lost count."

"I'm not a murderer!" I fiddled with the heart necklace, hoping it had some power to calm me down. After leaving the cottage, Mimsey had led me straight to the tiki bar. She said she wanted to show me around, but in retrospect, I'm nearly certain she just wanted to assign me babysitters. "I don't know anything about it."

"Ew." Poppy shuddered. "Murder. Blood. So gross."

"And sad," I added. "It's sad too."

"I *hate* blood." Poppy winced.

"Of all people to be born a vamp." Zin shook her head. "I can't believe it."

"You're just jealous because I *could* be dangerous. Watch—" Poppy paused a moment, closing her eyes and concentrating. After a moment of silence, she opened her eyes and jumped toward Zin with her fingers outstretched like a fake monster. "Boo!"

I started, stepping backward even though she didn't look in my direction. Poppy's not-fake-fangs extended beyond her lips, making her appearance legitimately scary.

A small *snap* sounded, the telltale sign of Zin shifting.

"Gotcha!" Poppy laughed. "Serves you right. Don't make fun of my blood intolerance. I can't help it."

I glanced at my feet, but instead of a turtle, there sat a cute little chipmunk.

"Hi there, Chippie," I said, bending and offering Zin my finger.

She completely ignored it, her little furry legs charging toward Poppy. Zin's small body scurried up her cousin's leg as Poppy giggled in uncontrollable fits.

"Get off, get off!" Poppy swiped at her back, where Zin danced on tiny chipmunk feet. "That tickles!"

I bent over, laughing just as hard, as Zin scampered up Poppy's neck and perched on top of Poppy's head. Just as Poppy swung at her own head, Zin took a flying leap, her chipmunk form sailing through the air.

I stopped laughing and dove forward in an attempt to catch Zin before she injured her small body with a crash landing. What I *didn't* anticipate was that Zin had planned her landing all along. As I hit the ground, arms outstretched and palms facing upward, another *snap* alerted me to Zin's changing figure. Before she landed, human Zin returned in a mass of sprawling limbs and bumbling legs.

Unfortunately, I hit the ground first.

Zin followed shortly after. Except instead of sitting on the ground, she landed smack dab on me.

"Ow!" I grunted. Even though Zin was petite and thin, the impact of a hundred pounds falling straight onto my rear end was enough to knock the wind out of me.

Meanwhile, another *thunk* sounded, this one due to Poppy's body hitting the floor as she burst into howls of laughter. Zin sat in stunned silence.

I moaned. "I can't breathe."

"Why in the world would you do that?" Zin shifted her weight to the floor, situating herself between Poppy and me. "Why did you try to catch me?"

"I didn't want you to get hurt!" I massaged my stomach as I

rolled onto my side. "You took a flying leap. I thought maybe you'd lost it and were trying to… I dunno… end it all."

This time, both of my cousins fell silent, looking at me with astounded gazes.

"You know chipmunks can practically fly, right?" Poppy asked. "Not to mention she was transforming back to normal size."

I groaned. "Yes, I realize that *now*."

Poppy and Zin shot each other a look that bordered on amusement, before the both of them lost it again, writhing in unstoppable giggle-convulsions.

My face flamed, and I almost opened my mouth to argue. Thankfully, I held off a moment, considering the situation, and replayed the events in my mind. Then the funnies hit me as hard as they'd hit my cousins. The three of us rolled with laughter until my abs ached and tears streamed down our cheeks.

We laughed, hee-hawing until we'd dried the well of funniness. Just as we had begun to gather ourselves after the last wave of laughter—thanks to a reenactment by Poppy—a shadow appeared, looming over us.

We fell silent, and my eyes slid upward hesitantly. I lay sprawled on the ground, trying to catch my breath from a combination of laughter and being squashed. At the same time I looked up, I realized I'd twisted about so much, my dress had gotten caught far too high up my thighs to be appropriate. I tugged it down before shading my eyes from the sun and looking up again.

"I'm beginning to think you have a *thing* against pants."

The low, rumbling voice made a shudder rock my body, his seductive tone bringing back memories from the first time we'd met—on my porch. The Ranger who'd stopped by and scared me off my hammock was back, his face as stern as ever.

"I'm beginning to think you have a thing for creeping up on unsuspecting girls." I yanked on my dress while getting to my feet.

"Oh, snap," Poppy whispered. "Burn."

I ignored my cousin's color commentary and stepped toward Ranger X, taking in the scar next to his eye and the tailored white shirt buttoned over a thick, muscled chest. The shocking whiteness of the fabric contrasted against his deep tan, while the breeze coming off the lake ruffled his dark, unruly hair.

I could see objectively why other girls might throw themselves at him on a regular basis, but not this girl. He'd invaded my space on two occasions now, and he had the annoying habit of popping up when my dress was all out of whack.

He watched me with a relaxed expression, a lazy smile tugging at his lips. "That's the first time I've been accused of *creeping*."

"Well, keep it up, and it won't be the last." I crossed my arms and took a few deep breaths. Maybe I was overreacting a bit, but that cocky smirk on his face, the easy handsomeness of his features, the smart remarks he always had ready—the whole *package* had my blood boiling.

He blinked. "It's my duty to keep watch. I'm just doing my job."

"Bam, point for X," Poppy said, as if keeping score.

This time, Ranger X and I both looked in her direction.

"Do you mind?" I asked. "I'm busy putting him in his place."

"You're doing a great job of it." Poppy winked. Adopting an English accent, she did a half bow and waved for me to continue. "Carry on, carry on."

"Yes, do carry on." Ranger X stepped forward, closing the gap between us.

Dang it. I'd lost my train of thought. "You... well, you." I poked his chest. "What is your real name?"

"How is that relevant?" he asked.

"I need something to call you if I'm going to tell you off," I said.

"Ranger X works just fine," he said. "As it seems the gossip queens have shared with you already."

"Ranger X —what sort of name is that?" I extended a hand, my pointer finger jabbed against his chest. "That's a title. Not a name."

"For me, it's both."

"I don't believe you. You had a mom at one time, and she gave you a name. Didn't she?" I poked him a few more times. Mostly because my fingertip was already there against his chest, and I didn't know what else to do with it.

Before I could process his movements, Mr. Tall, Tan, and Tempting grasped my wrist hard and twisted me so close my chest pressed against his. I felt the distant *thud* of his heart as it raced against mine, a battle of wills.

"I do have a name," he said, his voice so low that Poppy and Zin had to lean in to hear. "But I'm not going to tell you."

"Why?" My skin rippled in reaction to his proximity. I couldn't help it. Even if the man made me madder than anyone else on this island, I couldn't deny the effect he had on me. Goose bumps prickled my arms and legs, and my stomach flip-flopped as he grasped my other wrist and pulled me even tighter to his body.

"Do you ladies *mind*?" Ranger X looked over my shoulder at Poppy and Zin, who were probably watching with their jaws hanging open.

"Nope, go ahead. I'm liking what I'm seeing here." Poppy sighed. "Romance."

"C'mon, let's talk amongst ourselves," Zin, the smarter of the two, at least for now, said.

"If you mean eavesdrop from a few feet away, I'm in." Poppy's whisper was loud enough for everyone to hear.

Ranger X's hold on my wrists tightened. He leaned in, his voice dancing over my ear as he whispered, "I'm not telling you my name, so you can forget about it. Names are power, and I'll never trust you with mine."

"But you know mine."

"Whose fault is that?" Ranger X let my wrists fall to my sides, taking a step backward.

"Well, that's just not fair." I shook my head. "I'm going to give you a name, then."

"That right?"

"Yes. It's gonna be…" I frowned as I thought. "Well, I don't know yet. But I'll think of one."

"Chad!" Poppy called from the peanut gallery. "Or Larry. I've always had a thing for Larry."

I shook my head. "He's not a Larry."

"Trevor," Zin suggested. "Or something dark. Let's go dark."

I shook my head. "I've got to sleep on it."

"Keep me posted." A slightly amused look danced in his eyes. "Meanwhile, I've got work to do."

"Peeking up skirts?" I muttered.

"I came by to *warn* you," he said. "If you won't stay in The Twist for safety, then at least don't walk around alone."

"I'm not in danger," I said. "And I didn't do anything."

"I'm not so sure about either of those." Ranger X looked at my cousins. "Don't let her out of your sight."

"I don't need a babysitter. I didn't do anything wrong!"

"Is there a reason she's in danger?" Poppy asked. "I mean, aside from you peeking up her sundress?"

"I'm not peeking anywhere." Ranger X's voice turned exasperated. "But if she's flaunting it in plain sight, I won't say no to a glimpse."

I turned to face him, a retort hot on my tongue.

"He's just saying that to rile you up." Poppy rested a hand on my shoulder. "Don't take the bait."

"Am I?" His brows pinched together as he made eye contact with me, holding it until I looked away.

"You're annoying," was the only thing I could come up with as I stepped back to Poppy's side.

"Don't wander off." Ranger X turned on his heel and walked away.

"Dang, he's off duty now," Poppy said. "Something big must be brewing for him to come find you in his leisure clothes."

"Those are leisure clothes?" I snarled. "Looks like he's ready for a wedding."

"Yours?" she asked hopefully. "I can feel the heat radiating off you two."

"Angry heat," I corrected.

"Anger and lust are a fine line," Poppy said. "Could go either way. But let's forget about it. He seriously doesn't mess around with small-time crime. If he's warned you to look out, we'd better watch your back."

"I don't feel like watching my back," I said, still fueled from my exchange with Ranger X. "I feel like marching forward and finding out who is responsible for this mess."

"All right, honey. All right." Poppy patted my shoulder again. "Let's be smart about it, though. We're stopping by the supply store for a few things, then we'll start asking some questions."

"The supply store?" I asked.

"Well, no offense, but your magic is crap," Poppy said.

"And you might have killed somebody with your potions," Zin added. "So it's best if we get you some sort of third-party weapon for now. Just to have for backup."

"I didn't kill anyone!"

"We know, we know. The weapons are just like… hm. What do you have in the human world?" Poppy asked.

"Pepper spray?" I asked.

"Yes. Except we use much more awesome things." Poppy pulled me forward. "Let's go. We can talk about where we need to start asking questions along the way."

"I already know the answer to that," I said, my eyes narrowing as we marched toward the supply store. "I have a few questions for Mr. Harpin."

Chapter 16

"WHAT ARE THESE?" I HELD up a pair of sunglasses that belonged back in the eighties. Large, circular lenses were surrounded by heart-shaped frames made of a shiny pink plastic.

"They're sunglasses." Poppy looked at me as if I were an idiot. "You put them over your eyes."

"I know how to wear them." I slipped on the shades and found a mirror on a spinning carousel filled with more out-of-style sunglasses. "But I thought we were shopping for weapons."

"Not necessarily weapons." Poppy handed me another pair. "Try these. More like defense tools. You've already almost killed one person. I don't think it'd be a smart idea to put a weapon in your hand right now."

"I didn't kill anyone!" I ripped the shades from my face. "How many times do I have to tell you that?"

"This anger I'm sensing"—Poppy raised a hand and made circular motions in front of my body—"this is the reason we're not giving you weapons."

Zin rolled her eyes. "She's not going to kill anyone. She's far too honest."

"I'll, uh, take that as a compliment?" I shrugged. "I suppose."

"It wasn't meant to be one." Zin frowned.

"Zin *thinks* she likes dangerous, but she's just trying to overcompensate for her inability to shift into something beastly like a saber-toothed tiger-bird," Poppy said with a smirk.

"First of all, that's not a real animal," Zin said. "Second of all—"

"The sunglasses," I said, interrupting their tiff. We'd never get out of here at the rate these two bickerers were going. "Why do I need them?"

"They're Uncloakers." Poppy pursed her lips, selecting a pair of green shades in the shape of four-leaf clovers. Leftover St. Patty's Day paraphernalia, if I had to guess. "They allow you to see straight through any basic illusion."

"Awesome!" I slipped on the pair. "What else you got? And... I'll go with those plain black ones. The least conspicuous of the bunch, please."

"Boring." Poppy handed over the least obnoxious rims. "Next, let's get you some perfume."

Walking behind my cousins down the supply store, a place that could be described as a cross between an ancient library and a cluttered storage barn, I tried to discreetly sniff my armpits, but I didn't smell anything out of the ordinary.

"Perfume?" I scurried to catch up. "May I ask for what purpose?"

"Well, we sell all sorts of stuff. For you, I was thinking of the EvilAway," Poppy mused. "What do you think?"

"That'd be good, or we could go with a TruthTeller." Zin pursed her lips as she eyed me up and down. "We definitely don't want to mix and match."

"What do they do?" I asked, scanning the piles upon piles of baskets and barrels, bookshelves and drawers, bottles and canisters, and sprays, spritzes, and sprucers. If my cousins hadn't been there to guide me through the maze of boxes and stacks, I'd never have found a thing.

"They do exactly what they say." Poppy waved before selecting a teensy black bottle. "Ah. EvilAway. All it does is avert those with ill intentions toward you. These are light spells, so they won't keep away an exceptionally determined person. But it's easy, cheap, and better than nothin'."

"Here's the TruthTeller." Zin took a sniff. "This one smells nice. Fruity, essence of orange, I think. It *encourages* those nearest you to tell the truth. Much like EvilAway—and all perfumes, really—it's not perfect. The determined liar will be able to detect and press through the spell, but it's a bit more draining for them."

"Can I smell?" I leaned in to take a whiff at the same time Zin depressed the squirt bottle. A shot of the stuff went straight into my face, cloaking the air around us.

"You have ugly underwear," Poppy blurted. Clasping a hand to her mouth, she glanced wide-eyed at me. "I didn't mean to say that, sorry. It's the TruthTeller acting up."

"How would you know?" I stood, waving the perfume out of my face.

"Well, your dress kind of hiked up high when Ranger X showed up," Poppy said almost apologetically. "Maybe next time you're going to run into him, think *lace*. He seems like a guy who appreciates the finer things in life."

"I don't have plans to see him again," I growled. "Especially not romantically."

"Well, you can't do much worse than you already have." Zin clasped a hand over her mouth. But even a hand couldn't stop the effects of the spell; she continued to babble.

"It wasn't on purpose!"

"It's the TruthTeller, darlin'," Poppy said. "We can't help it. Anyway, let's go with that. Seems to be working great."

"Plus, it's already all over my face." I took a few deep breaths. "In fact, I think it's burned off most of my nose hairs. By the way, Poppy, you're nice. Zin, you're rude. But I wish I looked as cool as you."

"Yep, it's working... guess we don't even need to buy it." Poppy waved an arm. "You'll be able to make it on your own soon enough, once you get the hang of mixing perfumes. Now, let's get out of here."

"I'll be able to make it?" I asked as soon as we'd checked out and added the sunglasses to Poppy's ever-growing tab. I'd offered to pay, but she waved it off and said we'd sort it out later. "I've been meaning to ask you guys more about that. Seems like some of the witches here just snap their fingers and things happen. Will I be able to do that someday?"

"Neither of us are witches," Zin said. "In case you forgot."

"How could she forget your cute little chipmunk chompers?" Poppy pinched Zin's cheek then leapt out of the way before Zin could retaliate. "Witches tend to have a strength. Like Zin said, we don't know from experience. But we're related to enough of 'em to have an idea."

"What's your—*our*—grandmother's strength?" I asked.

"Ah, you had the pleasure of meeting Hettie, eh?" Zin's eyebrows shot up. "She's a joy, huh?"

"She's interesting," I said cautiously.

"Interesting." Poppy snorted. "Your political correctness will wear off very quickly. She's bonkers."

"She seemed nice," I argued.

"She's not particularly nice, but we love her anyway." Poppy shrugged. "Suppose that's family, huh?"

I shrugged right back. I certainly wasn't the expert on family dynamics. I'd grown up an only child with a dad as helpful as a cardboard cutout. I'd take Hettie any day. She'd even complimented me already, which was more than I could say for my dad. He'd never once told me I wasn't a tomato. "Anyway, about these special talents?"

"Well, Hettie has never told us," Poppy said, seeming grateful for the change of subject as she led us toward the lower bridge. "But we all have assumed she has Seer tendencies."

"Like... psychic powers?" I slid the sunglasses onto my head, not feeling the need to see through illusions at the moment.

"Sort of. Like I said, she's not a full-on psychic—she's a witch with Seer tendencies, meaning I suspect she has hints or glimpses of impending events," Poppy said. "But it's hard to say for certain because as big of a mouth as Hettie has, she likes to keep certain things private."

"Like her house," I agreed. "It was a bear to get through The Twist. I don't think I could do it alone."

"You could, but it takes time," Zin said. "I got lost for three days the first time I went in alone."

My jaw dropped. "Nobody rescued you?"

"Well, I also sort of ran away from home and stormed off in a huff. I think my mom thought it'd teach me a lesson," Zin said.

"Plus, she was sixteen," Poppy said with an eye roll. "Plenty old enough to take care of herself. She realized she couldn't control her shifting powers like she should be able to, said she was going to Gran's, then just stormed out of the house. With seven kids running around, I don't blame Trinket for not being able to keep track of 'em all."

"My mom's not the most sympathetic," Zin said, her eyes darkening. "Life with six younger siblings isn't always *easy*."

"Yeah, she decided to go the *rebel* route instead of the overachiever route, right, Zin?" Poppy winked. "That's why we get along so well."

Zin scowled.

Poppy ignored the glare. "I wanted a sibling for a while, but it was more of a phase than anything else. Zin and I grew up together, and she had enough siblings for the both of us. At my house, it's just me and Mimsey."

"I don't know how to ask this politely," I said. "But is it normal here to live with your parents even when you're... you know, almost thirty?"

"I live with my mom because it's just the two of us. My dad took off when I was little, and I didn't have the heart to leave my mom alone." Poppy shrugged. "I'd move out if I had a reason to—it's not as if she's holding me hostage. But for now, it's not so bad. Zin stays at home to help with her siblings. But she'd probably move out too, if the opportunity arose."

"You guys could always live at the bungalow with me if you want. There're extra bedrooms."

Poppy raised an eyebrow. "That's a thought I like thinking about."

Zin raised an eyebrow. "Living with you two? I'd consider it. As long as we lay down some ground rules first. I can't live with Poppy being so happy all the time. She'd drive me nuts."

I grinned. "You don't have to answer now. Just a thought. By the way, what are your moms' special tendencies?"

"My mom's is yelling and color-coding every Tupperware container in our house," Zin mumbled. "She's a rock star at that."

Poppy frowned. "Your mother has a talent for auras. That's how she knows how to hit everyone's weak spots. And frankly, it's how she can manage seven kids."

Zin grudgingly nodded. "It's true."

"See, here's how magic works. We can all get to the same outcome, we just have to discover our own talents to get there." Poppy gestured to the large Isle. "For example, say we're going to have a tsunami tomorrow, and we all have to figure out how to survive."

"We're not really going to have a tsunami, are we?" I glanced up at the cloudless blue sky.

"This is an example," Zin snapped. "Of course not. We have protective spells against storms. And you don't find tsunamis in the *sky*."

"She didn't know," Poppy said. "Anyway, I have a better example. One time, Zin decided to sneak out of the house at night, despite Aunt Trinket's strict curfew."

I looked at Zin. "True story?"

"No," grumbled Zin at the same time Poppy said, "Yep!"

"Hettie knew Zin was going to sneak out before she did it,

since she can see the future. Aunt Trinket, however, knew Zin was up to something because she had a black aura with a red outline, which signals a liar." Poppy glanced in my direction to see if I was following. I nodded, and she continued. "My mother has a penchant for ghosts. So all she had to do was chat with the departed to find out that Zin was off sneaking into The Forest, hoping for a glimpse of a Werewolf."

"A saber-toothed tiger," Zin corrected under her breath. "It had been spotted in the woods around our house."

"Then, there's you." Poppy scanned me up and down. "You still have to discover your tendency—nobody can do that for you. But if I had to guess, it'd be something with Mixology. You could've whipped up a Frothy Forecaster for a hint at the future, or a Truthful Tea to get Zin to spill the beans."

"Wow, I never expected witchcraft to be so complicated," I said. "Then again, I never expected it to be real either."

"It's really not that complicated," Poppy said. "It's quite simple once you figure out your tendencies. It's kind of like that college thing you human folks believe in, though I don't understand that. Explain to me how you expect an eighteen-year-old to decide—out of all the options in the world—what they want to do for the rest of their life?"

"That is a great question." I bit my lip. "And I don't have an answer. But if I wanted to get started, how would I go about figuring out my tendency?"

"I'm a vamp, and she's a shifter who can't figure out her form." Poppy looked at me with a smile. "We're the last people you want to ask. We can ask my mom later. For now though, we're almost back to the tea shop. Shall we go in?"

I shook my head. "Would you girls mind if I went in alone? I don't particularly want to, but I feel like it should be me. By myself. It's not you guys he has a problem with."

"We're not supposed to leave your side." Zin pulled a small

switchblade from her pocket and balanced it against her chin. "And I take my defensive duties seriously."

"She wants to become a Ranger," Poppy whispered. "But they don't let shifters become Rangers until they find their Final Form."

My heart twisted a bit as Zin's face fell.

"I'm sorry," I said, wanting to reach out to her.

"I don't want your sympathy," Zin said. "I didn't ask for this babysitting job. You do it, then, Poppy."

I hung my head, looking at the ground as Zin's footsteps faded into the distance. "I didn't realize I was such a burden. I'm sorry, you can go... I never meant to, uh, bother you guys."

"We were having a good time," Poppy said, her voice soft. "I shouldn't have said that stuff to her. I meant it as a joke, but sometimes I take things a little too far. I should apologize. The Rangers rejected her latest application just last week, so that was a cheap shot on my part."

"Listen, you go talk to her. I don't want to cause any wedges between you guys." Poppy didn't look convinced, so I pressed on. "Honestly. I really do want to speak to Harpin alone and see if he has anything else to say after the recent developments with Leonard."

"I can apologize later. I should stay..." Poppy watched as Zin hung her head, her figure getting smaller and smaller in the distance by the second.

"Go." I gave my cousin a push. "I'm not going anywhere, else I'd get lost. If I get done talking to Harpin before you're back, I'll wait out front. Right here."

"Right here? Sitting on the ground?" Poppy forced a small smile.

"If that's what it takes. Now *go*." I gave her another push, this time a bit harder. "Bring Zin back. Tell her I don't feel safe without her."

"That's a big fat lie," Poppy said. "But thank you. I'll let her know."

I stood still for a moment, watching with an easy smile as Poppy shifted into a jog, struggling to catch up to Zin's lithe frame. Zin would make an excellent Ranger, no doubt. Maybe the next time Ranger X came snooping around my private property, I'd have a few more words for him. It wouldn't hurt to see if he could use his influence to give Zin a leg up during the interview process.

When Poppy finally caught up to Zin, I waited a second longer to watch. I laughed as Poppy took a flying leap and tackled her cousin to the ground. As they righted themselves and brushed one another off, Zin's look of anger faded. The two looked as if they were fast on their way to making up, so I turned and entered the dank, musty tea shop. The smile wiped straight off my face.

"Ah… Lily." Harpin sat on the desk in the front of the room, his black robe long and swishing in the dim light as he shifted slightly. "Do come in. I've been expecting you."

CHAPTER 17

MY BODY STIFFENED, FIRST IN shock then disdain as Harpin's oily gaze slid over my body from head to toe, not missing a single part in between.

I struggled to hide my shiver. "How could you know I'd be coming here?"

"How do we know anything?"

"Do you have Seer tendencies?" I realized a beat too late what Harpin's question was—a dodge from my question.

"Ah, I see they've finally begun teaching you *infant* levels of magical knowledge." He stood, balancing his weight against the desk. "About time."

"Why do you hate me so much?" I hadn't meant to cut right to the chase, but something about the look on his face ruffled my feathers the wrong way. "I've only just arrived."

"Exactly." He shook his head. "Yet here you are, the new Mixologist."

"This is all about my job, isn't it?"

"Whatever you'd like to tell yourself, Miss Locke. It's not personal—if that's what you'd like to believe."

"That's what I'll believe until you tell me otherwise." Despite every atom in my body telling me to turn around, run back to the sunlight, and hide with Gran in The Twist, I forced my legs to move me farther inside. "Do you want my job enough to kill for it?"

Harpin didn't look the least bit shocked. His mouth twisted into an ugly smile. "Would I be so obvious about it if I did?"

My skin grew cool, and goose bumps prickled my flesh. The more Harpin spoke, the more I believed him capable of murder. He didn't show a trace of compassion, an ounce of sadness over a fellow islander's death. I'd been on The Isle for mere days, and even I'd felt the deep sense of loss at Leonard's death.

"I don't know, would you?" I stopped my forward progress.

The two of us stood facing one another, six feet apart, surrounded by heavy barrels stacked on heavy barrels. The scent of tea leaves was more overwhelming than before, and I pressed my hands to my temples to stem an oncoming headache.

"Is that smell getting to you?" he asked. "Maybe you shouldn't come in here accusing me of things you know nothing about."

"What does my accusing you have anything to do with the smell?" I asked, the headache worsening by the second.

"That's the problem. You forget you now live in a world of magic. You can't fight magic as a human."

"That sounds dangerously close to Faction talk." I glanced around the room, looking for a chair, any place to sit down. I spotted a barrel with a closed lid a few feet away, and I leaned against it, my body feeling weaker by the second. "You're not associated with The Faction, are you?"

"Stop accusing me of things you know nothing about!" Harpin's voice came out in a roar, so loud it bounced off the many surfaces of the shop. He raised his hands by his sides slowly, as if gesturing for someone to stand.

I buckled in half, the smell increasing by the second. "Stop it." I coughed. "I can't breathe."

"Then don't forget we have magical defenses, *human*." Harpin continued to raise his arms as if raising a zombie. The smell worsened. "I have the right to protect myself from your lies."

"I'm not..." My head grew light, and I couldn't remember the words to the sentence I had begun. "Please."

"If you were a *witch,* you'd be able to fight back." Harpin's arms were at shoulder height now, his hands palm down as if playing with a puppet. His fingers twitched, and I could no longer breathe.

I flipped the sunglasses onto my face, choking from a lack of air, but of course the Uncloaker did nothing now. The smell wasn't an illusion—it was real. *If only I had a canister of good old-fashioned pepper spray right about now.*

Remembering the sprays I did have, I groped in the pocket on the front of my sundress. I pulled out the TruthTeller, remembering far too late that we'd decided against EvilAway. Stars winked around my eyes.

What am I doing here? I'd die in a tea shop, suffocated by an oily, jealous man who may have killed my first Mixology patient. I hadn't even had the chance to learn magic, to spend time with my new family, to discover the truth behind my mother's tendencies and powers.

A burn deep inside my soul kept me from blacking out. I struggled to stand, but Harpin's eyes turned to glittering black buttons as he raised his hands above my head.

"Where do you think you're going?" he asked.

I leapt forward, but the lack of oxygen made my body too weak to continue. I stumbled halfway through my leap, my outstretched arms reaching for him. I wanted to rip, claw, drag his arms from his sides, but I fell short. My efforts weren't enough…

I clawed at my throat, struggling to breathe. My gasps brought in nothing but more toxic, tea-scented non-air. My wheezes became louder, my breathing shallower, and blackness crept around the edges of my mind. My body shuddered, an involuntary convulsion. Just as I decided to let myself sink into the darkness… an unfamiliar voice spoke from the door of the tea shop.

"What the hell are you doing, Harpin?"

I struggled to blink through the fog, but I was too far gone. I closed my eyes, laying my head on the floor.

Harpin responded, though I couldn't make out his words. He

must have dropped his hands to his sides, because my next breath contained traces of oxygen, and the breath after that was nearly a full gulp of air.

Like a fish drowning out of water then suddenly tossed back into an ocean, I sucked in one gulp of air after another, my body still weak from the spell. I coughed, spluttered, continued to heave. It took too much effort to pay attention to the conversation between the men—the two of them shouting loudly over my body—so I focused on breathing *in* and *out*, *in* and *out*.

"Are you okay?" the strange man's voice asked near my ear. His hands danced over my forehead, his palms resting gently on my back, probably feeling if I could breathe.

I managed a nod. I tried to speak, but my throat was in too much pain.

"We need to get you out of here," he said. "I'd recommend taking you to the Mixologist for an oxygen-infused cocktail, combined with some sort of throat soother."

I coughed through a wry laugh. "You're looking at her."

"Let's get you home." He helped me to my feet. "Don't get ideas about disappearing, Harpin."

"I didn't do anything wrong." The tea shop owner walked behind his desk, pulled a piece of parchment from a drawer, and set it nonchalantly on his desk. "I'm going to balance my books now."

"You nearly killed her," the man said, lifting me to my feet. "I'd call that wrong."

"I have the right to defend my shop." Harpin's pen scratched along the page, and he looked as unfazed as if he'd just gotten up to change a load of laundry.

"From an infant witch?" The man shook his head in incredulous disbelief. "I do believe you've made yourself an enemy, Harpin, and she has more power in her blood than you could ever *dream* of having."

Despite my burning throat, I warmed inside. I wasn't sure what to make of my valiant stranger, except that I liked him. I liked him a whole lot more than Harpin, that was for certain.

Harpin's face grew pale, though he didn't look up from his bookkeeping. "If she survives to use it, that is."

"Why wouldn't she survive?" The man slipped his arm under mine, propping me up against his body. "Hm, Harpin? I know you don't have Seer powers, so if you know something's going to happen, it's because you've planned it."

"Get out of here, Aarik." Harpin scratched a letter so deep into the parchment I could hear the tear of paper, and I imagined the ink bleeding through onto his desk. "Now."

"Why do you want to kill me?" I whispered. That was all I could manage. My voice broke when I tried to speak at a normal volume.

"I'm just showing you the dangers of the magical world," Harpin said. "If you can't survive a visit to my tea shop, you sure as heck won't last long on the West Isle. I give you a week."

"I may not know magic yet." My voice cracked. "But I'm learning. I have friends. I have family. I'm not alone."

The words, or the sentiment behind them, must have cut Harpin. He stood, jerking one arm upward in rage. The scent of the smothering tea leaves flared as he shouted, "Get out! Both of you. Get out of here!"

"Watch yourself, Harpin." My rescuer helped me hobble from the tea shop. "And remember what I said. I'd try to stay on her good side because when she comes into power, not a soul on this island—magic or otherwise—will be able to stop her."

CHAPTER 18

A FEW MINUTES OF AWKWARD STUMBLING later, the mystery Good Samaritan led me to a bench just north of the tea shop, out of sight of the front entrance and away from the stench of tea leaves.

"I don't know how to thank you." My voice had partially returned, though it was still scratchy. "So I guess thank you will have to do for now."

"That's more than enough. I just did what anyone else would've done."

"Not anyone," I said, meeting his gaze. "Not Harpin."

Now that the threat of my immediate death had been avoided, I took a moment to study the man before me. All at once, I remembered where I'd seen him. He'd been lounging on the beach when Poppy pointed him out, saying that he smoked a few of the special leaves Hettie grew in The Twist.

"Your name is Aarik?" I asked, remembering Harpin's words.

He nodded, his blue eyes a bit foggy now that I looked closer. He was handsome in a surfer boy sort of way—sandy hair cut short, tan skin that brought out his sky-blue eyes, the bulkiness of a man who carried heavy things—like a surfboard—regularly.

"I don't know how to thank you," I said again.

"Don't worry about it, really. How are you feeling now?" Aarik asked. "I live right around the block. I think I have some leftover ThroatSoother from the last Mixologist in the medicine cabinet if you want it. We can stop by, and I can give you one on the way home. It'll hold the pain off until your assistant can help you whip up a new batch."

I shook my head. "I should really get back to my cousins. They'll be waiting for me in front of the tea shop."

But as I looked in the direction of Harpin's store, I couldn't make my feet move. Maybe I could meet up with them elsewhere. I looked into Aarik's semi-unfocused eyes, saw the goofy smile on his face, and another rush of gratitude hit me in the stomach.

His brow crinkled with concern. "If you're not feeling up to walking, maybe you can wait here while I run back to grab the lozenge. I really think it'll help get the healing process started on your throat. You have red marks..."

I stiffened as Aarik raised a hand, but when he set his fingers against my neck, the touch was so soft, I immediately relaxed.

"I'll be right back. Wait here." Aarik stood, a concerned look on his face. At my worried expression, he smiled. "Harpin will leave you alone. He won't come outside after you."

"I should go find my cousins." Mostly because I didn't want to be alone.

"All right, I see them over by the bridge. I'll walk you to them." Aarik extended a hand, helping me to my feet. "You're okay to walk?"

I nodded. "Do you live in the houses by the canal?"

"No, I'm more of a free bird, I suppose you could say." He nodded toward the beach. "I have a cozy little hut a few paces up that way, which is why I'd be able to run home and back in a jiffy."

Squinting into the distance, I could barely make out Poppy and Zin chatting by the lower bridge. We were in for a decently long walk. My throat burned, and my eyes watered every time I tried to swallow.

"You said the lozenge will help with the pain?" I asked, wrapping my hands loosely around my neck.

He nodded.

"Maybe we can stop by your hut and pick one up on the way to Poppy and Zin?" I asked. "If you don't mind, of course. My throat is raw."

"Of course. It's a two-minute walk from the shop, and your cousins look occupied. Here, lean on me."

I took Aarik up on his offer, blushing as he slid his arm around my back. "You're a godsend, I hope you know that. I'll do whatever I can to make it up to you. Unlimited Mixes, once I learn how to mix anything."

"You don't have to do a single thing. Like I said, I didn't do anything any decent person wouldn't do. I heard Harpin yelling, smelled something strange, and popped my head inside. I was only headed to the library." Aarik gave me a wry smile. "Most interesting library trip I've ever had."

"That's one for the *books*." My cheeks turned warm as Aarik laughed at my dumb joke.

"It'll make for a good *story* someday," he said.

"You make 'dad jokes' just like me." I grinned.

"I hate to say this"—Aarik scrunched up his face—"but I'm really glad we had the opportunity to meet."

A small smile tugged at my lips. "I am too. And not only because I might still be choking on his floor if we hadn't ever met."

Aarik's easy laugh relaxed me. The tension left my shoulders, and some of the adrenaline surge from the shop evaporated. "You know, I've thought of one thing you could do to repay me."

"What's that?"

"Have a Caffeine Cup with me when we get back. Just you and me."

"Like a date?"

"Sort of. But it's just coffee." Aarik grinned. "Maybe if your throat feels better by then, we can chat for a bit. No pressure, though."

"I'd love to get to know you—" My words disappeared

as someone else's arm grabbed my wrist and yanked me from Aarik's grasp.

By the time I could collect my thoughts and look up, I was fuming. It was none other than my worst nightmare. I stuck a hand on my hip. "What do you think you're doing?"

Ranger X stood behind us, having once again appeared from thin air—or so it seemed. "What do *you* think you're doing? You're supposed to have a security detail with you at all times."

"I do have a security detail," I said, gesturing toward my rescuer. "Meet Aarik."

"Hey man," Aarik said raising a hand. "We're just chatting."

Ranger X ignored him. "Where are Poppy and Zin?"

"They're talking! They're just over by the bridge."

"Without you?"

"What, they can't have private time?" I crossed my arms. "I'm perfectly fine, thanks for asking."

Ranger X's eyes fell to my neck, and I shivered under his glance. Instead of commenting on the red marks, he very lightly ran his fingertips along my skin. My eyes closed and a tremor ran through my spine, in part due to his touch and in part due to the pain.

My eyes flashed open, and I stepped back. "That hurts."

"You are *not* perfectly fine." His voice held a warning. "Who did this to you?"

"Harpin," I said. "And if Aarik hadn't wandered into the shop when he did, I would've turned out a lot worse for the wear."

Ranger X's eyes flicked toward Aarik then back to me in the time it took me to inhale. "Come with me."

"I don't want to come with you." I took a step toward Aarik. "We're going to grab a lozenge from his house, then he's going to walk me back to my cousins. I'm *fine*."

"A quick afternoon *lozenge*." Ranger X's eyes narrowed. "I didn't think you were the type to go home with a stranger, darlin'."

"Don't call me darlin'."

"Princess?"

"Stop it!" I crossed my arms. "I can take care of myself."

Ranger X blinked. "So that's a *no* to Princess."

I let out a sigh of annoyance, hoping he'd get the picture and go back to wherever he'd come from.

Instead, he missed the picture completely. He winked, heat erupting in my stomach at his playful expression. "I'm here to keep you safe, since apparently your family-assigned bodyguards are doing a terrible job of it."

"I can keep myself safe just fine." I considered the recent events and decided my statement needed a bit of revising. "Well, I have Aarik here, and I'll stay by Zin and Poppy from now on. It's not their fault. I told them I wanted to speak to Harpin alone."

"Why would you do that?"

"I had questions for him," I said, shifting my weight from one leg to another.

Ranger X shook his head in disbelief. "Someone has been murdered. I tell you to be careful. So the first thing you do is ditch your bodyguards and go talk to a wizard on a power trip?"

"Well, when you say it like that…" I drew a circle on the sandy walkway with my toe. "I didn't know he was powerful."

"He's out for your job," Ranger X said. "And—"

"Hey, man, she said she didn't know." Aarik stepped forward, taking my wrist. "Relax, dude."

"Last time I '*relaxed, dude,*' she almost got herself killed." Ranger X watched as I stepped closer to Aarik. "So I'd say that didn't work out so hot."

"My throat hurts," I said. "I just want to go home, and you're making me feel like I'm the one who's done something wrong. I didn't do anything."

Ranger X's voice dropped low. "What didn't you do?"

"L-Leonard's death. You haven't heard about it?" I asked.

Ranger X raised his eyebrows. "I have. Is it true he stopped by your bungalow and had a Caffeine Cup the morning he died?"

"Yes, but—"

"Is it true you left the store and mixed the drink in your bar—alone?"

"Yes, but I didn't—"

"So you could have added a little extra something—a pinch of a certain powder or a spritz of a special solution, something that might cause Leonard's throat to close up?"

"I didn't use magic!" I tried to shout, but my voice came out as a feeble warble.

Aarik stepped forward, pushing me behind him. "Listen, bro—"

"Call me *bro* one more time." Ranger X stepped up, nose to nose with Aarik, making the latter look like a Ken doll, while the Ranger looked more like G.I. Joe.

"Aarik," I whispered, tugging on his shoulder to pull him a step back. "Don't."

"I'm not looking for trouble," Aarik said. "I'm just trying to walk this lady home."

"I *am* looking for trouble," Ranger X said. "And I've found her. Some folks call her Lily. I prefer Princess, since she nixed darlin'. Here's what's going to happen, *bro*: I'm going to walk her home, and you're going to go back to the beach. That way, I'll forget about your stash of 'special leaves' I can smell a mile away."

Aarik looked down at the ground. Eventually, he slid his gaze over to me. "What about our coffee date?"

"Raincheck," I said with a smile. "Now's not really a good time."

Ranger X gave me an extra second to thank Aarik again, and sent him on his way. As his shaggy blonde hair disappeared into the distance, I turned around and glared at the Ranger.

"You didn't have to be so rude."

"Come on," he said, taking me by the elbow. "You've got some explaining to do."

CHAPTER 19

"WHAT IS THIS PLACE?" I asked as we approached a small, out-of-the-way cabin. My hands were bound behind my back, probably because I'd threatened to run away enough on the walk over that Ranger X decided not to take any chances. "There's no way I could ever find my way back here on my own. It's hidden."

"That's not a problem," Ranger X said. "I don't want you to find it again."

"There you go, sounding all creepy again."

"It's not personal, Princess. I prefer nobody finds this place."

"What is it, your secret lair?"

"Something like that." Ranger X led me up a small stone path that twisted through dark, overhanging branches. "Nobody should come up this way without training."

"Are we in The Forest?" I looked around, and the question practically answered itself. We'd crossed the Upper Bridge, but I'd been so livid about my handcuffs I'd barely paused to notice my surroundings. "Can you take these cuffs off?"

"I will," he said. "After you tell me what I need to know. Technically, I should be arresting you. But I'm not taking you in for questioning at the station, so let's call it a compromise. I'll remove them after we talk."

Now that I'd stopped moving for a moment, I noticed the eerie silence surrounding us. We moved in near darkness, the sunlight obscured by a roof of branches wound around one another. The leaves created a twisting path through the underbrush to the front door of a structure that could hardly be called a hut, it was so bare.

"You live like a king," I said dryly. "Look at this luxury."

"It's got four walls, a fireplace, and a comfortable bed—what more do I need?" He glanced my way. "I'm a simple guy."

"Mmm." I didn't respond, mostly because as he'd mentioned *the bed*, my insides had twisted in strange ways, and I found myself wanting things I didn't care to admit. I blamed it on frayed nerves and a man who was, though sometimes a pain in the neck, undeniably handsome.

My murmur brought a hint of a smile to his lips. "If I let you go, you're not going to do something silly like run away now, are you?"

"Depends. Looks like my choices are you or The Forest." I pretended to think a minute. "I think I'd rather try my luck at the dangers in The Forest."

"Shame. Then I'll have to do this." Ranger X swooped a hand behind my knees, scooping me up against his chest and marching the both of us right into his cabin.

"I was joking!" I wriggled against his arms but gave up just as quickly. It was as useless as trying to get out of a straitjacket—impossible without some limber movements and a special tool. I had no tools and wasn't particularly flexible, so just biding my time was easier.

He dropped me, rather unceremoniously, on the bed. Thank goodness my dress remained firmly over my knees for now. Especially since Poppy had pointed out so *kindly* that my underclothing was ugly.

"What?" Ranger X stepped back. "What are you muttering about?"

My face turned red. "Nothing."

"What isn't ugly... ?" He waved. "Never mind. I don't want to know."

I tried to play it cool but failed miserably. My cheeks were hot, and even my ears warmed. "Nothing."

"I changed my mind about not wanting to know."

"Unbind me." I shifted on the bed. "Please."

"You told me you were going to run."

"I was *joking*." I took a deep breath and glanced around the bare cabin. Simple was an understatement. A fireplace sat along the far wall, a table and two chairs that might've been handcrafted stood in the middle of the room, and I had been plopped on the bed against the far wall. He'd also been accurate about his bed being comfortable. If he'd just remove my handcuffs, I had no doubt I'd be able to sleep like a baby.

Ranger X didn't comment, instead walking into a small corner that hardly qualified as a kitchen. A sink, stove, and a few pots and pans did not a kitchen make.

"Where are you going?" I started to stand but then thought better of it.

I didn't *actually* want to take my chances with The Forest. So instead of fighting my bindings, I decided to embrace them. And try for that nap. Crumpling over on the bed, I relaxed against the soft sheets, the luxurious fabric smooth against my skin. Ranger X didn't seem like the fancy-thread-count sort of guy—more of a rough flannel sort of man—so the silky satin caught me off guard.

"These sheets are nice," I murmured, my eyes already drooping. What with Gus waking me at the crack of dawn, coupled with a day filled with shocking news, murder, attempts on my life, and adrenaline that had come and gone, I was exhausted.

"Yes, I happen to like them too. And no, you can't have them." Ranger X kneeled next to the bed, his eyes level with mine. "Can you sit up?"

"It's a bit tricky." I let my eyes close all the way. "See, I'm really tired. Plus, there's that whole thing where you tied my hands behind my back."

Ranger X reached over my body, and his forearm brushed against my ribs, as he did something behind my back. A second later, my bindings vanished. I sat up, rubbing my wrists.

"Did I hurt you?" Ranger X's eyes clouded, an underlying anger to his voice.

"No, no. Just making sure I still have circulation." I managed a smile, but Ranger X didn't seem amused. I set my hands by my sides. "I'm joking, really. I'm fine."

Ranger X spun my legs to face the front of the bed. Still kneeling, he rested his chest against my knees, one of his arms on either side of my body.

He still didn't seem particularly amused, but the anger in his eyes had faded, replaced by a murky darkness that made his expression difficult to read. He looked at me with a sharp, intelligent gaze, scanning my face, my arms, and eventually my neck.

"I'd never hurt you." Ranger X cleared his throat. "I hope you know that."

I gave a hesitant nod. "I think so."

"You don't know so?"

"I hardly know you at all."

Ranger X leaned forward, his lips hovering over mine and teasing me with the threat of a kiss. All at once, I found myself wanting it, wanting him, and hating that very same fact. He was rude, arrogant... but when his breath danced across my neck, I couldn't help the shivers that went straight down my spine.

"I can change that," he said, "if you would like to get to know me better."

"No," I murmured, losing the words as they fell from my tongue. "I mean..."

"I gave you two options: me or The Forest." Ranger X pulled back, his eyes locking on mine. "You chose to stay here instead of take your chances in The Forest." He blinked. "But Princess, I promise I'm a whole other kind of dangerous."

"Then I should stay far away from you. Because I'm trouble, and you're dangerous."

"Danger and trouble don't mix."

I shook my head. "We can't…"

"We shouldn't…" He looked down.

My chest rose and fell, my palms sweating with his proximity. Magic—it was the only explanation. Because something drew us together despite every logical thread in my brain screaming at me to stay far, far away from him.

"Your undies aren't ugly," he said, finally breaking the heady silence. It was as if the words had tumbled out of his mouth without him having a say in the matter.

"Excuse me?" I blinked.

Mr. Tough Guy looked away, and I'd never in a million years have guessed that this would be the subject matter to embarrass Ranger X. After listening to Poppy's gossip, I was sure he'd had *plenty* of experience with the island ladies.

"I heard you mumbling. I just thought you should know they're not ugly."

"And I don't think you'll hurt me." I gave a lopsided smile to complete the awkward moment.

"I brought you some food. I thought you might be hungry." He produced a plate of bread and some sort of grayish blob that looked like a mutant meatball.

"What the heck is that?"

"Meatball," he confirmed.

"It looks like brains."

"Well, it's not."

I shook my head. "I'll stick with the bread."

"Sorry, I'm not a Michelin chef."

"You know Michelin? I'm surprised. I didn't know The Isle studied human culture."

"Yes, well, some of us are aware." Ranger X gestured toward a cup of bubbling yellowish liquid that reminded me of fermented lemonade. "Drink that. It'll help your throat."

"I don't trust it."

"I said I'd never hurt you."

"Yes, but I don't trust my stomach to handle it." I wrinkled my nose. "It smells somewhat like cat puke."

"Does your throat hurt or not?" Ranger X's patience was wearing thin, and quite quickly, it appeared.

I pinched my nose, reached for the glass, and downed the entire thing.

"That's completely nasty," I said.

"When you come into your Mixology role, you can make something that tastes like fruit and top it with a twist of lemon, for all the hell I care." He shook his head, moving to sit next to me. "But for now, beggars can't be choosers."

"I'm not begging *anyone*, I'd like to make that clear."

"Not yet."

"What's that supposed to mean?" I put a hand under Ranger X's chin and tilted his face toward mine, forcing our eyes to meet.

They twinkled, dark and dangerous, but his lips remained sealed shut. We froze that way for a long second.

"Let me see what happened here." Ranger X wrapped his large hand around my smaller wrist and pulled it away from his chin. His dark eyes roved my neck and darkened with a frightening cloudiness.

"I'm *fine*," I said once more. I still hadn't looked in a mirror, so I had no idea how bad the marks on my neck looked. "It's already feeling better after that disgusting beverage."

"That was for the pain in your throat, not the marks on the outside." He stood, moved to a different drawer in the kitchen, and removed a small jar. "But you're in luck. I have something for that too."

"Seems you can heal anything! Aren't you just a jack-of-all-trades."

"My name's not Jack."

"I know that. It's a saying."

"A saying?" He knelt once more, his chest pressed against my knees.

"Yes." I shot a skeptical glance at the jar, which looked more like rubber cement than any sort of medicine. "So what is this you're using on me now?"

"It's a salve. It'll soothe your skin, help the marks fade faster and heal quicker." Ranger X removed the lid. "May I?"

I nodded, my hesitation less than before.

He dipped his fingers in the salve, a honey-like substance, and brought his hand up to my neck. His fingers hovered over my skin for a long moment as he made eye contact with me.

With a touch as gentle as a butterfly, he applied the salve to my sore neck. His gaze hesitated for a moment on my necklace, then he lightly lifted it and moved his fingers around it. Instead of feeling sticky and gooey as I'd imagined, it was light and airy against my skin. But even as the weightless salve soothed and cooled my skin, his fingers set fire to the same spot. The hot and cold made me shudder from head to toe.

"Does this hurt?" he asked.

"It feels nice. It's just cold."

"It'll help numb the pain and begin the healing process. Would you like me to continue?"

I nodded. *Continue with what?* I would've liked him to specify. Because if his hands crept to other parts of my body or his lips fell onto mine, well... I wasn't sure I'd be able to resist that, either.

"All done." He stood and stepped back, screwing the lid onto the jar. "How do you feel?"

I moved my head back and forth, testing the functionality of my neck. It was a good thing the TruthTeller was wearing off. I couldn't bear to tell him that I hadn't noticed all that much of a difference. "Good as new."

"That's a lie. It takes at least ten minutes to sink in. Try not to brush up against anything in the meantime."

"Okay." I couldn't describe the empty sensation that took over once he'd removed his hands from my body. "What's next?"

His shoulders stiffened as he walked over to the sink. "What do you mean?"

"I *mean...* are you taking me back to my cousins?"

"I was thinking you could stay here."

It was my turn to freeze. "*Why?*"

"Because look at the whole lot of good your cousins did as your bodyguards. No offense to Poppy or Zin, but"—he gestured to my neck as an explanation—"I'd prefer if I can keep an eye on you as much as possible."

"Of course you would." For some indescribable reason, my heart sank a few more notches. But only because I sensed his reason for wanting me to stay had everything to do with his job and nothing to do with his feelings. Everything was so clinical with him, down to his lack of a real name.

"You're not arguing," he said.

"I just haven't gotten around to it yet."

"So you're okay with this arrangement?" He gestured to me on his bed.

"If you mean me being your prisoner, then no, I'm not."

"I figured." He sighed. "Don't make me lock you up again."

"Don't make me..." I considered a few threats but couldn't come up with one good enough to say. "I'm going to put a pin in that threat and come back to it."

His lips flicked into a brief grin before settling back into *business mode.*

"How long do you anticipate having to babysit me?" I asked.

"Assuming it wasn't *you,* then until we find whoever killed Leonard."

"But that could be days, weeks... who knows, even months."

"Not if I have any say in the matter."

I cleared my throat. "I have a question for you."

He raised an eyebrow. "That's never stopped you from asking questions before."

"I'm just warning you." I looked at my feet and ran light fingers over my neck. My fingertips detected the tiniest bit of salve residue, but the substance had begun to sink in nicely. "It's a bit of a strange question."

"Like I said, that's never stopped you before." His eyes fixed on my fingers as they ran over my neck. "Feeling at all better?"

I nodded, though I wasn't really listening. I was more focused on my own question. "You don't seem as set on the same conclusion as everyone else. You accused me of it before, but… for some reason, I get the feeling you don't believe it. Why?"

Ranger X watched me with a level gaze. He didn't look surprised. "What conclusion is that?"

I scowled. "You know what I mean. The conclusion where you think I killed Leonard—either by accident or on purpose."

"Why would you kill him on purpose?"

"That's exactly my point—I have no reason to kill him."

"I'm explaining," Ranger X said. "You asked the question. If you want to hear the answer, then listen."

I debated between lecturing him about rudeness once more then decided I'd rather hear what he had to say. Sealing my lips, I looked toward the ceiling before eventually settling my gaze on his and nodding for him to continue.

"The possibility of you being the murderer jumped into my mind, of course." Ranger X stood, clasping his hands behind his back. "How could it not? You're a newcomer to the island, playing with magic though you don't fully understand it, and our victim visited you the day he died. All the indicators make you the perfect prime suspect."

"But—"

"Listening is not your forte, is it, Miss Locke?"

I closed my mouth again.

Ranger X resumed talking once he seemed sure I'd listen. "My job is to consider every possibility. You were one possibility but not the only one."

I scooched forward on the bed, listening closer.

"First of all, why would you kill him? A bit of digging told me it was the first time you'd met Leonard. Now, he rubbed many people on this Isle the wrong way, but not in the sense he'd be murdered for it. And you had even less of a reason since you hadn't been here long enough for him to annoy you."

My eyes followed Ranger X as he strolled around the table in the middle of the room, talking as much to himself as to me.

"I struggled with your motive. Which made me pursue other, more likely theories. For example, the theory that you made a mistake with the potion you gave to Leonard." Ranger X looked up. "It was your first Mix. I found that out from asking around a bit, and I *also* found out that the chance you'd made an innocent mistake was entirely possible. You could've accidentally Mixed in a poison powder or combined an herb and flower to make a toxic combination. I've seen you only on a handful of occasions, and each time has given me more of a reason to believe you're entirely capable of making a mistake."

"Hey—"

"It would make sense. You've got a bit of clumsiness, an overeager desire to learn your trade, a need to *prove* yourself, and a vast array of Mixers, herbs, and flowers at your disposal." Ranger X crossed his arms. "I have to say, I'm still not convinced it wasn't a mistake on your part."

"But I didn't use magic," I said, forgetting I wasn't supposed to be speaking.

"That's also what I heard. And if you didn't use magic, that's where we have a problem."

I frowned. "What sort of problem?"

"Magic is meant to enhance, not harm. It's against the nature of pure magic to be used for evil." Ranger X unclasped his arms, letting them fall loosely at his sides. "Which makes magic used for evil a far more draining process than using it for good, for healing. Magic sort of... *fights back* against the evil user, I guess you could say."

"Is that true for The Faction?" I asked. "These witches and wizards who want to take over the world with magic... is that part of the reason they haven't succeeded yet? Because magic is more difficult to use for evil than good?"

"It's one of the reasons." Ranger X eyed me in a new light, as if surprised I knew about The Faction. "It doesn't hurt our cause, that's for certain. Magic is *always* draining to the user, but more so when it's used maliciously."

"Is that enough to stop them?" I asked. "Or is that not enough?"

"That's a chat for a different day." Ranger X crossed his arms. "We're focused on you, on Leonard, on local business for now."

"Are you involved in the fight against The Faction?"

"What did I just say?" Ranger X's voice turned hard.

I swallowed. "I want to help."

"We don't need your help."

"So you are involved with fighting The Faction?"

Ranger X ran a hand through his hair. "Why are you so difficult?"

"I didn't kill Leonard."

"I know that!" Ranger X's voice escalated in volume. "The glass you used was coated with poison. I discovered it when I stopped by the store to have a look, after they found Leonard. His death wasn't an accident, Lily. It was murder."

"But... why would someone want to murder Leonard?" I asked. "And how did they know which glass to use? I didn't even know he'd stop by. I could've selected any number of glasses."

"That's exactly what I wondered." Ranger X bent over and met my gaze. "Can you think of a single reason why someone would break into your bar, line a coffee cup with poison, and time it *just right* so that Leonard would stop by and drink from it before someone else did?"

"To try to frame me? But *why?* I'd used that coffee cup a few hours before. It was mine. I'd just washed it out after breakfast. There was no reason Leonard should've used it..." I looked up, a sinking sensation in the pit of my stomach as I realized Ranger X's conclusion. "*Oh.*"

He nodded and stood. "They weren't after Leonard. Lily, the murderer was after you."

CHAPTER 20

AN HOUR LATER, WE'D EXHAUSTED a hundred different reasons someone might want me dead.

I threw myself back on the bed. "I don't want to talk about it anymore. Someone wants my job or wants me off The Isle, most likely. But talking about it over and over again is getting depressing."

Ranger X sat next to me on the bed. "Take a nap. You look like you could use some rest."

"What are you trying to say?" I narrowed my eyes at him.

He stared at me. "Nothing?"

I let him off the hook for now, since we had more pressing matters. "I'm sure my cousins are worried. I should be getting back to them."

"You forgot the little detail that you're staying with me until we figure this out."

I shot right back up on the bed. "Nobody knows how long that'll take."

"It shouldn't be much longer. I have a few ideas of who might be behind this."

I raised an eyebrow. "Really? And who's on your short list?"

Ranger X shook his head. "Ranger business."

"Where are all your buddies?" I asked, looking around. "Shouldn't they be helping with 'Ranger' business?"

"Part of keeping you here is so that nobody *knows* where you are. Flaunting you would defeat the purpose of that secret."

"You'd flaunt me?" I winked. "That sounds like a date."

"I don't go on dates."

I sighed. "I'm going back to my cousins. I'm an adult, and you can't stop me unless you arrest me, which you've already done once today. In that case, I'd ask you to please make up your mind if you want me arrested or not."

"I want you safe." Ranger X swiveled toward me, our legs bumping into one another on his bed. The close proximity felt more intimate than it should have, given the circumstances. "I didn't arrest you because I thought you were guilty. I arrested you because it was the only way you'd let me protect you."

"I don't need you to protect me."

"Do you want to die?"

I shook my head. "Not today, if I can help it."

"Can you think of anyone else who would do a better job than me?"

I thought about mentioning Poppy or Zin, but their track record wasn't great. "Aarik was doing a fine job of it."

"I don't trust him."

"Why don't you trust him?" I raised my arms in exasperation. "He could've let me keep choking on the floor of Harpin's tea shop if he wanted."

"As I told you earlier, I don't believe Harpin was trying to kill you. Scare you to death, maybe... there's no way Harpin would've gotten away with killing the new Mixologist in plain daylight. He's not that stupid."

"I don't know about that," I said. "The only people who like me are the West Isle Witches. Even Gus doesn't seem to like me much."

"You're the center of gossip these days." Ranger X raised an eyebrow. "People are curious."

"I didn't picture you as one to keep up with the gossip."

"It's impossible to miss the rumors." Ranger X pressed a finger to his lip in thought. "People have been awaiting your arrival for *years*. Longer even, some of 'em. Neil, the previous Mixologist, held his own as a fill-in, but he was nothing compared to your skills once you've spent some time studying with Gus."

"People keep saying that." My shoulders slumped. "But they have no reason to think that's true. What if I fail?"

"You?" Ranger X scanned me incredulously. He shook his head. "No, not you. You're too stubborn to fail."

I looked at my hands. "I'm fairly certain that was some sort of compliment, and I... I really appreciate it."

It was Ranger X's turn to look away. "Stay away from Aarik."

"I think it's Harpin I should stay away from." Subconsciously I raised a hand to my neck and stroked the skin where the salve had been absorbed.

"Him too," Ranger X said. "He'll be reprimanded for what he's done to you."

"By the law?"

"I am the law." Ranger X swallowed. "So yes, you could say that."

I swallowed. "Don't hurt him. Not too badly."

Ranger X's hands closed into tight fists.

"Look, he hurt me, but I'm okay now." I rested a hand on Ranger X's thigh. "I'm more worried you'll do something *you'll* regret later. I don't care about Harpin. I'll just avoid him."

"He won't be bothering you anymore."

"And what about Aarik?" I asked, keeping the conversation business focused. "He did nothing wrong. Well, except for the smoking bit."

"I don't believe in coincidences."

"You think he rescued me because he was working with Harpin?"

"No, I don't." Ranger X shook his head. "Not in the slightest. But the man is high as a coconut most days."

I laughed. "High as a coconut?"

Ranger X looked confused. "It's a saying."

"We say high as a kite in human world."

"Well, here on the island, coconuts are usually the highest fruit on trees, so…" He shrugged. "Same thing, I suppose."

I grinned. "That's cute."

Ranger X's eyes turned dark for a moment. "Cute. Really?"

My heart sped up as he leaned close, his hands hovering just over my hips, never quite touching me.

"Call me cute one. More. Time."

I took deep breaths. Part of me wanted to provoke him. Another part of me knew that'd be a terrible idea. Thank goodness logic won out.

I cleared my throat. "So why don't you trust Aarik?"

"Besides the fact he smokes day in and day out?" Ranger X shrugged. "Not much. I'm not sure where he gets his stash. However, I do believe your grandmother might have a few in her gardens…"

My mouth hung open. "My grandma grows special leaves? Is that *legal*?"

Ranger X gave a wry smile. "She says she only grows them as fertilizer for her garden."

"I sense a 'but' in your words."

Ranger X laughed, the sound nice and happy for a change. "I have a strong, strong feeling she nips into the stash now and again."

I gasped. "You have evidence? Have you arrested Hettie for growing special plants?"

"You've met your grandmother." Ranger X shook his head. "I'd have to have a death wish to arrest that woman."

"Don't tell me she's the one witch in the world you're afraid of?" My cheeks hurt from smiling.

"I feel no shame in admitting that your grandmother terrifies the living daylights out of me." Ranger X stood. "I think admitting that makes me pretty manly, in fact. Because the only people *not* scared of her are idiots, and I don't fancy myself an idiot. I might be a lot of things that aren't nice, but I'm not an idiot."

"I propose a plan, then." I rose, planting my feet next to Ranger

X's. "I'd be a burden if I stayed here. I know you have work to do, and I don't want to be in the way. Can we strike a deal?"

"I'm open to options." Ranger X crossed his arms. "I like to negotiate."

"How about I hole up at Hettie's for now? The Twist provides a good defense. Plus, as you've proven, everyone is scared of my grandmother." I licked my lips, building steam for my case. "I accidentally left my book there earlier, so I can study. And my cousins can come by. And you don't have to feed me. Or give up your bed."

Ranger X looked torn.

"Look, I don't fancy myself an idiot *either*. A klutz sometimes, sure. But I don't want to end up dead. I won't do something stupid and wander off."

"I suppose I can work with that, if you *promise* to stay on your grandmother's land."

"I promise." I didn't want to leave his house. Not really. Something about Ranger X made me feel safe. But I also didn't want to be a burden. "Thank you for being reasonable."

"Let's go before I change my mind."

CHAPTER 21

MIMSEY FLUNG OPEN THE DOOR to Hettie's home and looked at the front steps where Zin, Poppy, and I stood, staring at our shoes. "What in *tarnation* were you—you *children* thinking? I asked you to do *one* job. Stay together, the three of you. But no, I have to hear from *everyone else* that you're wandering away…"

Mimsey shook with rage, while I wondered who counted as *everyone else*. I sneaked a glance out of the corner of my eye at Ranger X, who'd slunk into the background, though I didn't know how he'd gotten through The Twist. After we'd left his cabin, he agreed to swing by the bungalow to let my cousins know I was all right. They'd decided to come to Hettie's with us.

Trinket joined Mimsey, her frown so severe, her frown lines turned into anger lines. "You girls…" She shook her head. "I don't even know what to say."

"It's my fault," I said. "I asked them not to come into the store with me."

"Why would you do that?" Mimsey asked. "Actually, that doesn't even matter. They should know better than to listen to you. No offense, dear, but you're new here. Poppy and Zin should know better. We ask them to watch you, and what do they do? Wander off!"

"Really, it's my fault," I said again. "I forced them to wait outside."

"She's lying," Zin jumped in. "I walked away on purpose. It was my fault."

"They're both lying," Poppy piped up. "It's my fault. I dragged Zin away."

There was silence as the aunts rounded on Poppy. With Trinket's ability to read auras, I was surprised she hadn't already called out Zin and Poppy for lying. Then again, maybe we were talking too fast to make any sense at all.

"You're lying!" I nudged Poppy. "Don't cover up for me. I asked you to go away."

"Sure, you did." Poppy rolled her eyes. "We both know that's not true."

"I started it," Zin said. "Sorry, it was *my* fault."

"Sorry," Poppy echoed, "but it was *mine*."

I stared at my cousins, who stared back with expectant gazes.

"Oh," I said quickly. "Sorry, it was *my* fault."

"Grrrrahhh!" Mimsey let out a noise that was more beast than human. "Even as adults, you cause trouble. More trouble than any other witch to ever be born. I should ground you all."

"If I may?" Ranger X stepped forward. He bowed his head toward both aunts, acknowledging them each with a *ma'am*.

"What is it, X?" Mimsey asked. "Thank you for bringing our girls back, by the way. Seeing how they could've been *killed* wandering off like that."

He acknowledged their thanks with another nod. "As these ladies cannot keep their stories straight, I suggest a mandatory stay at Hettie's place until this case is wrapped up."

"You're *grounding* us?" Poppy's jaw dropped open. "Mother, he can't do that."

Mimsey crossed her arms. "He just suggested it, and I think it's a great suggestion. You all are grounded."

"Lily and I already have an... agreement about her whereabouts for the next few days." Ranger X glanced in my direction, and I did my best to avoid stares from the rest of the group. "She'll be living and studying here until further notice."

"Whose further notice?" Poppy asked.

"Mine." Ranger X leveled her with a gaze. "I think it'd be beneficial if you girls took a brief vacation from wreaking havoc on The Isle and relaxed here for a few days."

"First of all, we're not *girls*," Zin said. "We're ladies. And second—"

"If you're ladies, then act like them!" Trinket said, her voice clipped. "Ladies walk, talk, act the part. They don't go clowning around The Isle, showing their... their *lady business* to anyone who wants to see it!"

"Who's showing their lady business?" Mimsey faced her sister. "The ghosts haven't mentioned that."

Trinket's face turned the slightest bit pink. "Never mind. The way these girls have been acting though, it's as if they belong back in... what's that thing that comes after high school for humans?"

"College?" I filled in.

"Yes, that horrid place."

I raised a finger. "It's not so horrid. It's actually—"

"They'll be staying here, all of them. Mother will be fine with it, I'm sure. She'll love it, but I'll ask her later anyway," Mimsey said. "Poppy, a word?"

Before Poppy could respond, her mother grabbed my cousin by the ear and half-dragged her through the entryway. Mimsey's shrieks bounced off every surface of the hallway.

"What's all this racket?" Hettie, glammed out in a dandelion-yellow velour tracksuit, appeared in the doorway with a grin. "Someone's in trouble."

"You don't have to be so happy about it," Zin grumbled. To me, she whispered, "Gran loves to see people up to no good. Don't ask me why. Says it keeps her young or something."

"Must be real trouble for Mimsey to be shoutin' to the heavens.

Usually Mimsey's in on the shenanigans." Hettie clapped. "I can't wait to watch this play out."

"Tell me about it." Trinket crossed her arms. "I'm the only one who has rules around this place."

"So many rules," Zin muttered. "Endless rules."

"That's enough, young lady. You're grounded." Trinket glared at her daughter. "Get inside."

"I'm nearly thirty, Mom." Zin tried to look tough, but she dropped her gaze to her feet after one look from her mother.

"Get inside." Trinket turned and disappeared down the hallway, her head held high, nose in the air.

Zin gave the largest eye roll known to man before dragging her feet at a sloth's pace over the threshold. "If I don't go, I'll never hear the end of it. Lily, are you coming? I think I smell shrimp poppers."

"Your nose is right. I ordered them fresh from Sea Salt." Hettie crossed her arms. "And I ordered extra. I had a feeling we'd be having guests tonight... are you staying?"

Her last comment was directed at Ranger X.

"No, ma'am," he said. "I should be going."

"How old do you think I am?" Hettie asked, her gray hair wobbling. "Quit it with the *ma'ams*. Only Trinket likes that sort of hoity-toity junk."

"Sorry... Hettie." Ranger X's gaze flicked my way. "May I have a word alone with Lily?"

"No." Hettie folded her arms.

"It's about her safety."

"What do you think this is, a brothel?" Hettie stomped forward, her small frame about a tenth the size of Ranger X's. She stuck a bony finger right into his rib cage, which was about as high up as she could reach. "You come here, thinking you can frolic around with my girls?"

"Hettie, it's not like that," I said. "He's just doing his job."

"And is his job kissin' my granddaughters?" Hettie asked,

punctuating each of her words with a jab to Ranger X's chest. "It'd be smart of you to realize I have the gift of *Sight*. That means I can see into the future. You better take care of my girl, you hear me?"

Ranger X cleared his throat, apparently at a loss for words. Heat flamed in my face, and I wondered if she knew how close we'd come to kissing in his cabin. The thought made me nauseated.

Hettie let out a cackling laugh. "Ah, lighten up. I'm just messin' with you two lovebirds. I'll leave you alone." Hettie stepped inside the cottage, leaving the door wide open.

"For the record, we're not lovebirds," I called after her.

A long silence filled the gap as we waited for Hettie's footsteps to disappear around the corner.

"So that's a *no* to a kiss?" Ranger X asked, one of his eyebrows raised.

"Sorry, Charlie. Not in front of my grandma."

"My name's not Charlie."

"That was another saying." I sighed. "Never mind, I'll learn to hold back at some point."

"Or you could teach them to me," he said, his voice soft. Before I could agree to anything, he coughed. "Anyway I wanted to talk to you about this. This is how we're going to communicate."

I jumped half a foot as his hand grasped mine. He pressed a small object into my palm.

"What is this?" I tore my eyes from his face, looking at the small rubber band, which resembled a hair tie, he'd given me.

"Wear it on your wrist. It's like those... um, the dealie-bobs you put in your hair. Speak into it if you need me."

"Is there a button to turn it on?" I examined it closer. It was a solid rope of black. "Because things could get a bit awkward if the thing stays on all the time."

"There's no off button."

"What if I have to go to the bathroom?"

I must have looked mortified because a small smirk turned up the corners of his mouth. "I fully suspect you might. But it's built for that. It doesn't turn *on* unless you hold it to your mouth and speak into it. See? I have one too." He showed me a similar band wound around his right wrist.

"So only you can hear me?"

Ranger X straightened his arms, shaking out the sleeves of his white button-down shirt. "Yes. There's a spell that will recognize your voice and your breathing. It'll only turn on when it detects your breath on it. Otherwise, the device remains *off*, so long as your hand is more than a few inches away from your mouth."

"That's pretty neat," I said. "So it recognizes my breath?"

He nodded.

"Does my breath smell good?" I asked, suddenly self-conscious. "How'd you program it to do that?"

"It's a spell. I have no idea what your breath smells like." Ranger X stepped close. "But your grandmother thinks we should give it a shot. What do you say we just get that kiss thing out of the way? She gave us a free pass, the way I see it."

Ranger X stood so close to me, his chin just above my forehead, that his words sent tingles down my arms. I looked up, meeting his dark, brooding gaze filled with a mixture of amusement and something deeper. Something far more complicated.

"Do it!" squeaked a voice from behind the front door.

"Hettie!" I leapt away from Ranger X just as my grandmother popped her head outside.

"Pretend I'm not here," Hettie said. "I just wanted to make sure I was right about my vision. Kiss now so I know I'm right."

"You've ruined your own vision," I said, crossing my arms before turning to face Ranger X. "Because now I'm not kissing you just on principle."

"But you were considering it?" Ranger X asked.

"No. You arrested me today," I said.

"For your own safety," Hettie said. "Give him a break. I think it's romantic."

"Well, I don't." I sniffed. "I think dates and flowers are romantic."

"Who needs flowers when a man looks like that?" Hettie winked at me and leapt out of sight as I scowled at her.

"Good-bye, X." I glanced over my shoulder at him. "I've got to go have a talk with my grandmother."

"I'm glad to see you've become one of the family already." Ranger X winked. "I'll leave you be, then. Remember to Comm me if you need anything. Just say my name."

Ranger X turned and walked away. Although I was eager to have a word with Hettie, something kept me rooted to the spot. As I watched him disappear into The Twist, I wondered if he had any family to go home to or if he was all alone. Just as I'd been.

"He's a big ball of mysteries in a nice package, huh?" Hettie asked, moving to stand next to me. "You should've kissed him."

"About that," I said. "Can we establish some ground rules? I'm an adult, and my dating life is my own personal business."

Hettie let out a bark of laughter. "That's where you're mistaken. I see you must not have grown up with overbearing parents and a family who liked to meddle."

I didn't offer a response.

"Let me explain how this works." Hettie stopped me in the hall and looked into my eyes. "You *think* your dating life is your own business, but your man must pass all of our approvals, he must not call me ma'am, and he should have a nice body."

I frowned. "What about what I want?"

Hettie waved. "There's room for you to fit that in with all of our requirements. Oh, and you should expect plenty of advice from me and everyone else in this house. Advice that you don't want and opinions you don't need to hear."

"If I don't want the advice or the opinions, then why offer them?"

"Because that's what family's about, Lily!" Hettie shook her head. "Getting on each other's nerves then getting over it because you love each other. As a family, we *have* to love each other."

"You don't *have* to do anything."

"We might pretend we don't care, but we care more than you know, sugar-pop. Even if we *have* to. Because at the end of the day, if you don't have family... what *do* you have?"

We walked in silence down the hallway as I considered the old woman's nugget of wisdom. Just when I was coming to the realization that maybe my grandmother was wiser than she appeared, she had to go and shatter the illusion.

"Back to his package..." Hettie grinned. "It's nice, huh?"

"Excuse me?!"

"I said Ranger X came in a nice package. His body, I mean."

I frowned. "I suppose he's okay. But I'm still mad at him."

Hettie sighed. "That's how all the best romances start. Through anger."

"That seems counterintuitive."

"Love and hate are a fine line, dear, and I despised my husband when we first met." Hettie chortled. "He turned out to be the best thing that ever happened to me."

I didn't ask the unspoken question, though it burned at the tip of my tongue. *Where is he now?*

"Oh, by the way"—Hettie looked at me with a mischievous grin—"I couldn't see a darn thing about the future regarding you and that Ranger. My *Sight's* not that great. I just wanted to give you two the opportunity to kiss."

I closed my eyes.

"But that don't mean I'm blind either." Hettie patted my arm. "I see how you look at him like he's a hot fudge sundae."

"I do not. He makes me so livid, more angry than any person I know." I shook my head. "It's never gonna happen."

"Keep trying to convince yourself." Hettie smirked as if she knew something I didn't. "But if I don't get a great-grandbaby before I die, it's your fault."

"That's a horrible thing to say!" I took my grandmother by the shoulders. "Aren't you a witch? Don't you live forever?"

"Have some shrimp poppers." She gestured for me to step into the kitchen as we rounded a corner. "I can't eat 'em all. I'm never gettin' fat. Gotta keep things tight for all the suitors."

"Mother, you hate company. If you don't allow anyone to come to your house, you'll never find a suitor." Mimsey shook her head, apparently having calmed down a bit.

"You never know," Hettie said. "At least I haven't been flirting with that grouchy old Mixology assistant for twenty years without doing a single dang thing about it."

Mimsey's blush nearly glowed in the dark. "I *do not* flirt with Gus, Mother!"

"Let's eat," Trinket said, clapping. "Not a word spoken over dinner, unless it's something nice."

"Fine." Hettie sat down, flopping a napkin over her lap. "I think it'd be *nice* if Mimsey finally asked Gus out on a stupid date."

"*Mother!*" Mimsey and Trinket roared in sync.

Zin, Poppy, and I all helped ourselves to the basket of steaming popcorn shrimp, keeping our noses down as we let our aunts wage war against their mother.

CHAPTER 22

DINNER TURNED INTO A ROUND of homemade wine and eventually morphed into late-night hot chocolate in front of a fireplace in the den. Our chatter fell into an easy rhythm, almost friendly.

As the fire burned low in the grate, Hettie instructed my cousins to give me a tour of the guest bedrooms and choose one for my temporary stay. Though I hoped I'd only be a prisoner in my grandmother's home for a few days, I had to admit the lodgings were comfortable, the food incredible, and the company interesting. Prison could be a whole lot worse.

Bidding my cousins good night, I slipped into the bedroom I'd chosen—a cozy room barely larger than a shoebox. A twin bed was pushed against the far wall, a white antique dresser against the other. Someone—one of the maids working for Hettie, I assumed—had laid *The Magic of Mixology* on the ancient desk in the far corner.

I climbed into the squishy bed, running a hand over my throat. Ranger X's disgusting potion had done its job. The marks on my skin were gone, and it no longer hurt to swallow or speak.

Slipping under the covers, I replayed the day's events in my head, from Gus's announcement that Leonard had been found dead, to the strange incident with Harpin and ensuing rescue by Aarik. My last thoughts before drifting off to sleep centered around Ranger X's softer side. The one I'd seen at his cabin, and I wondered what I'd have to do to see the gentle side of him once more. To see the man who'd rubbed salve on my neck with a touch so gentle it made my heart flutter, who fed me bread though I was certain it was the only food he'd had left. The man who riled me up to the point of boiling then cooled me down with a single smile—that brief, fleeting smile was the last thing I saw before slipping into my dreams.

When I woke the next morning, I found myself wrapped in a ball of sheets, my body trapped so deeply in the fluffy mattress that I panicked. Worried I was suffocating, I sat up in a rush, wiping sweat from my forehead, my palms clammy. While I'd fallen asleep with pleasant thoughts, my dreams hadn't been nearly as enjoyable. Tea leaves—the scent of them, the look of them, the damp, dank feel of the shop—had me drowning in fear.

My hand clasped at my neck, my heart racing until I realized that it'd all been a dream. I was alive. I was safe. I was at Hettie's in The Twist, protected by family, friends, and spells. Harpin couldn't reach me here. Still shaky from my dreams, I leapt out of bed, practically banging my head on the ceiling at the sound of a knock on the door.

"Yes," I muttered, "coming!"

"Check your closet for clothes," Poppy said through the door, as if reading my mind. "Hettie set it up with your sizes early this morning. Pick something a size larger than you'd normally wear, because Hettie cooked her famous wild rice pancakes, and you'll need a little room for waist expansion. Then get your patootie downstairs and *eat!*"

My fingers still trembling, I yanked open the closet door and found all sorts of clothes that were in my size... but not my decade. The sequins and designs were something out of a bad eighties throwback catalogue—leg warmers and leotards and all sorts of crop tops.

I groaned, eventually selecting a simple jean skirt and the least glittery tank top I could find. The other options were far, far worse.

Good thing I had been instructed not to go out in public today. The sheen from my shirt would have blinded people.

"Aw, *man*, you went with the most boring option?" Hettie greeted me as I entered the kitchen. "All those leggings and leotards, and you went with *that*?"

Poppy and Zin—both dressed in incredibly normal jeans and shirts—snickered into their plate of pancakes.

I glared at them, sighing. "What's with the eighties attire?"

"I don't know what you wear over in human-land," Hettie said with a grin. "I was just trying to be thoughtful."

"Right. Thoughtful." I plopped down at the table. "Well, thank you. It's better than not having anything to wear, I suppose."

"Debatable." Poppy cough-laughed.

Zin snorted.

I ignored the two and gestured to the pancakes. "May I?"

"Next time you ask if you can eat something in this house, I will smack you," Hettie said, turning and putting a hand on her hip. "What do you think this is, a hotel? You're *family*. Get used to it. Make yourself at home. We don't ask before we eat. Plus, the other girls are animals. If you don't want to starve, you better move fast."

"It's too early to smack anyone, Mother," Trinket said with a haughty expression, striding into the room dressed as if heading to an interview. At some magical job. If that sort of thing existed. "Lily, eat up. I've arranged for Gus to arrive in ten minutes for your lesson."

"Spoilsport," Zin muttered.

"What's that?" Trinket swiveled on her daughter, who had the gall to look mystified.

"I don't know what you're talking about. I didn't say anything. More pancakes?" Zin scooped two more onto my plate before I could say otherwise. Then she lowered her voice and grumbled, "It's *never* too early to smack someone."

"Is Gus here for Lily or for Mimsey?" Hettie asked, looking far too excited by the prospect. "Or *both*? Maybe they could double-date—Mimsey for love, Lily to learn."

"*Mother!*" Mimsey stormed into the kitchen, all flowers and bright headbands and neon nails. "If you say one word to him about me or love or anything embarrassing—"

"Of course I won't say a word." Hettie frowned, looking around the room. "I'm discreet. Aren't I discreet?"

Everyone suddenly became very engrossed with their pancakes.

"Lot of ungrateful kids, you all…" Hettie turned back to the griddle, flipping pancakes so high in her annoyance that one of them got stuck on the ceiling.

Everyone fell silent, each of us watching the doughy ring slowly peel from the ceiling one inch at a time. Eventually, the pancake fell straight downward and landed on Mimsey's plate. Syrup spattered her face as she stared at the pancake.

"Breakfast is served," Hettie said, a slightly evil tone to her voice.

"*Mother!*"

"Serves you right," Hettie mumbled. Then she raised her voice and laced it with sweetness. "Yes, dear, is something wrong?"

Mimsey opened her mouth to respond just as the doorknocker rang louder than a gunshot, a thunderclap, and a church choir combined. The reverberations rippled through the house, shaking the entire kitchen.

"Don't complain about the noise." Hettie pointed a spatula at her daughters. "You're the ones who installed that god-awful knocker."

"She's just upset because she can't figure out the counter-curse to remove it," Poppy whispered to me. "Drives her batty."

"We wouldn't have installed a special doorknocker if you didn't ignore every person who knocked on your door." Mimsey stood. "I'll get it. You're welcome."

"No, *you're* welcome," Hettie said to Mimsey's back. "I'm sure it's your lover boy out there."

Mimsey stormed off, her flowery dress swishing faster than a flag in a hurricane. She returned a moment later, her voice even. "Lily, it's for you."

I thanked Hettie for breakfast then hightailed my sparkle-clad rear end toward the front door, where Gus waited with an angry expression.

"I've been waiting here for *two minutes.* Two minutes! Who do you think you are, keeping me waiting?" He shook his head. "Let's get to work. Just because you're staying at The Twist doesn't mean you're on vacation. Where's *The Magic of Mixology*? You better not've lost it. It's unique, none like it left."

"It's in my room. I'll grab it and meet you in the den," I said, wondering if Gus's extra-foul mood had anything to do with Mimsey.

"We haven't got all day," Gus snarled. "Move it."

Turned out, we *did* have all day. By the end of the day, I was more exhausted than ever. We still hadn't started Mixing, but I'd memorized most of the items in *The Magic of Mixology*. It'd take a few days for the knowledge to sink in and a few weeks before I was comfortable with the ingredients—knowing which combinations were for healing, and which potions could steal the drinker's breath and leave the user for dead.

"Don't stop studying just because I'm going home." Gus stood, his bones creaking after the all-day study session.

The sun had set ages ago, and we'd had dinner delivered to the den. The only exercise either of us had gotten was when I paced the room, struggling to remember herbs and flowers and powders galore.

"I'm exhausted, Gus." I flopped down on the couch. "Can't I continue tomorrow?"

"If you want to let every single person on The Isle down, then yes. Sleep now and study when you feel like it." Gus shook his head in disgust. "You don't *have* a choice."

"Just a quick nap. My eyelids weigh more than the rest of my body."

Gus gave me a light smack on the cheek. "Stand up. Study, girl."

I stood, tracing the same path I'd walked for most of the afternoon. If I continued at this rate, I'd wear grooves into the floor.

"Good work today," Gus grunted, barely audible.

Just like that, a flash of warmth flooded through me. However, before I could thank him, he clomped down the hallway, smacking his cane as loud as he could, probably trying to tick off Mimsey for some unknown reason.

Sure enough, a second later, my aunt's shout echoed down the hallway. "Shut that racket up, Gus, or you're not welcome back here!"

"I'm using a cane, lady!" Gus shouted back. "Need it to walk."

"Like hell you do," Mimsey shot back. "We all know you only carry that cane to hit people with it!"

I closed my eyes. I'd never get any studying done at this rate. Thankfully, the sparring match ended after another few insults. The *click* of the front door echoed through the otherwise silent hallway.

"Rough day?"

The voice came from behind me. From inside the room.

I whipped around, my hands up in a boxing stance and my startled heart doing flips.

"Gonna fight me?" Ranger X smirked.

At first, that smirk gave me a rush of relief when I realized the intruder had a familiar face. But soon after the realization hit, a rush of annoyance drowned out the relief. *How had he gotten in here?*

I lowered my fists. "It's you."

"Sure is, Princess."

"Why do you go around scaring me like that?" I let my hands fall to my sides, though my fingers remained clenched in fists. "It's annoying, and it's an invasion of my privacy. Why are you here anyway? And *how* do you keep getting in? I thought you needed West Isle Witch blood to navigate The Twist."

"Generally speaking, you do," Ranger X said. "But there are *some* ways around it. For example, The Ranger team has a limited amount of SeekerSolution—something you'll be replenishing for us once Gus shows you the proper method. It gives us immunity to the charms of the labyrinth. Before Hettie set up The Twist, the Ranger team required her to have an antidote—a master key, if you will—available in case something happened. Otherwise if *you* ladies were in trouble, how could we help you?"

I frowned. "Hettie never told me that."

"I'm not surprised. She doesn't make it public knowledge that there's an antidote available."

"Is anyone else aware of it?"

"Just the Rangers and the Mixologist, as far as I know. Hettie swore us to secrecy."

"But could someone else get it? The solution, I mean?"

He seemed confused by my question. "In theory."

I crossed my arms. "Interesting. What if she wants to have guests? Would she give them this antidote?"

Ranger X tilted his head. "If someone is with a West Isle Witch, they can be guided through The Twist. And I believe there's some sort of doorbell hooked up outside the maze. A visitor could ring it, and one of your family members could come and collect them."

"That sounds like a lot of work," I said. "I certainly wouldn't want to throw a party here."

"Yes, well, your grandmother is... something else." He raised his eyebrows. "Now, for the *why*. I thought I'd stop by to give you an update on the current situation. But if you don't want it, I can leave."

"What happened to the Comm devices?"

"Like I said, if you don't want to hear it, I can leave."

I made a conscious effort to relax my fists. "What sort of update?"

"The kind about Harpin."

My blood chilled nearly fifty degrees. "What about Harpin?"

"Do you have five minutes? Maybe we can sit. And talk."

I eyed him suspiciously, taking the farthest armchair from where he'd perched against the desk. "What update?"

"It's Harpin," Ranger X repeated. "He's disappeared."

"Disappeared?" My eyes nearly bugged out of my head. "What do you mean disappeared?"

"There're a few options." Ranger X crossed his arms. "Number one, he left for vacation and didn't tell anyone."

"Unlikely, considering recent events," I said. "Plus, this island *is* a vacation."

Ranger X nodded. "That, and the fact that his store was left open. Anyone could've waltzed in and taken things. As uncharming as the man may be, nobody can say he's not a shrewd businessman. He's got some expensive teas and ingredients in his stockroom, so it's unlikely he'd disappear without locking his store. The man secures it with six levels of hexes, spells, and charms just to use the restroom."

"I'm assuming you have other theories?"

"Three of them."

I was busy drawing my own conclusions but kept them to myself. I wanted to hear Ranger X's theories before I spewed my own.

"Number one, he's up to no good," Ranger X said. "He might be hiding out after yesterday's events. Waiting for the opportunity to pounce. He's smart—which could mean he's staging his own disappearance. That'd explain the unlocked store."

I tried my best to maintain composure. "That's number one. What are the other theories?"

"Number two is similar to the first. Harpin might be voluntarily hiding, but for different reasons. Maybe he's afraid someone's after him. Which, in the light of recent events, isn't entirely wrong."

"Who would be after him? Nobody else even knows about the stunt he pulled in the tea shop..." I looked up. "You're after him? I *told* you not to do anything to hurt him."

"I have grounds to arrest Harpin. Which I plan on doing when I find him. That brings us to the third theory—someone's already found him."

My jaw dropped. "Who else would be looking for him?"

"That's the million-dollar question, now isn't it?"

CHAPTER 23

RANGER X LEFT SOON AFTER he divulged his theories, but not before he set my skin on fire with a grasp of my arm and a murmur in my ear, reminding me to call him via the Comm device at the first sign of trouble. Though his whispers were nothing but business, they didn't help reduce the ever-growing list of emotions I associated with his presence. Anger, gratefulness, possibly a bit of desire, a touch of embarrassment.

"Cheer up, sugar plum," Poppy said, her cheerful voice brightening the dim room.

"Hey," I said, scooting over on the plush couch and patting the cushion next to me. The fire crackled in the hearth, the warmth combating the chill from an outside breeze. The windows were open, letting the salty sea air drift through the cottage. "How you doing? I missed you guys today. I can't believe Gus kept me locked up in here for ages."

"We missed you too." Poppy patted my leg. "But believe me, you didn't really *miss* anything if you catch my drift. I mean, I love this family to death, God help me. But we are *not* meant to live in the same house."

I offered a sympathetic wince. "Things got ugly?"

"Let's just say my mother's hair is orange, Trinket's hair is blue, and Hettie has locked herself in her room and been cackling nonstop for the past thirty minutes." Poppy shook her head. "And those are just the after-dinner stunts. It doesn't include the cooking fiasco. Don't ask."

"I'm glad you stopped by." I exhaled a long, slow breath. "Talk about a day."

"Tell me about it." Poppy sat back, kicking her legs up on the seat of the couch and leaning against my shoulder. "I don't have anything else to say except I'm getting antsy from being here, and it's hardly been twenty-four hours. They aren't allowing us outside. We can't even *look* at The Twist."

I hardly heard the second half of Poppy's sentence. I was too distracted by the easy familiarity with which my cousin laid her head on my shoulder, examined her fingernails, and curled up close without a second thought.

Having not grown up with siblings, or even much in the way of friends, I didn't know how to react. I liked it, her head resting on me, but it felt strange. I'd constructed a bubble of personal space so large I could take off like a hot air balloon.

Touching another person was such an intimate gesture, reserved only for a select few I'd invited into my bubble. Not that I'd invited anyone into my bubble for years. A few bad experiences had led to me constructing hard walls instead of a soft, pliable bubble, and I preferred to be alone.

"Are you falling asleep on me?" Poppy tilted her head to look at me. "Why'd you go quiet?"

"Oh, no, sorry. Just thinking—I have a lot in my brain right now." I laughed. "I've pretty much memorized that entire book."

"That fat thing?" She nodded toward *The Magic of Mixology*. "Dang, girlfriend. Your brain must weigh about thirty pounds to hold all that info."

"Feels like it." I sighed.

"C'mon, just start talking. It'll feel good," Poppy said. "Spill the beans about anything you want. Ready? Go."

"I don't want to bore you."

"I'll tell you if I'm bored. Start talking. Just go with it. Go until you can't talk anymore."

"What do I say?"

"You've never done this?" Poppy asked with incredulity. "Cripes. Say anything. Start with: *Poppy is making me do the stupidest exercise.*"

I laughed again.

"Don't laugh, just do it already."

"Poppy is making me do the stupidest exercise to ever have been invented," I said, the laughter still present in my voice. "Because the last thing I want to do is talk after a long day in which Gus banged my shins more times with his cane than I can count, and..." I paused for a breath.

"Keep going," Poppy prodded. "You're getting the hang of it."

Over the next ten minutes, I moaned and whined, griped and complained about everything I could think to say. At one point, I stopped thinking and let the words tumble like uncontrollable somersaults, cartwheeling off into every direction without a wisp of a filter.

"Dang," Poppy said once I'd finished. "That was a lot of word vomit. Feel better?"

"Wow." I stared at my cousin like a deer in headlights. "Yeah. I feel great."

I'd filled her in on everything from the first page of memorization to the last. I'd explained how Gus had pushed me to the edge of a mental breakdown, then just when I neared the edge of throwing my arms up and begging to quit, he'd give me the push I needed to keep going—a hint of positive reinforcement that gave me the strength to go on, to turn the page, to Mix one more imaginary drink.

Poppy had *awwed* with sympathy, grunted with frustration, *hmmed* with a thoughtful expression at all of the appropriate times. But when I got to the part about Ranger X appearing in this room, her jaw had dropped. Thankfully, she hadn't said anything.

"So Ranger X was in this room?" Poppy asked. "This very room?"

I nodded.

"I think it's cute. Y'all are like high schoolers, sneakin' through the windows to smooch each other." Poppy sighed. "High school, that's what the humans call it, yeah?"

"It's not *cute*," I said, and an eerie sense of déjà vu hit me. I realized I sounded like him. "He's not my type."

"Fine. Apparently your type is boring and ugly." Poppy swung her legs to the floor and sat up, staring at me. "What was he here for, anyway?"

I filled her in on the rest of the details, from Harpin's mysterious disappearance to Ranger X's warning to remain here and continue my studies. I skipped the part where he touched my wrist and sent ribbons of fire to my stomach, but she might've guessed anyway, since I looked away to hide my red cheeks.

"Sounds like you need a drink." Thankfully, Poppy didn't pester me about Ranger X and his lips any further.

"Wine?" I asked. "I think I saw some—"

"Better idea." Poppy hopped to her feet. "Has anyone explained to you about the Menu yet?"

I shook my head.

"Well, I can't think of a better time to do it." Poppy crossed her arms, her face taking on a teacher-esque expression. "It combines your studies, a bit of fun, and adult beverages."

"That sounds too good to be true."

"Well, it's not."

"Explain to me, then, Miss Poppy. What is a Menu?"

"Well, ever since the beginning of time, each Mixologist has created his own customized potion list." Poppy grinned. "They choose a theme. For example, one of them focused on creating love potions. Their menu has items like the Kissing Kup and the Sexy Spritzer. Another Mixologist was into fitness, so he created Muscle Milkshakes and Slimming Sunrises. That last one is awesome. I lost three pounds before my last date."

"What happens with these menus?"

"Think of it like a legacy." Poppy tapped her chin in thought. "I suppose you haven't seen the Menu board yet. Behind the bar, there's a huge chalkboard that populates as you create each drink. You wouldn't have noticed because the slate is wiped clean when each Mixologist passes on, leaving it blank for the next one."

"Can you still order their drinks? Or does their Menu retire when they... pass on?"

Poppy nodded. "You can get them, but it's sort of a specialty item. The main point of the Menu project is for the legacy—to leave something behind when you're gone. Sorry, that sounds morbid."

"It's life, I guess."

"What's your theme going to be?"

I bit my lip. "Well, seeing as how I didn't know these Menus were a thing, I haven't given it any thought."

"Well, what do you like? Let's brainstorm your theme."

"Hmm." My mind went blank.

"What do you like?" Poppy asked. "It's not that hard."

I blushed. "I like marketing. I was good at it. That was my last job."

"Huh. That's... cool." Poppy wrinkled her nose. "I don't really know what that means, but this is supposed to be fun. The way you say *marketing*, it doesn't sound enjoyable. What do you do for fun?"

"I'm not into fitness, or exercise of any sort really. My love life is crap, so that's out. I don't have a ton of hobbies... I always liked mixing drinks, but now that makes a whole ton more sense than it did when I was in the Twin Cities."

"What sort of drinks did you make there?"

"All the regulars. I like plain stuff—vodka and soda, wine, whiskey on the rocks..." I hesitated. "It was always more fun to make drinks for others, because they liked the fancy stuff. Margaritas, Cosmopolitans, Sex on the Beach—"

Poppy's eyes widened. "What? You're allowed to have sex on the beach? I mean, I can't lie, I've always wondered how that would work." She leaned in, dropping her voice to a whisper. "Doesn't sand just get... you know, *everywhere*? Like, all up in there?"

"It's just the name of a drink!" My face burned.

"Oh, cripes." Poppy fanned herself. "You didn't seem like the real exploratory type, but I suppose you never know. It's usually the quiet ones."

"*Poppy!*"

"What if you did some sort of human theme to your menu?" She looked at the ceiling. "I think... yes, I'm fairly certain you're the only Mixologist who has ever been off The Isle. Most of them were born here, and once it's confirmed they're next in line, they spend most of their lives training for the job. It can be your unique twist."

"A twist on human drinks..." I tapped my lip with my forefinger. "I like it."

"Just... I dunno, make your human drinks more magical, and *boom*. You're all set!"

I stood and paced the same circle I had walked a million times already today. By my fourth lap, I held up a finger. "I've got it. Know how we have Sex on the Beach?" I clarified quickly. "As a drink?"

Poppy nodded.

"*Hex on the Beach!*"

Poppy leapt up from the couch, clapping. "Excellent. Let's get started."

"Started on what?"

"Your drink, silly. What do you want it to do?"

"What do you mean... *do?*"

"It's magic." Poppy rolled her eyes. "Make it do *something*. Anything. You could make the drinker giggle uncontrollably, snort instead of laugh, bark like a dog—it doesn't have to be serious. In fact, why don't you make one for me? I want a potion to attract men."

"I don't want to attract men. I seem to attract the rude ones, and I want to get rid of them."

"Then make a man-repellent." Poppy smiled. "It's perfect! Say you want to run out to the grocery store in your sweat pants. You just put on this potion from a spray bottle, and the men stay away. You can call it… *Stay-Away Spray.* It doubles as the name and the description."

"I like where your head's at." I looked around the room. "Now, where do we start?"

"You're the Mixologist."

"I haven't mixed a single thing yet."

"How about that drink that killed Leonard?"

"I didn't kill Leonard!"

"Oh, right…" Poppy pursed her lips. "So you've really never done magic?"

I shook my head. "Gus says I have to learn all the rules first."

"Didn't you say you memorized that entire chunk of paper?" Poppy eyed the massive book on the table.

"Unfortunately, yes." I sighed. "Well, not unfortunately I suppose, but it sure would've been nice to spread it out over a few more days."

"Well, you know how the saying goes—you gotta learn the rules before you can break them."

"How does that apply?"

"You just learned all the rules!" Poppy clapped again. "Now you get to break them."

"I don't think that's a good idea."

"I'm going to dig up what Hettie has in the cupboards while you get cooking," Poppy said. "Time to sink or swim, my dear. Either Mix some drinks, or go study some more. You can't study for the rest of your life, can you?"

"It's only been a couple of days."

"Exactly. Time to get a move on." Poppy looked around the room. "This is the first time I've been glad we're locked up at this cottage. Hettie has spent *years* developing The Twist for moments just like this. If I sneak out fast, she won't notice. I've been perfecting a hidden route for years."

"And how do you see us using a maze to help create beverages?"

"The Twist is *so* much more than a labyrinth." Poppy grabbed my shoulders. "Hettie has been cultivating the rarest flowers, a variety of foreign herbs, a smorgasbord of specialty plants—whatever you need, it's all there. She won't notice if some goes missing. In fact, she'd love to give you some. She enjoys breaking the rules more than anyone."

"So that's where you get it from?" I smiled.

Poppy's eyes crinkled with her grin. "Possibly. Then again, you're related too."

"But—"

Poppy squished a finger against my lips. "*Shhhh.* Your job is simple. Just have a recipe ready to go by the time I get back, and holler if you think of something in particular you need. Otherwise, I'll just grab the basics and whatever else I can find."

Before I could protest again, Poppy was off to gather supplies. I sat alone, only a book the size of a couch to keep me company.

CHAPTER 24

A BOOK THE SIZE OF A couch makes for interesting company, it turned out, though creating a drink that repelled men was far more complicated than one might imagine.

By the time Poppy returned an hour later, I had ten separate recipes that could potentially start us off in the right direction.

"Hey, can you open up this door?" Poppy called from outside the den.

Frowning, I stood, turned the knob, and saw immediately why she couldn't do it herself. "Wow, Poppy, you shouldn't have."

"Oh, it's just the basics. I figured we might need some trial and error, so I got plenty of everything. But don't mess up more than three times, or we'll run out of ingredients."

Judging by the stack of ingredients in Poppy's arms, we'd never run out. She stood in the entryway looking like the Leaning Tower of Witchcraft—bottles and vials in one hand, leaves stuffed into pockets, plants balanced every which way in her arms.

I hustled to relieve her of the ingredients and spread them on the table in front of the couch.

"There." Poppy's chest heaved. "That should get ya started, huh?"

"You forgot one thing…" I eyed all the ingredients.

Poppy's face fell. "You've got to be kidding me. I spent forever gathering all that. I even asked Hettie for suggestions, and she was more than happy to load me up with the most dangerous ingredients."

I grinned at my cousin. "I'm just kidding. You wanted me to joke with you, right?"

"You learn quickly!"

"Okay, since you brought an entire garden, I have a few ideas. I've come up with a handful of starter potions that'll give us a good baseline. Shall we begin testing?"

Poppy's eyes glowed. "Well, I didn't haul this junk across The Twist for *fun*."

"Basil. Do you have basil? And garlic." I looked at my notes. "Those are the two consistent ingredients I have for each tester potion."

"Are you trying to scare men away with your *breath*?" Poppy shook her head. "If you're not careful, you might kill them. Garlic can be lethal."

"I've factored that in, you'll be happy to know, and I plan to include mint leaves to combat the dragon-breath issue." I smiled, pleased I'd had the foresight to address that tiny wrench. "But here're my thoughts. Basil has strong love properties and is used in a lot of spells to bring love to you."

Poppy's eyebrows cinched together as she listened.

"Garlic, however, has protective spells. I'm thinking if I can combine the two with a few other ingredients, the garlic might reverse the effects of the basil and instead of drawing love to us, it'll push it away." I finished speaking quickly, a thrill growing inside me. Mixing magical drinks was like solving a problem and putting a puzzle together.

"You're going to make this potion temporary, right?" Poppy bit her lip. "I'm just saying... I'm only looking for a quick fix in case I'm having a no-makeup sort of day and want to sunbathe on the beach. I don't want my ovaries drying up forever. I think I'd like a man at some point."

I frowned. "It'll be temporary."

"Well, I'm not testing it until you can prove it's temporary."

"I have dandelion powder for that." I selected a small vial and held it up for Poppy to see. "Dandelions come and go so quickly, so I'm thinking their short lifespan will give the formula properties of a temporary potion."

"Test it on Zin. I don't think she's into men," Poppy said. "At least not romantically. She's still bitter they won't let her become a Ranger, so she's sort of sworn off boys."

"It's unfair," Zin said from the doorway, having crept in while I laid out my plan for the potion. "I heard you guys talking about me."

"It's nothing we wouldn't have said to your face," Poppy said. "You don't like men because they won't let you be a Ranger."

"I still don't want to test the potion," Zin said. "Maybe someday I won't dislike men so much, and I'd like the *option* of them being around."

"I'll test it on myself. I don't have luck with the male species anyway," I said. "Now, I need a pot, a burner, and a few stir sticks. Where can I find those?"

Another hour and three failed potions—which bubbled puke-green, sunflower-yellow, and then murky-brown—later, I came up with one that didn't smell like feet. We had potential.

"Look at this one." I spun the violet concoction with the long stir stick. "I think the salt made all the difference. Pinch of salt. Gotta remember that."

Neither Poppy nor Zin paid me any attention whatsoever. They'd grown bored after the second failed concoction. Poppy thumbed through a magazine while Zin sharpened a long, scary-looking knife.

"You guys, I think I've got it." Excitement simmered, my gut telling me that this formula was the correct one.

The Mix was finally working. As the potion bubbled in the cauldron, I understood what everyone had been trying to tell me— Mixology ran in my veins. I could inherently sense the ingredient needed for a concoction, I could tell when the potion had failed, and best of all, I knew when it worked.

This time, something had changed. My fingers tingled with

anticipation, and butterflies fluttered in my stomach. The air crackled, the presence of magic impossible to deny, although Zin and Poppy didn't appear to notice a difference.

"It's working," I whispered. "Magic."

"How does it feel?" Poppy glanced up from her magazine with a smile. "Betcha can't go back to working as an accountant now."

I shook my head, ignoring the fact I'd never once been an accountant. After one teensy victory as a Mixologist, already I knew I'd never return to my days as a normal human. The thrill of magic, the excitement, the passion—it permeated every atom of my body.

Finally I understood that I'd not only come home, but I belonged.

CHAPTER 25

THE KNOCK ON THE DOOR almost caused me to dump my newly created *Hex on the Beach* right on top of myself. I'd lined up a small vial and was carefully funneling the purple potion from the cauldron into a portable container when the knock sounded.

I hadn't decided if I'd let Gus know about our experiments, but I wanted to keep an extra sample on hand, just in case I wanted to show off for him. Even though I'd broken his rules about learning the facts before messing with magic, I thought my first Menu item was something to be proud of, something Gus deserved to see. After all, he'd given me the tools to create magic in the first place.

The knock sounded again, and I glanced up, annoyed.

Poppy froze with a look of trepidation on her face. "Remember how I said Hettie fixed us up with some extra ingredients?"

I fixed a *look* on Poppy.

"Well..." She wrung her hands. "I might not have told her *exactly* what we were going to use it for."

"Then we better hide this stuff." Zin stood, gesturing toward the ingredients spread across the table, the simmering cauldron, the containers of failed experiments. "And quickly, since I'm sick of getting into trouble. If we're going to keep breaking rules, we really have to learn to be better about hiding the evidence."

"Where can we put it?" I asked, panic lacing my voice. "It's all—"

The knock turned into a pound, interrupting my concerns.

"Lily, come out here," Mimsey's voice rang sweetly through the kitchen door.

Too sweetly. I looked at my cousins with raised eyebrows. They shrugged.

"You have a visitor," she clarified. "Come on out and say hello."

I exhaled a sigh—the last thing I wanted at the moment was a visitor. "It's late, Mimsey. Why are you up? Can't it wait until tomorrow?"

That sugary sweetness seeped through her voice again. "Oh, I was just cleaning up in the kitchen. He didn't bother me. Don't be rude to your guest. It might be important."

"This is good," Poppy whispered. "You slip out, we'll clean up here. Store the stuff over in the chest in the corner under the blankets."

"Thank you," I mouthed, slipping toward the door. I pocketed the vial of extra *Hex on the Beach,* finger-combed my hair, and straightened my jean skirt. Putting a hand on the doorknob, I made sure my cousins were mostly out of sight before I twisted the handle. "Coming!"

"There you are, dear, I was starting to think you were sleeping." Mimsey tittered. "You have a visitor. He's waiting just round the corner in the front hall."

I took quick steps down the hallway, my mouth parting in surprise at the unexpected guest. "Aarik, hello! What brings you 'round The Twist?"

"I just wanted to make sure you were okay." Aarik's sky-blue eyes met mine before he glanced away, demurely looking at his shoes.

"I'm doing just fine." I smiled, gesturing toward my body. "Thanks to you."

Mimsey stood a foot away, watching the exchange with a dreamy expression. "How romantic."

"Mimsey?" I raised my eyebrows. "Don't you have... sewing to do?"

"I don't sew." She grinned more broadly.

"Cooking?"

"I hate cooking."

"Mimsey!" My voice finally broke her out of a daydream.

"Oh, er. Right. I was just having a cup of tea. Would you two like some?" She tore her gaze away from Aarik and looked toward me.

I shook my head. "No, we're okay. Do you mind?"

"Oh, I don't need to stay long." Aarik offered a shy glance in my direction before clearing his throat and explaining to Mimsey. "Lily and I parted on, uh, interesting terms, and I just wanted to make sure Lily had made it home. When you weren't at the bungalow, I stopped here, figuring you might be with your family."

"He's the one who helped me out already." I stepped forward, resting a hand on Aarik's shoulder. "Are you sure you wouldn't like a glass of wine or a cup of tea before you're off? Just a small thank you. After all, it's a long way to come just to turn around and leave."

"I'm really fine," Aarik said, waving in a *no thanks* gesture. "I just wanted to see you. Make sure you were safe."

"Fancy a walk?" Mimsey asked him. "Lily, maybe you should take him through the lilac bushes. They're in full bloom now. You can lead him back through The Twist afterward. I let him in, and he'll need a guide out."

"We can skip the walk. I'm sure Aarik's tired." Turning to Aarik, I gave an apologetic shrug. "But I'd be happy to lead you back. I think I should be able to get the route straight this time."

"That would be great. I don't want to take up any more of your time." Aarik gave a long nod toward Mimsey. "Thank you for your hospitality."

"Oh, it was nothing." Mimsey blushed profusely, fanning her face. "Lily, can I see you a moment?"

Before I could respond, my aunt yanked me around the corner so quickly my arm was in danger of dislocation.

"When you walk him through The Twist, take a left at the apple tree instead of a right," Mimsey spoke in hushed tones. "It's a bit longer a route but scenic. Very pretty at night, especially when we have such a bright moon."

"Why do I sense you have an ulterior motive?" I whispered back. "There's nothing romantic between Aarik and me. We don't need scenic."

"Not yet, but there could be." Mimsey bit her lip, as if debating whether or not to continue speaking.

"Spill the beans."

"*Fine!* The lilacs have a bit of a lust tendency when combined with moonlight. It won't make you fall in love, but if there's something there underneath, it might help things along."

"Mimsey..."

She pouted. "I'm just trying to help."

"I'm not interested in romance whatsoever. I'm more interested in finding out why I'm in danger, who killed Leonard—you know, important things like that."

"Love is important. Do you want to go through life and end up alone like—" She stopped, having worked herself into a fit. "Never mind. Do whatever you like. You're not listening anyway."

I wondered if Mimsey had meant to say "alone like me," but I pushed the thought away. I didn't want to see her upset, but I also didn't want a pile of pressure heaped on Aarik and me, who were nothing more than acquaintances at best. First order of business was figuring out where Harpin had gone.

I returned around the corner, finding Aarik standing with his hands at awkward angles to his sides, a pained expression on his face.

"I'm sorry if you heard that," I said, squinting at my sequined shirt.

"I tried not to listen." He grimaced. "Neither of you have particularly quiet *inside voices.*"

I laughed. "It's nothing against you. I like you, it's just... I'm new here, still getting my bearings. You don't mind if we take the shortcut and skip the lilac bushes for now, do you?"

He breathed a sigh of relief. "No offense, but I was hoping you'd say that. I'd rather get a Caffeine Cup with you before your aunt puts a spell on us." He gave a quick shake of his head. "That sounds wrong, I suppose. All I meant was that I'd like to get to know you without magic interfering."

"I agree." I smiled as I gently touched his arm, leading him toward the front door. "Thanks for stopping by. Maybe we can do coffee tomorrow?"

"I'd like that."

The stroll through The Twist was far more pleasant than I'd expected. Neither Aarik nor I felt the need to continually speak, and we fell into an easy silence. A few late-night birds chirped, insects buzzed, and light glinted off beautiful blossoms and shining leaves. The floral scent added a nice touch, and before I knew it, we'd reached the entrance.

"This is it." I stopped short of the entrance to The Twist, where the hidden garden path met up with the rest of local civilization. "Thanks for stopping by. I really appreciate it."

Aarik stepped toward me, and for a second, I thought he just might kiss me. A subtle whiff of smoke caught me off guard, though it wasn't unpleasant—it had a floral quality, easy on the lungs, unlike the harsh menthol of cigarettes. His warm body stood inches from mine, his blue eyes a bit hazy.

"About that Caffeine Cup tomorrow…" His breath danced softly on my cheek, the scent unusual but not unpleasant.

"I'd love to," I said.

"That's the thing." His face tensed, his eyebrows knitted together. "I'm afraid I won't be able to make it."

"Oh." I tried to hide my surprise while wondering what had changed during our midnight stroll. "That's no problem. We can always reschedule… er, if you'd like, that is."

"I'm afraid that's not going to be possible." His hand cupped the side of my neck, his fingers weaving into my hair.

I looked into his eyes, his tone setting off the first set of alarm bells in my defense system. "Why is that—"

Before I could finish the question, my eyesight became hazy.

The look in Aarik's expression turned glazed and barren. "Because you won't be able to make it either."

I opened my mouth to respond but couldn't speak. My body, my mouth, my tongue—it'd all become paralyzed. Only a second later did I feel the *zap* of magic snaking through my veins, and I realized seconds too late that he must have used a spell as he touched my neck.

Hot threads of magic—evil magic, by the feel of it—wound through my body. One by one, I lost the ability to move, to speak, to stand. I collapsed in his arms.

As the spell darkened the edges of my mind, sending me reeling toward a cliff of blackness, he muttered, "I'm sorry."

CHAPTER 26

I'M SORRY.
Who's sorry?
Where am I?
Aarik.

Aarik. This was all because of Aarik. But that didn't make sense…

My brain fought to piece together the snippets of puzzle that didn't connect, made more difficult by the lingering grogginess from unconsciousness. I kept my eyes tightly closed, testing out various body parts. Tugging on my arms, I realized they were bound behind my back. My legs were heavy as sandbags, probably still suffering from the aftereffects of the spell that'd knocked me out cold.

I kept my eyes firmly shut, giving my mind as much time as possible to recuperate before Aarik—or whoever was now holding me captive—noticed I was awake.

My stomach churned uncomfortably, and I prayed I wouldn't puke and give away my consciousness. *What sort of spell had he used?* My body was so wobbly it was almost as if I were…

Wait.

It wasn't my body trembling—it was the entire floor. They'd brought me to a boat. I relaxed my limbs completely, listening, waiting. Sure enough, the slight *thwap* of water against the edge of the boat drifted through the air, and I licked my lips, tasting salt.

We were at sea.

Unfortunately, the discovery didn't give me a sense of

accomplishment, only trepidation. If we were on a boat traveling away from The Isle, we were heading in the exact opposite direction from everything and everyone who might be able to help me.

"You understand what these do?" Aarik's voice startled me.

He must not have been looking in my direction, however, because he didn't acknowledge my reflexive twitch. At least not yet. But as I focused on his words, I heard something else—the sound of a second body moving. Two people were on this boat besides me.

"Kenny, talk to me," Aarik said. "You understand these?"

Silence ensued.

I wondered if Aarik *knew* Kenny didn't talk and was trying to convince him to answer, or if Aarik was oblivious. I found myself hoping that if Kenny could speak, he would. I couldn't help feeling somewhat responsible for what happened to the non-speaking man. Maybe if he'd just pipe up and offer Aarik information, he'd be let go, unharmed. *Speak, Kenny. Speak.*

Still nothing.

"How on earth did those witches think it was a good idea to give someone as stupid as you responsibility for the boat?" Aarik mumbled, more to himself than anyone else. "Well, you probably can't understand me, you oaf, but in case you can… these handcuffs are magic resistant. You try anything, and the spell backfires, got it? So the harder you struggle, the more you hurt yourself."

The clink of handcuffs followed, but not a peep from Kenny.

"Guess you'll figure it out soon enough if you're tempted to try something on me." Aarik's toe nudged my leg. "You awake?"

I also didn't respond.

"Quiet bunch tonight, huh?" Aarik murmured. "Fine by me."

A *thud* like rope hitting the floor sent tremors through the bottom of the dinky boat, and the next thing I knew, the waves intensified. We were off.

I tried to feel for the Comm band around my wrist, but I couldn't tell if Aarik had left it intact. The bindings around my arms were too tight for me to tell a difference between the Comm band and the rope. Even if the Comm band was still functioning, it wouldn't help me now. The thing needed my breath and my voice to work. Since my hands were bound behind my back, unless I could twist my head halfway around my body, I was stuck.

Minutes passed, the silence accompanied only by the light *huffs* of Aarik and Kenny breathing, the *ping* of water slicing against the boat, and the occasional *splash* in the distance.

My mind raced with escape plans, none of them particularly promising. But then again, nothing really made sense at the moment. If Aarik was out to get me, then why had he saved me from Harpin? Were they working together? And if not, was Aarik the one who'd made the tea shop owner vanish?

I couldn't connect the dots no matter how hard I tried. My biggest problem was a motive. Or rather, a *lack* of motive. What linked me to Harpin? And more importantly, why was I worth kidnapping?

CHAPTER 27

I HAD NO IDEA HOW MUCH time had passed when a foot nudged me in the stomach.

"How long have you been faking it?" Aarik's voice sounded more curious than anything. "You had me fooled for a while, but no one breathes that evenly in sleep. Nice try."

"Thanks for the insight," I said wryly. "I'll remember that for the next time I'm kidnapped."

"Look, I knew you'd be angry with me," Aarik said. "I'm sorry."

"Sorry?" My voice cracked. "*Sorry?* Apologizing doesn't make everything right in the world, you know."

"Hey, don't shoot the messenger." I opened my eyes just in time to see Aarik's shrug. "I'm just doing my job."

"Your job is kidnapping people?"

"Not usually." Aarik had the grace to look uncomfortable. "You're a special case."

"Should I be thanking you?" Sarcasm dripped from my voice. "At least have the nerve to tell me what's going on—who you work for, what they want with me."

Aarik fell silent, glancing over toward Kenny.

"What do you care if he hears?" I said. "You put those magical cuffs on him, and you already said you think he's stupid. Plus, after kidnapping me, it's not like you can just return to The Isle."

"Of course I can." Aarik looked annoyed. "No one's going to know I did it. I'll be back in time to report you missing."

"My aunts know I walked you out of the cottage just before I disappeared. They're bound to put two and two together."

"Not if they find me knocked out at the edge of The Twist," Aarik said. "I'll hit your little doorbell then give myself an injection of the same stuff I gave you. When they show up, they'll find me unconscious. Genius, huh?"

I didn't answer.

"They'll think I'm a hero for remembering to hit the doorbell before passing out. I'll be the first person warning everyone you're gone." Aarik looked at me with renewed interest. "I can say someone knocked me out from behind, and I didn't see a thing. Or better yet, I can say the figure looked like Harpin. That'll work better. He's disappeared, so everyone will assume he made off with you—not hard to believe after the scene in the tea shop yesterday."

"Why'd you rescue me if you were just going to kidnap me anyway?"

"Same reason I had to get rid of Harpin. I needed you alive." Aarik looked at me. "Nothing personal. It's just... if I don't bring you in alive, I don't get paid."

"What do you need the money for?" I asked, my voice heated. "That stuff you're smoking all the time?"

"Of course not." Aarik's eyes shifted from mine to focus on the water. I'd hit the nail on the head. "Living expenses."

"Sure. Right. What are you gonna do with Kenny?"

Aarik bit his lip. "Hadn't really factored the oaf in, so I don't know yet. None of your business anyway—you'll be gone before I have to deal with him."

"I'll make *you* a deal. Let him go free, and I'll go peacefully with you."

Kenny gave no sign he heard anything happening on the boat, staring serenely into the sky.

"You're already going peacefully with me." Aarik nodded toward my bindings. "And if you struggle against those, I'll just knock you out again. I'm being real nice letting you stay conscious right now."

"Where are we going?"

"Doesn't matter. You'll find out soon enough."

"Who do you work for?"

"Same answer as above." Aarik's face pinched, however.

"Why are you doing this, Aarik?"

With each of my questions, he shifted a bit in his seat. It was obvious he didn't like the rapid-fire questions. If I could just push him over the edge...

"You don't know what it's like."

"I don't know what... *what* is like?" I asked. "Try me."

"Shut up."

"Why are you doing this, Aarik? Did you kill Harpin?"

"I never meant to kill anyone!" Aarik leapt to his feet, and the boat rocked so precariously, my nerves rattled and my body tensed. If we tipped over, there was no way I'd survive without the use of my hands.

"Who did you kill, Aarik?" I asked once the boat had settled, my voice so quiet the sound of the waves nearly swallowed it. "Harpin?"

"Harpin's not dead. But that's all I'm saying."

My glance traveled briefly toward Kenny, who sat silently at the rear of the boat, his gaze almost eerily locked on my face. At the front, Aarik stood with his arms crossed, watching as the Great Lake picked up momentum.

"How do you know Harpin's not dead?" I asked.

Aarik's back stiffened, though he pretended he hadn't heard anything. He hugged his arms tighter, and from my spot on the floor, I could see his face harden with anger. I guessed it was mostly anger at himself, anger that he'd already shared too much information.

"Who'd you kill? If it's not Harpin, who else could it be— Leonard? Was he involved somehow?" I wriggled, trying a new tactic when he didn't respond. I lowered my voice, infusing sympathy into my words. "It's not your fault, you know. Are they blackmailing you? Who do you work for?"

Aarik's jaw worked up and down on that last part. He didn't confirm or deny my theory, but his nervous tic gave me enough to suspect I might be onto something.

"Just tell me, Aarik. We can get you help. We can keep you safe, protect you."

"You can't. Nobody can." Aarik turned, his arms flying up in protest, his eyes flashing with anger. "Not you, not your stupid boyfriend, not anyone else. You're no match for these people."

"I don't have a boyfriend."

Aarik's eyes blazed, first in anger then in a mocking disbelief. "Right."

"I swear to you! I don't have a boyfriend."

"That's not what it looked like the other day."

"You don't know what you're talking about," I said, my own anger building. "If you're talking about Ranger X, he was just doing his job. And apparently his intuition is better than mine, because he didn't trust you, unlike *me*. I stuck up for you, Aarik."

That pained expression creeped back across his face, making me suspect that just maybe he *wasn't* lying. Maybe he was just the messenger, some sort of a pawn in a much larger game. Maybe he was scared for his own life. Maybe he was a decent person who'd been sucked into a bad situation.

"I don't think you're a bad person, Aarik. Just tell me who you're working for, and maybe we can work out a deal."

"*Shut up!*" Aarik turned to me, extending a hand in my direction. A bright glow surrounded his fingers, and though I didn't have much experience with magic of any sort, my gut twisted, and something told me he wasn't doing anything *nice*. His spell was meant to harm, not to help.

"I'm sorry," I said, backtracking quickly. "I'll be quiet from here on out under one condition."

The glow surrounding Aarik's fingers wavered a bit. "What's that?"

"Can I please sit on a seat instead of the floor?"

Aarik took a deep breath, dropping his hand to his side, the glow fading as he scanned the boat. He glanced at Kenny, who was still cuffed by magic.

"Sit in front of him. Any funny business, and one of you is going over the side of the boat." His gaze flicked between us quickly. "The water is cold this time of year. Understood?"

"Yes," I murmured.

Aarik waited a moment for Kenny's response, but unsurprisingly, there was none.

"Get up." Aarik flicked his wrist in my direction. "You've got thirty seconds to get situated."

Sitting up with bound hands and wobbly legs was more difficult than I'd anticipated. Thirty seconds wasn't long enough.

"Better hurry," Aarik said, his voice lazy again.

Something about the shift in his voice gave me the idea there were two sides to Aarik. One version spoke too much and let his anger get the best of him. The other version of Aarik was relaxed, indifferent, and spoke with a flat, emotionless tone. The latter was far more frightening.

All at once, Kenny stood, his big form rocking the boat. Aarik watched the silent man, another spell burning on his fingertips. However, Kenny ignored Aarik, instead bending over and hauling me up as if I were a sack of feathers. Even though his arms were cuffed before him, he hooked his hands onto my clothes and gave me a lift onto the seat in front of him. Then he sat right back down.

"Looks like you made yourself a friend." Aarik's lips curled up, eying my new spot on the boat bench. "Aren't you Little Miss Social Butterfly."

"That's what happens when you don't kidnap people," I said,

unable to help myself. "You make *friends*. I liked you, Aarik. My family trusted you."

The flash of uncertainty in his eyes was back, but just for a passing moment. The calm, collected Aarik took over in a second. "Like you said, that was a mistake."

"What about your family, Aarik? Where are they?"

Aarik looked away.

"Are they in trouble?" Then I threw my next question out of left field. "Who did you kill, Aarik?"

Aarik, the controlled version of himself, turned his back to me.

My shoulders sagged. I wasn't getting any answers. We also couldn't see either shore anymore, which meant we were too far away to get help from The Isle. My options were running out.

Just as I was considering contortionist ways to get my mouth near the Comm device in order to call for help, a light touch surprised me.

I twitched but didn't look back. I sensed Kenny had leaned forward, and I felt his proximity without seeing him. His hands worked at my bindings, his fingers delicate and nimble in a way I'd never expected. Then again, he worked on boats for a living and probably tied endless knots. My heart rate sped up. Maybe he could free me—maybe Kenny was my only hope.

My heart sank just as fast when I realized that even if Kenny did free me, my options still weren't rosy. My captor had much more powerful magic than I did, along with years of experience. The best I could hope for would be to call for help before it was too late.

Kenny then pressed something into my hand, and I realized he hadn't been working at my bindings—he'd been working at the Comm device. Which was unfortunate, because I couldn't use it until he untied my wrists. Without my breath on the device, it would be in a constant *Off* state. But I couldn't exactly turn around and explain...

Thankfully, his hands went back to work on the bindings,

pausing only for a second as Aarik looked back. But as soon as our captor's gaze turned forward again, focusing on the waves, Kenny was back at it.

Until Aarik whirled about, his hand accusingly held out while magic danced at his fingertips. "I warned you," he growled. "No funny business."

Aarik had been just a second too slow to catch Kenny in the act, but something—our expressions, the situation of our bodies, the shuffling in our seats—had put him on edge.

"What do you have in your hand?" Aarik asked quietly, stepping toward us.

I scrunched the Comm device tight in my palm.

But Aarik wasn't taking silence for an answer. His fingers closed on the outside of my fist. His touch burned hot, sizzling, and I dropped the device. Aarik scooped it up, looked at it for a moment, then tossed it into the waves.

My last shred of hope disappeared as the Comm device sank below the water.

"Shame on you," Aarik said, shaking his finger in Kenny's direction. "I warned you…"

"Don't! It's my fault," I said. "Leave Kenny be. If you're going to throw someone overboard, let it be me."

"I don't think that'd be a smart decision, since my employer would like you alive." The cold gaze had returned. "Which leaves me with only one option."

"You've already killed one person," I said, struggling to hide the panic in my voice. "Don't make it another. Kenny is innocent."

"You're not?" Aarik raised an amused eyebrow.

"Yes, I am, but Kenny has even less to do with all this than me. He's just collateral damage. I have no idea why you're after me, but I'm assuming it has something to do with Mixology… *oh my gosh!*" My head shot up so fast I nearly cricked my neck. "You murdered Leonard. Or the last Mixologist. Gus was right—it wasn't an accident!"

Judging by Aarik's surprised expression, I'd caught him off guard. In that second of uncertainty, he was unable to mask the twinge of guilt in his expression, the twitch of a muscle in his jaw.

"I didn't kill either," Aarik said. "It was an accident."

I shook my head. "It wasn't. Stop lying to me, Aarik. It's too late. I'm probably as good as dead now anyway. Ranger X found residue on the glass that Leonard drank from, a poison, and I didn't put it there."

Aarik looked as if he wanted to argue, but he met my gaze, and the fight whooshed right out of him—his face sagged, his lips turned down, his eyes focused on the bottom of the boat. "It wasn't supposed to kill him. The last Mixologist. I didn't have anything to do with Leonard."

"What was it supposed to do?" I kept my voice as quiet, as non-judgmental as possible, though I wanted nothing more than to shake him, shout at him, ask him why he'd ever done such a thing.

"They gave me a powder. Said it should knock Neil out, that I could slip it onto his glass, and when he drank it, he'd pass out. My instructions were to kidnap him." Aarik shifted his gaze to me. "Much like I'm doing now."

"But he didn't wake up," I said softly.

"I think it was poison, and I think my employers lied to me." Aarik's voice was barely audible, filled with pain. "They tricked me."

"Did you do the same thing to Leonard?"

"I refused, but I'm sure it was one of them."

"And Harpin too?"

Aarik shook his head. "I kidnapped Harpin, but he's safe."

I frowned. "Why did you do that?"

"My employer needed you alive, and Harpin was a wildcard. I couldn't tell if he meant to kill you or not at the tea shop." Aarik shot me a pleading look. "I kidnapped Harpin to keep you safe. I knocked him out with his own tea, but he'll be fine, I made sure of it. He'll come around in a few days and call for help."

"Why are these people killing—and kidnapping—the Mixologists?" I asked.

"They're not," Aarik said. "When I explained to my employer he'd given me the wrong powder for Neil—that it'd killed him—he smiled. Said that they weren't after him, not really, so it wasn't a big deal. I *know* they gave me poison on purpose. They wanted him dead."

"I still don't understand why."

"Because they wanted *you!*" Aarik's face clouded. "Neil wasn't the real Mixologist by blood. There's only one Mixologist alive, and that's you."

"But if they kill me, there will still be another Mixologist eventually. They can't stop the cycle."

"They don't want to." Aarik shook his head. "They want to change the cycle. Have you work for them."

"The Faction," I said, understanding. "I can't believe it. They killed the last Mixologist so The Isle would be forced to find me. Leonard, Harpin, Kenny, the previous Mixologist—they're all collateral damage."

"I didn't kill Leonard. I don't know who offed him, but that was someone else. They wanted me to do it, but I said no."

"What did he have to do with anything?"

"I don't know. Maybe they wanted to frame you. Maybe the poison was meant for you, but it was only supposed to make you sick and not kill you. *I don't know.*"

"You don't have to do this anymore," I said, my voice firm. "Aarik, let me go."

When his gaze returned to me, the calm was back. "If you tell my employers that I breathed a word of this to you, you're dead. I don't care about your life nearly as much as they do. I'll find you."

Aarik's words set a shiver down my spine. "Look." I nodded

over his shoulder as the opposite shore loomed into view. "We're almost there."

Our captor turned to glance at the shore, and just as I'd hoped, Kenny was ready. His nimble fingers got to work, pausing only when Aarik glanced back at us.

"Is that a person?" I asked, nodding once more to a shadowy object on the shore. It could just as easily be a bush or a tree, but I didn't say that.

Aarik turned forward and squinted as well. Kenny's hands got back to work. The bindings on my hands slipped away after a few more seconds of Kenny's quick work, and I caught them before they fell, keeping my wrists hidden behind my back.

I considered my options. Magic wouldn't work—I didn't know a single spell. I could lunge at Aarik, but I didn't hold out much hope for the success of that plan. First of all, he was much bigger than me. Second, my jean skirt didn't exactly promote nimble movements.

As I glanced at my out-of-style eighties clothing, I noticed the teensy bulge in my pocket, the outline of a vial. *Hex on the Beach*. It wasn't much, but maybe, just maybe, a bit of magical potion could help. I had no idea how the spell might work, or even if it *would* work, but it was my only option.

"I think it's a person on the shore," I said, leaning forward. The more I looked, the more I realized it might actually be a real person. Probably a late-night fisherman, but at this point, I'd take anyone. "Look there, can't you see a hat?"

Aarik leaned forward, and I took the opportunity to slip the vial out of my pocket. In one fluid motion, I uncapped the cork and downed the liquid in one gulp. I had my hands behind my back before Aarik stood up straight.

The potion burned on the way down. But then I started to feel stronger. More... confident.

At the same time, Aarik's hands went to his throat. "Is it getting harder to breathe?"

I shook my head. "I don't feel anything."

Behind me, Kenny coughed. He didn't seem to be struggling as much as Aarik though. I felt bad Kenny had to be involved, but there was no way around it.

"What did you do?" He turned toward me. "Magic, I feel it."

"I don't know magic," I said. "I've never used it."

"Lies!" Clutching his throat, Aarik lunged at me. "What did you do?"

I cried out in surprise, the vial dropping to the floor of the boat and shattering. Aarik crashed into me, and the two of us tangled on the floor. I let my bindings fall away, struggling for a way out from underneath my attacker.

But I was smaller than him by half. I'd never been in a fight, never taken tae kwon do, never thrown a punch in my life. I was vastly unprepared, and it showed. Aarik held me down easily, his hands tightening around my throat while he coughed, struggling to breathe. The tighter his hands got around my neck, the more he gasped for breath.

Blackness curled around the edges of my brain, my consciousness fading as erratic thoughts crossed my mind. As stars burst in my vision, I had the sudden realization that at least I could say one of my spells had worked. Aarik wasn't choking on accident. That was *my* potion. My creation. My *Hex on the Beach*.

The harder Aarik squeezed, the redder his face became.

Kenny leapt to his feet and lunged in our direction. Aarik's eyes shot up, noticing Kenny's movements, and a dark expression crossed his face.

Before Kenny could reach us, Aarik made the boat rock violently, so hard that Kenny lost his footing and toppled over the edge. From what I could see of his fingertips, Kenny'd barely managed to hang on to the boat. As he struggled to pull himself up, the watercraft rocked, its edges dipping into the lake.

Waves built up quickly—dark, stormy, thrashing waves—

tossing us with a fervor. It was only a matter of time before the vicious swells threw Aarik across the boat, his fingers releasing my throat.

Wobbly, weak, and light-headed, I sat up, sucking in air. The oxygen burned on its way down. I reached for Kenny, who was still dangling from the edge of the boat, his legs in the water, the rest of his body drenched. Just before I could reach his hand, Aarik snatched my leg and pulled me back. I missed Kenny's hand, screaming as I flew backward.

I kicked, connecting with Aarik's gut, and scuttled to the back of the boat all in one moment. I couldn't last all day dipping, dodging, fighting, but as I looked up, I realized I might not have to. If I could just hang on until we reached land…

The boat hurtled toward the shore, tossing and dipping every which way. My head knocked from side to side, the cold water stealing my breath and freezing my skin. If I could just last a bit longer… maybe, just maybe, the figure on the shore would be able to help.

The shadow raised both arms. He had a large, stoic form, his fingers alight with magic. I could just make out his glittering eyes, black as the deepest depths of the lake. His determined expression was as full of rage as the thrashing, biting waves.

I made eye contact with the figure just as the moon came out from behind the clouds, the light bathing him. But I couldn't make out a face. The person—a man, I was guessing, judging by his size and stature—wore a cloak that obscured my view.

The cloaked shadow twitched his fingers upward, and a tsunami rose before the boat. My heart sped up, trepidation heavy in the air as my breathing came in gulps.

Aarik's face filled with horror as he noticed the wave trembling above us, disaster seconds away. The water hovered for a moment. In that second of calm, I realized I wouldn't make it out alive.

Then the tip of the wave curled into an icicle, the water freezing—sharp, glittering, lethal.

The figure moved his hands downward.

The icy wave plummeted straight toward us.

I stood, held my breath, and took a flying dive into the frigid, unforgiving water. As I sank, I grabbed Kenny's waist and yanked him down with me into the deep, black depths of the Great Lake.

CHAPTER 28

A SENSE OF DÉJÀ VU HIT me once more, this time before I even opened my eyes.

The sound of a wind chime tinkled merrily in the distance. A soft breeze danced across my face, the floral scent fresh and warm. My skin touched something smooth—sheets maybe, or a nice blanket. I inhaled a deep breath, basking in the simple fact I was breathing oxygen, not cold, painful gasps of Lake Superior.

I had yet to open my eyes. I didn't want to ruin the moment. What if I opened my eyes and discovered I was dead? Or what if I'd been captured by The Faction?

I inhaled and exhaled evenly, realizing how much I'd failed to appreciate the simple act of breathing. Never again would I take a pleasant, fresh gulp of air for granted. My throat didn't hurt, and my body wasn't decorated with goose bumps. I was comfortable. Which meant I might just keep my eyes closed forever, lying here, basking in the scent of... *lilacs*? I groaned, already piecing together the familiar scent with the footsteps approaching.

One second later, Mimsey's voice filtered through my daydreams. "Are you awake, dear?"

I scrunched my eyes shut tighter. More familiar footsteps. Hettie's, I thought.

"Don't you even dare pretend to be asleep, young lady." Hettie's petite frame made surprisingly loud stomps. "You think you can fool a house full of witches with your fake sleeping? Playing the old *I'm sleeping* trick hasn't worked for fifty years in this house."

"Ma, she's fragile," Mimsey said. "Be gentle, for crying out loud. She's been through an ordeal."

"She's a strong one, this girl," Hettie said without an ounce of sympathy. "This one don't need babying, am I right?"

Reluctantly, I opened my eyes. "I'm all right."

"You are not all right." Mimsey bustled about, fluffing the pillow beneath my shoulders, resting the back of her hand against my forehead, pulling sheets up to my chin. "You need rest, relaxation, and food."

"To heck she does," Hettie said. "She needs a pat on the back and some answers."

I grinned. "Actually, I'd love some answers."

Mimsey frowned. "Not *now*."

"Why not?" Hettie crossed her arms. "Don't be a wimp, Mimsey. You're a sap."

Mimsey wrung her hands. "I led him right to her. This is all my fault. That man—I suggested you go with him past the lilacs... I wanted you to *kiss* him."

"It's not your fault," I said. "Please, don't blame yourself."

"It is too her fault," Hettie said. "But it don't do any good feelin' sorry for yourself. Look, everything turned out all right. You're alive."

Mimsey burst into tears.

"Hettie, stop it," I said. "Mimsey, come here."

My plump, huggable aunt hesitantly sat next to me, the bed curving under her weight. I drew her in for a long, squishy hug. By the time we separated, she was sniffling but no longer crying.

"I'm so sorry. I walked that man right up to our doorstep. To think, if you hadn't returned... if you..." Mimsey nearly relapsed into tears.

Hettie gave her daughter a light *thunk* on the side of her head with an open palm. "Stop your crying! You apologized. She said it's okay. I don't like whimpering in my home."

I patted Mimsey's back. "It's really okay. I know you didn't mean any harm. If it helps you feel better, I trusted Aarik. I chose to walk him out. In fact, I thought… I thought…"

"Oh for goodness's sake, spit it out," Hettie said.

"I thought he'd stopped by because he liked me." I looked down, playing with the end of the comforter. "When we got to the edge of The Twist, I thought he was going to kiss me."

"Oh, this is just gross," Hettie said. "I thought you had the hots for that Ranger? I like Ranger X much better. I bet Aarik has gross breath."

"You told me you wanted great-grandkids, and you can't get great-grandkids without being… gross!" I said, feeling my ears turn red. "But that's irrelevant, since I don't have the hots for anyone. It's dangerous."

"You don't have to explain how to make children," Hettie grumbled. "I had a few of my own."

"You seemed quite keen to see how it happened with Ranger X," I said. "So keen, in fact, you waited in the hallway and spied on us!"

"I didn't spy." Hettie shook her head. "Plus, he's smokin' good-looking. I'd have to be dead not to appreciate that man. Do I look dead to you?"

I looked at my tiny, wrinkled grandmother, all attitude and sass—hands on her hips, pointy elbows out in every direction. I burst into laughter. "You definitely don't look dead. You guys are funny. I can't even be mad you spied on my love life. Er… not love life, my business life."

Mimsey lips curved into a shy smile, but just as quickly, it was replaced by uncertainty. "I'm sorry about everything, dear. We love you, we really do."

"Stop sniveling," Hettie said as Mimsey's eyes welled up with tears once more.

"It's not *wrong* to tell your granddaughter you love her," Mimsey said. "For crying out loud, Hettie, you just met her. It wouldn't hurt you to say a nice thing once in a while."

After a moment, Hettie spoke, her voice holding a note of begrudging agreement. "I'm not *sad* you found us, and I don't want you to leave. Is that better?"

"That's sort of sweet," I said, nodding. I would pretend she'd said something more along the lines of "I love you, granddaughter, and we couldn't bear to be without you now that we've met you."

Mimsey glowered at her mother, but when she turned her gaze on me, it softened. "I'm sorry about today, and I'm sorry about the rest of it. I'm sorry we missed out on your childhood."

"We can't change the past." I planted a kiss on her cheek. "I'm happy to be here now, and I don't blame you for anything that happened. Please don't blame yourself."

Mimsey nodded, a look of relief covering her face.

"I do have one question for you. About that curse, the one you say prevented me from coming here a long time ago," I said. "Is it a curse *on* me? Is it still... around?"

My aunt stood, bustling as she pulled the sheets back up to my chin. "That's a conversation for a different day."

"But—"

"A different day." For the first time since I'd woken, Mimsey sounded like her motherly self once again. "You need rest."

"I don't—"

"You have a visitor." Hettie clapped. "A very nice tush is here to see you."

I groaned.

Hettie stuck her head outside the bedroom door and shouted down the hallway. "Hey, you. I'm talking about you. Get in here. Yes, you... who else would I be talking about?"

I closed my eyes. Hettie had shouted so loudly, I was sure the entire house had heard her.

"I have a nice butt," Poppy yelled back from somewhere far down the hall. "Can I come in and see my cousin?"

"No," Hettie yelled back. "I'm not talking about you. I'm talking about *you*. Yes, *you*."

I couldn't see Hettie's hands, but I imagined she was poking her finger in someone's face.

"Here he is." Hettie pulled her head back into the room, smiling devilishly at me. "Smile, granddaughter."

Mimsey leaned in to give me one more squeeze, whispering, "I left lilacs on the table."

"Already with the matchmaking?" I whispered back. "I'm still not recovered from the last one. Can't you wait a few days?"

"But this one's a *Ranger*. That's different." She winked, grabbing her mother by the wrist and yanking her from the room as she made an exit.

Hettie wouldn't be outfoxed, however, and got in one quick pinch to the Ranger's backside on the way out. She winked at me. "Ignore my hands. They're just feeling a little... *cheeky*."

"I'm *so* sorry about that." My face flamed as I stared at a very unamused Ranger X. "She's feeling the effects of the lilacs, probably. Her hands must have flown out of control."

Ranger X cleared his throat.

I gestured toward them. "In fact, do you mind getting rid of the lilacs? You can just toss them in the garbage. And close the lid, and burn the whole thing, and throw it out of the window. They're sort of what got me into trouble in the first place, my family's whole matchmaking business."

"I know the power of lilacs." Ranger X finally moved, closing the door and muttering something as he rested his fingers against the wood, his forehead leaning against the door.

I frowned at his words. Then I realized it was a spell. All at once, the wooden door turned transparent, revealing four sets of ears—Hettie, Mimsey, Zin, and Poppy—pressed tight against the door.

"You guys!" I shook my head. "Have you ever heard of privacy? Stop eavesdropping."

Having the gall to look sheepish, my family dispersed down the hall, Hettie mumbling about magic.

"Family is so embarrassing," I said. "I never realized it when I didn't have any..."

Ranger X pressed his fingers to the door once more and murmured another incantation. The door returned to its normal state. "Door's soundproofed now."

"Thanks." I glanced down, suddenly aware that the thin silk nightie I was wearing had the thinnest of shoulder straps. I pulled the comforter tighter. "I love my family, but... well, you know how it is."

Ranger X didn't respond.

"Or maybe you don't," I babbled. "Do you have family nearby?"

He stepped closer.

"I'm sorry..." I flailed my arms wide on the bed. "Can you just say something so I don't feel like an idiot talking to myself?"

He stepped close enough to the bed so that if I reached out, I could touch him. "Did that man do anything to hurt you?"

Without thinking, I raised a hand to my neck. "Aarik? No... nothing, I'm fine." I bit my lip, remembering the figure who'd quite possibly saved my life. "Was that you on the shore?"

Ranger X's fingers gently caressed the outside of my throat. "Does this hurt?"

I shook my head.

"I'm sorry I put you in danger." An emotion that looked like fury darted through Ranger X's eyes before he composed himself. "I should never have left you here alone."

"You couldn't have known I'd walk myself right into a trap." I gave a half smile. "Nobody suspected him. He walked right up to the door next to Mimsey. Not her fault, of course. Then I volunteered to walk him out alone. It was an unfortunate mistake."

"I don't like *unfortunate,* especially if I have the ability to prevent it." Ranger X crossed his arms, pacing next to my bed. "You're trouble for me. I should never have listened to you. I should've just kept you at my cabin. Alone. Safe, with me."

"No sense looking back now. Hindsight is twenty-twenty."

Ranger X stopped his pacing. His gaze met mine, his lips tightening into a thin line. Eventually, he shook his head. When he resumed his pacing, I breathed again.

"My job, first and foremost, is to protect you and everyone on this Isle," he said. "I can't let... *things* get in the way anymore."

"Are you calling me a thing?" My eyebrows crinkled. "I'm confused."

He pressed both hands to his forehead, kneading his temples. "No."

"Sit down and explain, then. You don't have to mince words around me." I patted the bed until he gave in and perched as far away from me as possible.

"As a Ranger, I'm not allowed to get married. We don't have relationships."

"I know that. Why are you telling me this?"

"Because I like you." Ranger X crossed his arms. "You waltz onto this island smelling like honeysuckle... with skin so soft I want to hold you close, even when you get mad. *Especially* when you get mad."

I swallowed hard. I didn't know where to look.

"But for me to continue doing a successful job as a Ranger, I *can't* care about any one person more than another." He blinked, shifting his gaze to mine. "We chose the job over our own lives."

I said quietly, "I understand."

He stood, the bed shifting as he moved. "Well, I put you before my job this time. Listened to you despite my better judgment."

"I'm sorry I asked to leave your hut. Is that what you want to hear?"

"No, it's not that, Lily." Ranger X turned to face me. "I couldn't keep you in my cabin where you would have been safe, because I wouldn't have been able to avoid kissing you."

Both of us fell into silence. Seconds, minutes passed, neither of us speaking.

"Was that you out on the lake?" I asked quietly. "How did you find me?"

Ranger X didn't answer. Instead he strode with purpose toward me, clasped my cheeks, and pressed his lips to mine in a possessive, deep kiss.

His mouth roved mine hungrily, his hands sliding back into my hair and gripping the strands tightly. Though his actions were firm and demanding, his lips became pliable and tender. My world disappeared, my chest rising and falling as my mind faded to black. All that existed was him, me, and the kiss that stole the breath straight from my body.

When he pulled away, ending the kiss all too soon, our gazes met in a fiery stare. His shoulders rose in defense, and mine huddled in vulnerability.

"That *has* to be the end of this." He gestured between us. "Understood?"

My body screamed for more, begged for his touch, his fingers clasped in mine. I wanted him to hug me and tell me everything would be okay, even if it was a lie. I wanted his hands to run through my hair, his eyes to lock on mine alone, his body to lie next to mine as night became morning. But he'd made it clear that none of that could happen. Never, so if I was smart, I'd move on sooner rather than later.

Unfortunately, I wasn't very smart when it came to matters of the heart. I looked up, ready to argue and tell him I wouldn't give up just because he already had.

But something in his eyes—a sorrowful expression—stopped

me. I couldn't bring myself to make the situation more difficult on him.

I coughed. "Why'd you kiss me, then?"

His eyes turned dark, a soft grayish color. "Because I wanted to, and you wanted to, and we're adults. Better to get it out of our systems."

"It's probably the lilacs' fault."

"Most likely." He crossed his arms and smiled. "So can we be civil? And friends?"

"Are you gonna keep going around kissing girls left and right?"

"I don't kiss girls... *left and right*."

The expression sounded funny coming from his lips, and as I looked at his face, I couldn't stifle my laugh.

"So we can call a truce?" He grinned.

I nodded. "Fine. But no more kissing each other, got it?"

He looked relieved. "Got it."

"Don't look so relieved."

Ranger X's eyes filled with confusion. "How should I look?"

"Sad. Very, very sad."

He laughed. "I'm utterly miserable. Is that better?"

"Much." I crossed my arms, and as the room regained its easy, comfortable feel, I remembered something else. "How's Kenny?"

"Kenny's perfectly fine. He's back to work already, as a matter of fact." Ranger X gave an approving nod. "He's tough. The whole thing didn't seem to faze him in the slightest."

"And Aarik?"

"He's in jail. Not going anywhere," he said. "I made sure of it."

I pondered that development. "Have you spoken with him?"

"Yes, a bit."

"And? Did he say why he did any of this?"

"It's been an interesting few days at the jailhouse..." Ranger X shook his head. "We gave Aarik an accidental detox. See, we don't let inmates smoke anything at all, let alone that junk Aarik's always huffing and puffing. It turns out Aarik's brain cleared up a bit without the constant smoke in his lungs."

I tapped my lip in thought. "You know, he said some interesting things on the boat." I quickly filled Ranger X in on the conversation that'd taken place during my kidnapping. "But there's one thing I can't put my finger on."

Ranger X raised an eyebrow.

"He apologized." I cleared my throat. "He said I'm sorry right before he tried to hurt me. Why would he apologize?"

A light clicked on behind Ranger X's dark eyes, illuminating them in a fascinating way I'd never seen before. "Those who hurt others are usually the most insecure of all of us, Lily. Often, the attacker is motivated by something other than the desire to just cause harm. I think that's what happened with Aarik."

I tapped his chest. "So what was Aarik motivated by?"

"I think it was more than motivation." Ranger X looked at me. "The smoke was enchanted. He wasn't *working* for somebody else. He was being controlled."

I began to connect the dots. "So whoever wanted to control Aarik realized he smoked like a chimney. Then they put a potion into his special leaves stash, and he unwillingly fell under their spell."

"Exactly. Now that he's detoxed, he's experiencing disorientation, lapses in memory, et cetera. Aarik claims he has no recollection of walking with you back through the maze or bringing you onto the boat. I didn't believe him at first." Ranger X pursed his lips. "But if his leaves were magically enhanced, it'd be enough for someone to control him. Mind magic, of sorts."

"He told me that he poisoned Neil. That it was an accident," I said. "I believe he didn't kill him on purpose."

Ranger X sighed. "That doesn't absolve him, but maybe we can work with Aarik to reach the people who are responsible for controlling him."

"The Faction?"

"Most likely." Ranger X breathed hard. "This fight has hardly begun, Lily."

"One more thing—when Aarik apologized on the boat, do you think he might have meant it?"

Ranger X nodded. "The spell might have been wearing thin by that time. It's difficult to maintain harmful magic for a long period of time, or over a very long distance, and this situation had both obstacles when you were in the middle of the lake."

My shoulders slumped. Aarik had been as much of a victim as me.

Ranger X looked away, as if sensing my disappointment, my embarrassment at being fooled. "It's not your fault, you know. To control someone's mind is a powerful and illegal form of magic."

"Still, how could I ever have thought he *liked* me?"

"It's *not* your fault." He rested his hands on my shoulder. "Far greater witches and wizards than you have fallen from less. You're new, but you're strong. And you'll get stronger every day. What sort of spell did you hit him with, by the way? Aarik was gulping for air, trying to recover, when he came to jail."

I grinned. "I call it *Hex on the Beach*. It repels unwanted men."

Ranger X scooched a few feet down the bed. "Should I be worried?"

"Only if you plan on ticking me off." I winked. "Or kissing me. If you try that again, then yes… you should be very, very afraid."

We fell into an easy silence.

"Did you ever find Harpin?" To be honest, I didn't really care, but it was polite to ask.

"Yeah, I found him, all right." Ranger X grinned.

"What are you smiling about?"

"Turned out Aarik locked him in his own tea barrel." Ranger X leaned back with a pleased expression. "I left him in there for an extra few hours and told him to think about what he'd done to you."

"You shouldn't have done that!" I tried to sound upset but couldn't hide my grin. "Shame on you."

Ranger X's grin melted into a more serious, thoughtful expression. "I don't have sympathy for any man who thinks it's acceptable to hurt a woman. Especially a woman I care about."

"You care about me?"

Ranger X blinked. "Don't push me."

I raised my hands. "Hey, your words, not mine."

He sighed. "You confuse me."

"So do you," I said, playing with a stray thread on the comforter. "So now that we've got everything straightened out, can we agree to be confused friends? No kissing. No... no flirting."

"No peeking under your dress?" He raised an eyebrow, an amused quirk to his lips.

"Absolutely not."

"Shame."

"Though in my defense, that never happened on purpose."

"Shame again."

I narrowed my eyes at him. "Are you flirting? Because if so, you're already breaking the rules."

"Fine, fine. You caught me." He held out a hand. "Truce?"

"Truce." I held out mine, and we shook on it.

Except he didn't pull his hand away, and neither did I. His thumb rubbed a soothing circle over the back of my hand. My eyes fell toward our clasped fingers in a daze.

I snapped out of it first. "Stop that."

"This might be the most difficult agreement I've ever made."

I pulled back my arm. "It's for the best. For both our sakes. You... you have your job to consider, and I need to study. I can't focus on becoming the Mixologist if I'm too busy showing you my lingerie."

Ranger X groaned. "You're sure this is for the best?"

"Yes!" I nodded. "I think so."

A knock sounded on the door. A second later, a squeal and some shouting filtered through, leading me to wonder about one-way soundproofing.

"I should probably get going." Ranger X stood. "I don't know how I'll be able to look your grandmother in the eye after your descriptive images."

I gave him a wave. "Thank you for everything."

"You should be safe now. Stay near the bungalow. Don't provoke Harpin. Let Gus know what you're up to at all times. And for God's sake, don't create any more dangerous potions geared against men. You did a number on Aarik."

"I can't make any promises," I said with a cheeky grin. "I'm told I have to come up with a Menu. There's no saying what'll appear on that menu."

"I'd stop by to try it sometime, but like I said—I don't want to end up dead. Or worse."

"Worse than dead?"

"I wouldn't put it past you." Ranger X gave a good-natured shake of his head. "Good-bye, Lily. Don't hesitate to get in touch if you need anything."

I followed his gaze down to my wrist, where someone—probably Ranger X himself—had reattached the Comm band.

"Good-bye." He left the room, the door closing on his way out, and took a piece of my smile with him.

For some reason, his good-bye felt more final than it should have. But in his words—maybe it was for the best.

CHAPTER 29

MY CHEERFULNESS BOUNCED BACK AS soon as Poppy poked her head into the room. "You *dog*, you."

"What?" I asked.

"You've got suitors coming here left and right. First Aarik, then Ranger X. Wowzers, is all I have to say." Poppy shook her head. "Share the wealth. I mean, come on. We live on an island. There're only so many available men to go around."

Zin joined us shortly, and the three of us formed a cozy bundle on the bed as they wrapped themselves in bits of my comforter.

"Aarik was trying to kidnap me, so you can have him." I laughed. "As for the Ranger... there's nothing romantic between us."

"You're telling me he didn't kiss you, not even once?" Zin asked, looking skeptical.

I fell silent.

"He *did* kiss you!" Poppy's voice squeaked with excitement.

"It was an accident," I said. "And it was the last time."

"But not the first?" Poppy's jaw dropped, incredulity scribbled across her face.

I waved. "I'm focused on my studies from now on. Just me, Gus, and my books. Don't tell Mimsey."

Poppy pouted. "And us. Don't forget us."

"And your aunts will force themselves into your life, don't you forget." Zin shrugged. "Hettie, too. Oh, the joys of family."

We shared a knowing silence.

"We're all really glad you're safe, Lily." Poppy looked at me.

"And we're all so glad you're here. Honest. It already feels as if we've known you forever. Please stay with us. I'm not sure if you've been thinking about leaving after this... this ordeal, but—"

"But please don't," Zin finished. "It's simple. Just say you'll stay."

My eyes smarted, the sting coming from nowhere. Luckily, I managed to swallow and not let the tears fall. "You're in luck. I'm here to stay."

Poppy did a huge fist pump, unabashed excitement on her face. "Awesome. You know what that means!"

"What does that mean?" I asked, playing with the heart around my neck, wondering about my mother and if she might still be alive.

"Well..." It was Zin's turn to chuckle. "We heard you really pummeled Aarik with your *Hex on the Beach* concoction."

"People are whispering that you're the strongest Mixologist in a long time... maybe *ever*," Poppy said in low tones. "Most people take ages for their spells to have any sort of effect. I heard yours did a number on him."

"It worked okay." I cocked my head to the side. "Enough to do the trick, I'd say."

"Come on, spill the beans. We've been dying to know." Zin looked at me. "What's next on the Menu?"

"I've been thinking about this a little bit, ever since you gave me that theme idea." I sat back, fluffed my pillows, and made eye contact with both my cousins. "How does a *Jinx and Tonic* sound to you? I'm also contemplating *Witchy Sour*."

Poppy clapped. "Why not both?"

EPILOGUE

MY COUSINS STAYED WITH ME at the bungalow that first night, chatting until they couldn't keep their eyes open any longer. They dozed off mid-conversation, their heads resting on the extra pillows in the bed. Gus stopped by in the late hours of the night, slinking into the room under the cover of darkness.

"Hi, Gus," I whispered, careful not to wake my sleeping cousins. "Thanks for coming."

"You're alive?" He gave me a grizzled nod. "I suppose that's a stupid question, seeing as how you're talking to me."

"Alive and well!"

He grunted. "I'm supposed to give you three days off. Orders from the kitchen."

"Is that right?" I bit my lip in amusement.

He grunted again. "You ain't gonna stop studying, are you?"

"Of course not." I nodded toward *The Magic of Mixology* manuscript on my nightstand. "I'll resume tomorrow morning. Did you hear I created my first cocktail? All by myself. I call it *Hex on the Beach*."

Gus grunted once more.

"Use your words, Gus. I can't understand all your noises."

"Then learn." He walked forward and gave me a single pat on the head. "Good job, kid."

"Thank you," I said, my voice hushed in disbelief. His

compliments came few and far between, and I intended to savor every moment of it.

"Get your rear end back in the store three days from now. You've got to learn how to control your power." Gus shook his head. "You almost killed Aarik, I heard, with that repellent stuff. Vicious stuff."

"Sorry." I looked down. "I didn't mean to make it so strong."

"Don't apologize."

When I met Gus's gaze, his eyes sparkled with a brightness, an intensity I hadn't yet seen.

"I almost killed someone," I said. "Or at least seriously injured them. That's not a cause for celebration."

"Your first potion was more powerful than anything I've seen for the last few decades, and you didn't even know what the heck you were doing. You've got something I can work with, kid. Something to work with." Gus shuffled to the door then turned to look back at me. "Three days, you hear? I don't teach wimps."

"Three days," I murmured. "I'll see you."

Gus left the room, and I took a moment to sit back and count my blessings. A compliment from Gus plus a sleepover with my long-lost cousins? An excellent day, if I said so myself.

⚬✕⚬

Three days flew by, and before I knew it, I was back in the bungalow, working my fingers to the bone grinding powders, hurling memorized herb and flower names at Gus, and poring over the golden pages of my trusty Mixology book.

"Again," Gus barked. "Again."

"Gus, I'm exhausted," I said, a few days after returning to the bar. "I've been working eighteen-hour days down here. I've barely eaten. I haven't seen anyone except for you in the last few days."

"Got a problem with me?"

"No." I sighed. "I need the morning off tomorrow. Just to

grab breakfast with my family, okay? Let's start after lunch. If we continue at this pace, my brain will explode."

Gus thought for a long, grudging moment. "It's getting late, I suppose. I'll tell you what—take the morning off and loop it in with an early lunch. Be back here immediately after. We'll start at noon."

I breathed a sigh of relief. "Thank you."

"I'm going to lock this up, then, and go home for the night. I'll be back late morning," Gus said. "You can go home now."

I didn't bother to correct Gus. I *was* home, here in my bungalow. I handed over *The Magic of Mixology* and watched Gus secure it in the magical safe along one wall of the store.

We normally didn't lock it up, but that was because we'd been working around the clock. In fact, I'd recently installed a foldout bed in the corner Gus had occupied for the last few days.

"Good night, Gus," I said, leaning in to give him a hug.

He grunted and backed away. "We don't hug."

I let my arms collapse to my sides. "Would it kill you to show a little bit of affection?"

"I did. I patted you on the head that one time. That's all I have in me." Gus shook his head. "Go to bed, Lily. I'll see you tomorrow at noon."

After Gus clicked his cane down the steps, muttering about "emotional types" and "hugging crap," I smiled and locked the door. Equal parts infuriating and adorable, Gus was, simply put, the best.

I took one last look around the store—*my* store—and soaked in the view. The shelves were full of ingredients, the golden book cover glinted behind a sturdy glass shield, the cozy folding bed sat in the corner of the room—all of it was more of a home than I'd ever known, and I hadn't even lived here a month.

I flicked off the light and made my way up the creaky old stairs, skipping the seventh one, which had a particularly loud *punch*.

After slipping into a nightgown, I crept under my covers with a book explaining the history of The Isle. I read and read until the book collapsed on my face, the pages imprinting on my cheeks in the wee hours of the morning.

When I woke a few hours later, I carefully peeled the book from my skin, slipped from the bed, and stretched, then I threw the curtains open. As the sunlight streamed into my lofty bedroom, I remembered all at once that this morning I had a few hours off. My heart leapt at the thought of spending time eating and chatting with my cousins.

I hurriedly dressed, rushed downstairs, slipped into my shoes, and grabbed a shoulder bag on my way out the door. But as I turned to lock up, I saw something that stopped me dead in my tracks.

An empty safe.

My stomach sank faster than a rock in Lake Superior as I crept back inside, my heart racing as I scanned the store.

Empty.

I left the door open, just in case I needed to scream for help, and approached the safe just above Gus's fold-out bed. The glass was protected by layers of hexes, charms, spells, and jinxes—if someone had broken in, I should have known. The alarms would have sounded, spells would've been triggered, and if nothing else, I should have found the intruder knocked unconscious by the magic. I looked toward the ground, not seeing anyone. Or *anything*. No trace that someone had been wandering around the bungalow as I slept.

The glass on the safe remained perfectly intact, the floor clear of footprints, and my front door had been locked. But inside the enchanted glass barrier, only the velvet cloth that lined the safe remained.

I lifted my wrist to my mouth and whispered against the Comm device, "Ranger X, we have a problem. Someone has stolen *The Magic of Mixology*."

Not only would Gus be furious, but the information inside that book could cause serious damage in the wrong hands.

My book was gone.

If I didn't find it, the entire Isle—plus the entire human race—would be in danger.

The End.

THANK YOU, ISLANDERS!

Dear Islanders,

Thank you for reading *Hex on the Beach*! If you enjoyed it, please stay tuned for the story to continue in book two, *Witchy Sour*! I appreciate all of my readers, and I love hearing from you! Email me anytime, or visit my website at www.ginalamana.com for more information on new releases!

Sincerely,
Gina

WEBSITES AND SOCIAL MEDIA

Find out more about the author and upcoming books online at www.ginalamanna.com or:

Email: gina.m.lamanna@gmail.com
Twitter: @Gina_LaManna
Facebook: facebook.com/GinaLaMannaAuthor
Website: www.ginalamanna.com

About the Author

Originally from St. Paul, Minnesota, Gina LaManna began writing with the intention of making others smile. At the moment, she lives in Los Angeles and spends her days writing short stories, long stories, and all sizes in-between stories. She publishes under a variety of pen names, including a children's mystery series titled Mini Pie the Spy!

In her spare time, Gina has been known to run the occasional marathon, accidentally set fire to her own bathroom, and survive days on end eating only sprinkles, cappuccino foam and ice cream. She enjoys spending time with her family and friends most of all.

Made in the USA
San Bernardino, CA
20 August 2018